NINE THOUSAND FEET UP . . .

and Brady eased the small plane's climb. The sun
had sunk below the horizon, and the eastern sky
was dark, showing its early stars. Brady looked
about him, enjoying the relaxation the flight gave
him. He saw a light high above and to his left,
descending slowly . . .

He knew it couldn't be a satellite when it continued to expand in brightness and size. At the
same moment he knew it was rushing directly
toward him.

Brady tensed, his mouth agape. Holding formation
off his left wing was a huge disc. It held position,
unmistakable, absolutely clear, unbelievably real.
He saw the rounded dome above the disc, a
wide-bellied protrusion beneath . . .

Brady felt the pounding of his heart, and he took
several deep breaths, forcing himself to calm down.
But now he knew he was right. *The discs were real!*

MARTIN CAIDIN

The Mendelov Conspiracy

PINNACLE BOOKS • **NEW YORK CITY**

This is a work of fiction. All the characters and events portrayed in this book are fictional, and any resemblance to real people or incidents is purely coincidental.

THE MENDELOV CONSPIRACY

Copyright © 1969 by Martin Caidin

A Pinnacle book, published by special arrangement with Hawthorn Books, Inc., New York.

ISBN: 0-523-00458-3

First printing, September 1974

Printed in the United States of America

PINNACLE BOOKS, INC.
275 Madison Avenue
New York, N.Y.

for
LES ROBERSON
just because

The Mendelov Conspiracy

CHAPTER I

"CRAP."

The word came out ugly and flat.

Cliff Brady watched for the reaction he knew would come. With a little more experience the man across the desk would have remained poker-faced. But the captain didn't know how to mask his emotions when someone called him a liar. A cheek muscle twitched and he tightened his lips. Brady smiled. The other man was fighting to keep in mind that he was an officer in the United States Air Force. As such—unless you're prepared to have your ass raked over hot coals—you don't get into a fight with a top newsman from World Press. Even when the son of a bitch is doing his best to provoke you.

Captain Walker remembered his orders. He leaned forward and slowly stubbed out his cigarette. "Maybe I don't read you right, Mr. Brady."

Brady snorted. "The hell you don't. I can recognize a snow job, Walker."

"I've told you everything I know," Walker broke in.

"That's a matter of opinion," Brady retorted, "and right now I don't mind telling you that mine isn't very high of you."

The officer shrugged. "That's up to you, Mr. Brady. Congress pays me to do a job. Including," he added sarcastically, "being insulted by influential newsmen."

Brady didn't take the bait. He knew better. He went back to worrying the bone. "What you're saying, in effect," he said smoothly, "is that half the people in Barstow are insane, or subject to hallucinations, or liars. Those people out there"—he stabbed a finger in the direction of the nearby town—"saw something. They saw it, Walker, they heard it. They know what happened. They weren't frightened by any mass hallucination. They—"

Walker threw up his hands. "Hold it right there, Brady," he snapped. "Don't put words in my mouth. I don't *know* what the people in Barstow saw or didn't see. I was sixty feet underground when this whole flap took place and—"

"WHAT flap?" Brady barked.

Walker eased back in his chair. "Nice try," he said. "The flap *you* are telling me about. Like I said, I was sixty feet straight down in a command post."

"Then how come I'm not talking to someone who *did* see what happened?"

"Because, Mr. Brady," Walker said, "we don't have anyone at this base who saw anything. At least not what you're claiming took place."

"I talked with forty people who saw it, Captain. Who saw it and who heard it and observed its effects. There must have been a few thousand more eyewitnesses. Hell, the town's only a dozen miles away—everybody here can't be deaf, dumb, and blind. Why the cover-up? What are you people so afraid of?"

A blank look appeared on Walker's face. "Afraid?"

"Yeah, afraid," Brady said dryly. "The symptoms are all over the place. I've never seen so many people so determined to deny that something happened."

"Look, Brady, we're not denying anything," Walker said. "We simply aren't going to confirm what we didn't see—even if you

4

tell me the whole town saw your UFO. I give you my word *I* didn't see anything at all." Walker sat back and glared at Brady.

"So you've told me a couple of times," Brady replied. "Sure, you're telling the truth. *You* were sixty feet down. *You* didn't see anything." Brady held the eyes of the other man and then dropped his trump card.

"How about my talking to some of the men who made up that combat team?"

Walker's eyes were unmoved. "What combat team, Mr. Brady?"

"The team you sent out by helicopter and ground vehicles to find whatever it was that landed about eight miles from here."

The silence held between the two men. Brady realized that Walker's instructions to deny everything didn't cover this sort of thing. Brady knew far more than the captain had realized; he knew far more than he should have known. And the captain didn't know what to do. He was a missile-control officer who spent most of his time riding herd on a group of Minuteman missiles buried in silos that were shotgun-scattered across the Nebraska hills and mountains. Walker didn't like newsmen. He wondered just how much Brady did know.

Brady knew enough to make a good story—but for a wire-service story he wanted hard facts, something definitive. He wanted confirmation from experienced observers. He wanted something official into which he could sink his teeth. He wasn't getting what he wanted. The captain in whose office he sat was making sure of that.

Barstow Auxiliary Air Force Base was essentially a command nerve center for an unspecified number of missile silos spread out in all directions. The town of Barstow, twelve miles distant, had learned to live with the presence of the missile-command sites. The Air Force people mostly kept to themselves, and those who came to town were pleasant, intelligent people. They should have been; they were handpicked for the job.

5

Nobody rocked the boat. Until a few days ago, when Barstow leaped onto the front pages as the center of a UFO flap. Brady had checked out the initial news reports. When the story failed to die down, World Press had packed him off to Barstow to see if he could make a wire-service feature out of it. Reliable UFO sightings were rare and they made good copy.

Brady expected one or two days of first-person interviews and that would be it. He hadn't figured on a town scared half to death. They weren't just excited. The people in Barstow had been frightened. The missile command post was involved. But Brady couldn't break through.

The first person he interviewed was the chief of police in Barstow. Brady's immediate impression of John Cotron was of a solid, reliable, phlegmatic man who knew his business and who wasn't likely to go off the deep end because of something he might have seen in the sky. Chief Cotron's first words made this clear.

"Maybe you want to call it a UFO," Cotron had said, measuring his words carefully. "I don't. UFO means 'unidentified.' This thing here was a disc. No doubt about it."

"You're certain of that?" Brady prodded.

Cotron nodded. "Yeah, no doubt in *my* mind. Course, it was a long ways off. But I saw it high up, when I could make out the disc shape easy enough. Then I saw it over the hills to the north, where it dropped below sight. The shape changed, but it was a disc, seen from the side."

"Could you make out any details?" Brady prodded.

"Uh-uh. Too far away. But it was a disc, all right."

"Anything in particular?" Brady knew enough to let the man respond to brief questions.

"Silver. It was silver. Metallic, I guess you might call it." Chief Cotron was emphatic. "The way it reflected light. Couldn't have been anything else."

"Could you see any markings, or windows? Perhaps a dome or control cabin?"

Cotron shook his head. "Like I say, it was too far away for that. And I know better than to try to guess."

Brady jotted down some notes. "Oh? Are you a pilot, Chief?"

"Was. During World War Two. Flew dive-bombers in the Navy, got a couple thousand hours before I quit. I got plenty of experience looking at things in the sky. It was a disc, all right. Nobody going to make me change my mind about *that*." He finished his final words with a snort of disdain.

"Anybody try changing your mind?" Brady asked.

The chief nodded. "Sure did," he said. "Bunch of professor types. Said they were from the Air Force, came out to investigate the UFO report. Told me I didn't see a disc at all. Said what I saw was probably a swept-wing airplane that reflected light to look like a disc." His gaze arrowed to Brady's face. "I *know* what I saw."

Brady thought quickly. Cotron's eyewitness report was strong enough to be worth something. But there was more. "Chief, what about those reports that the UFO—the disc, I mean—interfered with radios and electrical equipment? Is there anything to that?"

Again Cotron nodded. "Hell, anybody in town could tell you that. Never saw anything like it before. Every damned radio for miles around went crazy. Static. Like to drive us nuts. TV wouldn't work, radios just buzzing and sputtering. Half the lights in town were dimming, you know, like going on low power. Couple of people out in the hills called in later complaining that the thing, whatever it was, had killed their cars. Engines just quit, I mean. They saw the disc drop down below some hills to the north. A little while later it showed up again, this time going like hell. Faster than any airplane I ever saw. It climbed up real steep. Just kept on going until it disappeared from sight. Everything worked fine again."

"You said it landed beyond some hills to the north?" Brady queried.

"I didn't say it *landed*," Cotron said quickly. "I said it dropped

7

from sight. Long ways from here. I don't know if it landed or not. Maybe the Air Force people know."

"Why do you think they might know?"

Chief Cotron dug a black cigar from a shirt pocket, talking between puffs as he lit up. "They got combat teams—security teams, I guess you'd call them. They go out regularly to check the silos. Sometimes they get a report that someone's fooling around or something, and they get out there fast. Use helicopters. Well, they sent out a chopper from the main base to investigate. I wouldn't have known anything about it except that the chopper's engine quit. Just like that." Cotron snapped his fingers to emphasize his point. "Conked out. One of my men saw it go down and he got there right away. Pilot put it into a field without hurting it none. My man talked to the pilot. Said he couldn't figure out why the engine had quit. But you know something? His radio wasn't working either. Same thing with the radio in the police car. It wouldn't work. Not until"—Cotron spit out a piece of tobacco—"that damned disc left the area."

"What happened then?"

Cotron shrugged. "Pilot started up the chopper and took off. That's all."

Brady didn't learn much more. Hundreds of people had had a long, clear look at the UFO. Chief Cotron, an experienced observer, insisted it was a disc. Other witnesses insisted just as strongly it had a torpedo shape, or was curved in the form of a scythe. It was the same old eyewitness problem. They'd all seen something, but they had a dozen different descriptions.

But everyone agreed about the strange interference with mechanical equipment. That by itself didn't mean much. It had happened before, hundreds of times. Scientists explained it away as electrical discharges in the air, and there wasn't any reason to become hysterical over phenomena that were perfectly natural. Dead end. Except for the disc in the air.

Even *that* could be explained away. Plasmoids were weird

8

things. They were made up of a mass of ionized gas that formed into a visible shape for a few hours, held together by a self-generated magnetic field. While they lasted they shone brightly—and they took on a disc-shaped appearance. They also produced strong magnetic and electrical fields that screwed up radio and television and electrical systems. The plasmoid—the ionized gas—reflected both light and radar. It could move with tremendous speed. It was *real*. It was also perfectly natural.

Brady mentioned this to Chief Cotron. He wouldn't buy it. He'd seen electrical apparitions before; just about every pilot sees them, sooner or later. And this thing, Cotron said flatly, wasn't "no damned bunch of electricity. That was a solid object, and I don't give a damn what else anybody says about it."

The story would have died right there and then. Except for the combat team that had gone out in the helicopter and had lost all power without any known reason except that it was within a few miles of the strange object lost to sight beyond the hills. Even that, Brady admitted, could have been nothing more than coincidence.

But something was wrong. Two things, really. They irritated Brady, who didn't like loose pieces lying around.

First, the eyewitness reports that the UFO had been observed to *ascend* from behind the hills. Did ionized gas drop down from high altitude, wander about out of sight, and then take off again? Some scientists insisted it was perfectly natural. Okay. Brady would have relegated the story to just what it seemed to be—a good UFO feature with eyewitness reports.

But, second, the Air Force gave him the fast shuffle. Or tried to. They should have left Captain Everett Walker sixty feet below ground. He was a dead giveaway.

Brady didn't know *what* had the Air Force in such a snit that they would order an officer to throw up a wall of denials. Why should they be afraid to admit what they had seen? UFO's were common enough—birds, airplanes, planets, balloons, plasmoids, and a hundred other things in the sky had all been identified as strange and frightening objects. So why the sudden blanket refusal to admit *anything*?

Brady's sixth sense, his long experience as a newsman, jarred him.

Captain Everett Walker was, if not frightened, damned well shaken by something. Officers selected for missile-command duty do not rattle easily. Before they ever get near the red buttons with which they can send a dozen nuclear-tipped ICBM's racing toward the Soviet Union they go through intensive psychological screening. They live in a psychological glass cage. It takes a lot to rattle that cage.

Walker was rattled.

Brady wanted to know *why*.

And he couldn't find out.

CHAPTER II

CLIFF BRADY RIPPED THE PAPER FROM HIS TYPEWRITER AND CRUMpled it angrily. A quarter to four in the goddamned morning and he couldn't sleep. Worse, he couldn't write. At least thirty sheets of paper lay scattered about him in the wide first-class seat of the TWA jetliner.

Before he'd left New York to cover the UFO incident he'd virtually written the story in his mind. This wasn't his first UFO flap, and almost all of them turned out the same way in the end. He'd brought to mind the usual cutting phrases about the nuts and the thrill-seekers who kept seeing all sorts of things in the sky. Every so often they wandered into the press room in New York demanding protection from the government. Sometimes they brought photographs of strange lights and shapes in the sky as proof of a monstrous plot to take over the world. They'd been around for years.

There were the serious ones, of course. Experienced pilots who saw strange objects that appeared to defy all explanation. Sober observers in the air and on the ground who couldn't fathom shapes or lights in the sky. But they didn't leap to conclusions. They remembered that anything seen at night or at long range could *seem* to be anything but what it really was. St. Elmo's fire sometimes turned an airplane into a violent, multicolored fantasy of twisting light. Harmless enough when you knew what it was, but it could scare hell out of you if you didn't know what was happening. And if you were on the ground and looked up to see a plane wreathed in kaleidoscopic electrical violence, well, it was natural for a man to run for the nearest telephone.

But the pattern didn't fit what had happened at Barstow or at the ICBM command post twelve miles away. Before Brady left the area he had checked out a hunch. The military field would have its own source of electrical power for emergencies, the regular cut-in switches that were part of any emergency system. But for normal power, like most fields, they used the same electrical power source that fed the town of Barstow. That was Brady's lead. He visited the central power station. Within ten minutes he knew just how right he was. There had been serious interference with normal power outflow. So serious that the emergency systems at the missile-command center had kicked in and automatically set off the war-alert alarm.

That wasn't all. The communications center of the Minuteman command complex had almost been knocked out of touch with its remote command posts. Radio transmitters and receivers sixty feet below ground had thrown out so much static that for several minutes they were useless. The main power station in Barstow had automatic recorders that told Brady the exact times electrical current interference took place and just when the missile-command center radios started acting up. From that point on, the rest was checking out other figures. The results had Brady convinced he was on the brink of a story all out of proportion to the run-of-the-mill UFO flap.

No wonder that captain had been on edge! He'd been sixty feet down, shielded by steel and concrete, and all his critical communications had gone haywire. Cause? A strange unknown object in the sky, apparently.

12

Apparently. Brady warned himself not to jump to hasty conclusions. But why had Captain Walker played the role he'd presented to Brady? And what had happened to the combat team in the helicopter? Had they seen anything? Why should the Air Force be so hot and bothered over a UFO—which they claimed they had never seen in the first place?

The more he thought about it, the angrier he became. At the moment he didn't have his story. Nothing would fall into place so that he could turn in the copy that World Press expected later that day. At six hundred miles an hour, New York was coming up too damn fast.

He glared at the almost empty drink in his hand. It was time to stop chasing the shadows skipping just beyond his reach. He needed perspective. Shit, he needed another drink. He buzzed for the stewardess.

Ann Dallas looked up at the glowing light on the "alert" board and smiled. That would be Brady again, wanting another martini. He'd put away four already, double the quota she was permitted to serve. Even as she thought about not serving another drink, she twisted the cap loose from the small bottle to pour the martini over the ice. She dropped in two olives. With only two other passengers in the forward section, and both of them asleep, it really didn't matter.

She wondered about Brady. She knew of him through his column. Most of the crews did. Brady's byline was one of the few that promised accuracy in writing about the airlines. The pilots couldn't fault Brady when the newsman twisted their noses just a bit—not when Brady himself was a veteran at the controls.

She wondered about the man, and wondered equally at the fascination he held for her. She was twenty-six and knew from reading about Brady that he was about forty or forty-two, enough of a difference for her to dwell briefly on the matter before she dismissed it. He certainly wasn't physically attractive. For one thing he was too short. He made up for his lack of height with a body that might have been assembled from a tree trunk. He had thick sloping shoulders and powerful arms. You watched Brady walk and you expected the man to go charging right through a wall rather than to follow an aisle.

She'd felt an electric shock when he boarded the airplane. No smile. He was very clearly *not* in a smiling mood when he stomped his way up the ramp into the cabin. He stopped in the doorway and she stared into startling, clear black eyes. For a moment he didn't say a word, and in that instant she studied him. Not the casual appraising glance with which she judged boarding passengers. She was studying, evaluating. Not for TWA. For herself. His eyes held her fast. His face was a guide to years of violent battering. Somewhere in his past Mr. Brady had taken a right to the nose that left a thin white scar running from the bridge down across the side of his nose almost to his cheek. His chin and one side of his forehead showed the knotty bumps of scar tissue. She was startled to notice his lips, not quite full, strangely sensuous to her against that battered face.

His voice came straight, deep, and demanding. "Who are you?"

Experience came to her aid. "Miss Dallas, sir. Welcome aboard. May I help you with—"

"No. You can't help me with my things. I'm in first class. I have work to do." No nonsense with him. "Soon as Captain Marvel or whoever it is up front gets this thing in the air, bring me a martini."

He started past her before she could issue another automatic, if not shocked, "Yes, sir." Then he stopped and turned. "Miss Dallas . . . Make that a double." She nodded, afraid to say a word. His face split in a wide grin. "You're a beautiful thing, just in case no one ever told you."

And he was gone to his seat. Before she had collected her thoughts she heard the typewriter clattering.

14

The fierce intensity Ann Dallas noticed in her first meeting with Cliff Brady was a characteristic that marked him well throughout his profession. To his peers and those who wished to emulate him Brady was intense, confident, knowledgeable and possessed of brawling cynicism. He was also one hell of a good writer. Brady's physical appearance and belligerent demeanor masked an incisive mind. He didn't simply report his subjects; he *knew* whereof he wrote. It gave him a powerful calling card in the industry, and his rapier slashing of individuals and agencies made his column "essential reading" to millions of people daily.

As a war correspondent early in his career, Brady had carved a mild fame for his in-depth reporting from the thick of battle in Indo-China, and had become known as the most heavily armed noncombatant in any war. He had sworn never to be taken alive by Communist troops. From the debacle of Indo-China Brady had followed a natural evolution to covering military hot spots as they erupted around the world. He had reported on the testing of atomic and hydrogen bombs, missile and space shots, and become an expert on new developments in science, war, aviation and space.

Brady's marriage never really had a chance. News came first and his wife a poor second. Perhaps if Greta had known the art of "staying loose" rather than fighting for her own conception of wedded bliss, it might have worked. Perhaps not. Too quickly Brady discovered he didn't care. After their divorce something of Greta remained with him, but he knew he never really missed her; in the long run she just wasn't his cup of tea.

As a professional newsman Brady strove for perfection and accepted nothing less than the attempt to reach that state. Thus his growing irritation with the UFO incident at Barstow. He could easily have put together a story wholly acceptable to the wire service. He could make light of the affair and apply the screws to the Air Force for its inexplicable censorship. Safety lay in that direction.

15

But there was a story, significant and meaningful, behind what had happened at Barstow. The elusive nature of that story rankled every professional fiber in his system. And there was more. Deception, deliberate misinformation, and fear. The wrong people were afraid. Men in charge of nuclear-packed missiles aren't those you expect to . . .

Where the hell was that drink?

He really hadn't looked at her before. Now he stared. She sat on the armrest of the aisle seat, the overhead light a halo glow through the edges of her hair—raven hair . . . And full lips, a delightful, friendly smile . . . Without speaking, he reached out slowly for the drink.

Brady saw that her nose was perfect. Why the hell her nose meant so much eluded him, but it was perfect for her dark eyes and delicate brows. He looked and admired. He had remembered Ann Dallas when he climbed the boarding steps. He judged the legs of stewardesses with epicurean zeal. Hers made him want to snort and paw the ground. She was also as well proportioned as any female he had ever known. The curving lines of her bust, her waist, her hips and legs . . . everything was just right. "Thank God," he murmured to himself, "she isn't too stacked." Proportion was everything in a woman.

The stewardess gestured to the paper strewn about the seat. "You seem to need this." She smiled, looking again at the glass she was offering. "Trouble finding the right words?"

His fingers closed around hers for several seconds before he accepted the drink.

"Uh-huh." He mumbled his acknowledgment with the glass to his lips, drank deeply, and sighed. "Jesus, that's good."

She smiled again. "I've heard my father say the same thing when he was fighting a story."

Brady glanced up.

"Westerns," she anticipated the question. "Brawling, horsey

16

Westerns of the old school. Dad always believed in martinis and typewriters."

Brady raised the glass in a toast. "Smart man." He searched his memory. "Dallas, Dallas. Hmm." He looked up at her. "*Sam Dallas?*"

She was delighted with his recognition. "One and the same," she said.

"Hell, I know him. He's one of the best."

"I always thought so," she said. He liked that. She was proud of her old man and didn't hide it.

"I read him for years," Brady continued. "Sam Dallas . . . sure, he believed that cowboys and horses went together and women in the West should be kept for occasional thumping, cooking, and doing the laundry. Right?"

"You're very good, you know." She shifted the conversation to him without pause.

He raised his brows in surprise. "I didn't know that girls read my column," he said. "No sex, no scandal. Hardly interesting to a beautiful young thing like you."

"You're interesting," she persisted. "That's the second time to-night you've called me a beautiful young thing. Thank you."

"It's true."

She nodded. "I know."

The frankness of her words caught him off balance. She said it with quiet pride in herself, not ego. He couldn't believe it. He didn't think there were such women. His interest in her grew swiftly.

She glanced at his typewriter. "Problems?"

He closed the case on the machine and dropped it heavily to the floor by his feet.

"All writers have problems," he snorted. "Ask your old man."

"I don't need to. Remember, I made his martinis." She laughed quietly. "The more problems, the more martinis. What's your problem, Mr. Writer?"

He sighed and mumbled a curse. "It's a will-o'-the-wisp."

"A what?"

He glanced up. "You could also call it a UFO." In the dim light of the cabin he would have missed it. But the reading light was still on. The moment he said UFO she stiffened. He couldn't have been mistaken.

"You act as if I said something dirty."

She moved her hand in a sign of agitation. "UFO," she said. "In this business that's a dirty word."

He waited for her to continue but she kept silent. "Going to tell me why?" he asked finally.

This time the smile was guarded. "You're putting me on," she said softly. "You know what the papers have done to pilots who've reported seeing UFO's."

He nodded.

"Everything but castration," she continued with a flash of temper. "The way those stories are printed, you'd think the people flying airliners were all crazy." She looked about the cabin to confirm the other passengers were still asleep, and asked Brady for a cigarette. He held a match for her and she inhaled deeply. "As far as the crews are concerned, when it comes to talking about UFO's, newsmen are lower than dirt." She held his gaze.

He grinned. "Including me?"

She was still on the defensive.

"That depends, I suppose, on how you treat the report of a competent and serious man. That's for starters."

Brady shrugged. "You read my column. Apologies don't go along with it."

She nodded. *"Touché."*

"Think nothing of it." He grinned again. "Anyway, according to some people, I'm the one who's going off the deep end."

"Did you see—"

"Uh-uh," he said quickly. "Nothing *I* saw. But a few hundred people, including some very solid citizens, saw something. They saw it clearly, they know what they're talking about. Some other people, however . . ." He let his words trail off. "You really interested? Seriously, I mean?"

"I am." She stubbed out her cigarette. "Tell me about it, please."

He told her what had happened. As much as he was enjoying talking with her, being with her, he was also interested in her reaction. By the time he'd related the events of the past few days, the SEAT BELT sign was on.

"We're starting down for JFK," she said.

"Wait a moment." He held her wrist. "I don't want this to just break off and . . ." He finished his meaning without words. She nodded. "I couldn't sleep now," he added quickly. "Not with this" —he tapped the typewriter—"bugging me. Besides, I don't want you to disappear. How about a dinner-breakfast or whatever they call it at this ungodly hour? I know a great all-night restaurant in the city. Chef's a great friend, make you anything you like. Date?"

"Date." She smiled.

"Where do I pick you up?"

"You know the Lexington Hotel?"

"Uh-huh."

"I have work to finish after we land," she explained. "I'll go into town with the rest of the crew. Six o'clock? In the lobby?"

"Great."

"See you there."

He was surprised with himself. He was eager for six o'clock to roll around.

Breakfast was more than he had bargained for. At six o'clock sharp he walked into the hotel lobby, where he found Ann with another stewardess and a man wearing the three stripes of a co-pilot on his sleeve. Ann introduced Keith Johnson, the copilot of the jetliner in which Brady had flown. Brady looked at Johnson carefully.

19

"Chaperon?"

The others laughed. "No, not really," Ann explained quickly. "Those two are engaged, and you and I are keeping them out of bed." The other girl showed pink on her cheeks and smiled at Brady. He liked these people; they were crisp and clean-cut and honest. "But Keith wanted to meet you," Ann was saying.

"That's right, Mr. Brady. I've been a fan of yours for a long time. I wanted to see if there really could be a newsman who didn't have horns," Johnson said with a smile.

Brady pawed at his forehead. "Not yet, anyway."

Keith then became serious. "Ann mentioned you were on a UFO story."

Brady nodded and waited to see the point of Keith's seriousness.

"It would mean something to a lot of us if a writer . . . I mean, a writer with your background and scientific knowledge—you're an airplane driver, aren't you?—well, someone with *your* qualifications . . . we'd like to see your reactions to what we've got to say. That is, if we can agree ahead of time on . . ."

"Ann's told me about your problem," Brady said. "I don't blame you."

"No names?" Johnson queried.

"No names," he promised as they shook hands.

The copilot took a deep breath. "Okay, Mr. Brady. Let's go to breakfast."

An hour later Brady said good-bye to the others and walked Ann to her hotel room. He hesitated at the door.

"I'm leaving for three or four days, but dinner's open tonight."

"It's a date. I'll call you later and let you know what time." She kissed him lightly on the cheek.

He hesitated. "Ann, I want to ask you something. . . . What Johnson said, during breakfast, I mean. Is all that for real?"

"It's for real, Cliff. He was very serious. So are the others."

He rubbed his chin. "If what they say is true . . ." He realized his words could be taken two ways. "I don't mean their honesty or integrity," he added quickly. "It's a matter of interpretation, I suppose. But if what they've seen is what it seems to be, and there are more cases like Barstow—" Abruptly he cut short his own thoughts, self-conscious for keeping her in the hall. "I'm too tired for all that right now, anyway."

"Do you want them to join us for dinner?" she asked.

"The hell I do," he said with mock anger. "Tonight's for me and thee. Strictly. Music and flowers and all that."

She kissed him again.

Brady went to his apartment to wrestle with his typewriter.

CHAPTER III

MILT PARRISH SUCKED NOISILY AT HIS PIPE. HE WITHHELD IT FROM his mouth and tapped the stem against the story on his desk.

"You're putting me on, Cliff," he said, glancing at the typewritten pages. "At least—I *hope* you're putting me on."

Brady's response was tense. "That story is straight."

"But everyone knows this UFO stuff is bullshit!" Parrish snorted.

"Who the hell is 'everyone,' goddamn it!" Brady shouted. "You? The guy in the next block? Your sainted aunt? Where are all your experts coming from? What the hell do they know about this stuff?" Brady jammed his cigarette in the ashtray, scattering ashes across the editor's desk. "I don't get you, Milt. You never tried to second-guess me on a story before."

"You never gave me drivel before," Parrish retorted.

Brady came slowly to his feet. His voice dropped to an angry growl. "Drivel? You're sitting here on your fat ass. I was there and suddenly you're an expert—"

"Now hold on!" Parrish cut in. "You know I'm responsible for what passes this desk. It's got to carry my personal okay, and that means I'm supporting what the story says. Not this time, Cliff."

Brady returned to his chair and studied his editor. "You canning the story?" It was a challenge, and Parrish knew it.

"I didn't say that." He frowned, hesitating on Brady's demand for a decision.

Brady rolled his eyes. "Then what's this all about?"

Parrish picked up the story and thumbed through the pages. He was friendly and concerned. "Cliff, according to this, the Air Force people you talked to are liars who are—"

"Goddamn right they are," Brady snapped.

"Who are," Parrish continued, "deliberately concealing information from the public about a UFO, or a disc, or whatever it is—"

"That's what the story says," Brady threw at him.

"Will you shut up and let me finish? You're saying that not only are UFO's real but that they're threatening our missile bases and—"

Brady couldn't remain quiet. "That is *not* what I said!" he shouted. "I've given you a report on what happened at Barstow. I didn't say UFO's, plural. I said a disc. *One*, singular, disc. Not strange things buzzing around in the air. A disc. With eyewitnesses, with—oh, hell, it's all there and you're interpreting it the way you see fit."

Parrish's eyes gleamed. "That's right," he said softly. "That's the way I interpreted it. How do you think everyone else is going to see it? The same way I did."

"Then you've got a streak of stupidity I never saw in you before," Brady retorted, still unmoved.

Parrish dropped the story back on his desk and spent several moments stacking the pages neatly. "All right." He sighed. "Let me ask you some questions."

Brady gave him an unintelligible grumble in reply.

"You quoted the eyewitnesses. Right?"

"You know how to read," Brady said ungraciously.

"Never mind the wisecracks. You quoted eyewitnesses, but

23

the Air Force will not admit to seeing anything. That's true, isn't it?"

"I *told* you what happened with—"

"Stay with me, damn you," Parrish broke in. "Isn't that true? I'm talking about what we're going to put on the wires."

"Yeah."

"Okay. So as far as the Air Force is concerned, the people in Barstow saw what thousands of other people all over the country have seen. Strange lights or shapes in the sky. Right?"

Brady's eyes narrowed. "Go on."

"All right. There isn't any way for you to disprove what the Air Force says. It's your word against theirs."

"What's that got to do with—"

"It's your word against theirs," Parrish hammered at him, "and you weren't there. You got there when it was all over. Anything you've got to go against the Air Force is so much hearsay."

"You're twisting the facts and you know it, Milt."

Parrish slammed his hand against his desk. "You're damned right I am! And so will everyone else who reads this copy." He took a deep breath. "Now let me ask you something else." Brady didn't comment and Parrish went on.

"Were the missile sites damaged in any way?"

"I told you about the readings at the power station. It's right there—"

"Please. Answer the question. Do you know, do you have any *proof*, that the missile sites were damaged? Do you have anything else except some squiggles from a civilian power station?"

"No."

"So. There's no *proof*—nothing to show that the missile sites were damaged. If you can't show that, if all you've got are those squiggles and a power-station engineer with a vivid imagination, *why* should the Air Force lie to you or anyone else?"

"That's what I would damn well like to know."

Parrish sighed with relief. "But you *don't* know, do you?" He

24

held up his hand to forestall a reply. "Hold it, Cliff. That's my whole point. Your story is based on inference. You're drawing conclusions without meat to them." He tapped the story with his fingers. "It won't hold up. More than that, it's not like you to turn in something you can't back up. And you *can't* support what you say in here."

Brady dug in his shirt pocket for his cigarettes. Jesus Christ. What the hell was he supposed to do? Out there at Barstow it was clear as ice. No mistakes. It came up and belted you right in the face. But the way Parrish threw the story back at him . . . Of course he couldn't *prove* . . .

"We're right back where we were before," Brady said. "I'll ask you again. You canning the story?"

Parrish shook his head. "No, I'm not. There's nothing wrong with the story. It's the conclusions that bother me." He looked directly at Brady. "I want you to run this through the typewriter again. You don't need to change much. Write it as it was, as it is. Tell what happened. Let it wind up as a mystery. Just don't end it with a warning that the Martians are invading us."

Brady thought back to his conversation with Keith Johnson. He recalled what the veteran airlines pilot had said about the discs he and his pilot had seen, on at least three occasions. Clear sightings. Unmistakable. Not a doubt in their minds. And when they tried to explain it to someone else, it was all a big joke. Very funny. Now he knew how they felt.

He climbed heavily to his feet and picked up the story. "All right, Milt. I'll do it the way you want. I *know* I'm right, but apparently that's not enough."

"It is for me, but not for the wires." Parrish felt grateful the session was over. A lopsided grin appeared on his face. "You pissed at me?"

"Go screw yourself."

"How about a drink when you're through?"

"You buying?"

25

"We'll toss for it."

Silence.

Parrish sighed. "Okay. I'm buying."

The cab pulled up before the hotel and Brady saw Ann waiting for him. "Hold it here a moment," he told the driver. He climbed out and helped Ann into the cab and leaned forward. "Make it Sixty-Seventh and Third," he said.

Ann leaned over to kiss Brady lightly on the lips. "Hi, there," she said. It came out light and with a musical sound to her voice and Brady felt better than he had all day. He held her hand tightly and sighed.

"Oh, my. Bad day at the office?"

"Yeah," he grunted. "Did the Barstow piece over again to please an editor who thinks UFO's show up only on mornings after. And then—oh shit, it's not worth recapping." He waved his hand to dismiss what had happened as unimportant.

Ann laughed. "Welcome to the crowd," she said. "Now you know what it's like. I saw one of your mysterious visitors one night, you know."

"Oh? You didn't tell me."

"Keith told you about it. The time we were flying through high clouds. You know, those cumulus buildups at night. Bright moon and it's all so lovely, like flying in the midst of clouds made of marble." He nodded; he knew the sights and the sensations. "Remember? He told you that something—no lights, just reflecting the moon like polished silver . . . when it came around, *not* through, but around, a cloud?"

"Sure," he said. "Took up formation with you."

"The pilots called us in the back and told us to look. Wanted proof that they weren't drunk or something like that. We had plenty of witnesses. Half the passengers were glued to the windows. 'It' stayed with us for several minutes."

"You see anything the pilots didn't?"

She shook her head. Brady didn't reply and Ann studied the passing crowds. The streets were filled on the warm summer evening.

The cab pulled to the corner of Sixty-Seventh and Third. Ann looked out and exclaimed. "Oh, Oscar's! I've heard about this place—"

"Out, out," he broke in. "Let us rather have at it."

Ann looked up at the sign. "Salt of the Sea," she read aloud. "Is Oscar real, or is it just a name?"

Brady opened the door for her. "It's real—I mean, *he's* real, all right. I used to eat here when this place was only a seafood bar. Now look at the damned thing."

Ann looked with dismay at the people crowding together behind a rope barrier, waiting for tables. "Oh, Cliff, it'll take us hours."

He ignored her, waving vigorously to someone beyond the crowd. A heavy-set man in dark slacks and an open black shirt pushed through to them. Before Ann could collect her senses, Oscar had them seated. He waved off a waitress approaching with menus. Their host cracked Brady smartly on the back and was off again toward the impatient crowd waiting to be seated.

"Is it always crowded like this?" she exclaimed.

"Always."

"The food must be marvelous."

"Better than that," he said. "No one does lobster like you get it here."

"But you didn't ask me if I like lobster."

"You do, don't you?"

"Yes, but—"

"So what's the bitch?"

"Cliff, you're impossible. Aren't you going to ask me if I want a drink?"

"Nope."

"Are you always this uncooperative?"

27

"Sure," he said.

She studied him carefully. She wasn't accustomed to someone like him. It tugged at her vanity, but at the same time Brady was accepting her as a woman who didn't need the standard routine of boy-meets-girl. That pleased her.

Oscar reappeared and vanished as quickly. Brady was pouring wine into a glass that seemed mysteriously to have leaped into existence on the table. She held up the wine and studied the gold liquid in the light.

"What is it, Cliff?"

"Taste. Don't talk." He filled his glass and brought it against hers.

"I've never had anything like it," she marveled. "Going to tell me what—"

He didn't let her finish. "To be honest, I don't know. It's private stock, and Oscar never tells. I don't know a damn thing about wines or vintages or what's a good year or anything else, Ann. All I know is what I like, and Oscar keeps his private stock close to the vest. Except," he said, smiling, "when I show up with a beautiful girl."

She drank to that.

Dinner, he told her while he slowly tore his lobster to small pieces of claw and shell, was celebrating a small victory.

"Did you shoot your editor, Mr. What's-his-name?"

"Parrish."

"Well, did you?"

"Milt's all right, and no, I didn't shoot him."

"All right?" She shook her head. "That's not the impression you've given me. A while ago you sounded as if you'd like to boil him in oil. Slowly."

"Not really. Milt backed me against the wall. But he's fair. He put me on the spot and told me to prove what I'd written." Brady shrugged. "The long and short of it is I couldn't prove—and the emphasis is on the word *proof*—anything."

She slammed a lobster claw to her dish. "Cliff, you're the most exasperating man I've ever known. What are we supposed to be celebrating?"

He looked smug. "I did some backing against the wall myself," he replied. "Had a couple of drinks and a long talk with Parrish after I did the rewrite. I got the okay to do an in-depth series on UFO's."

"That's marvelous," she said. "How did you manage it?"

"I told you Parrish was a square shooter. Although," he hastened to add, "he's not exactly doing handsprings about the idea. He thinks this whole thing with UFO's is really way out. Kooksville and all that."

"He hasn't flown in formation with one of them," Ann said grimly.

"Of course not," Brady agreed. "That's the trouble. You go along for years laughing and pointing the finger at the people who insist something screwy's going on in the skies. Then one day a UFO comes along and kicks you in the slats and *whap!* just like that you're a believer."

"And everyone else then thinks *you're* a nut," she added.

"Uh-huh. Right now Parrish is, like I said, against the idea."

"Then how did you—"

"News," he said brusquely. "No matter what else it is, a good UFO story is news. Get enough people seeing swamp gas under their beds or chasing them down country roads, and you've got news. Parrish is a newsman first and an editor second. He can smell the stories. I made a deal with him."

"Go on."

"Well," Brady shrugged, "I backed off today. I don't do that very often, and Milt appreciates that fact. I met him halfway. It was up to him to do the same. He had me down to cover a meet-

29

ing of atomic scientists in England, but I got him to assign some-one else to that. He knows this Barstow thing's got me bugged. Which it certainly has." He emptied the remains of the wine bottle in his glass and toyed with the stem.

"I'm in something of a quandary," he said, suddenly moody. "I know how I feel about the Barstow story, but I can't pin it down. It's the sort of thing you know absolutely, but if you were to tell your case from a witness stand in a courtroom, you'd sound like an idiot."

"Is that how you feel, Cliff?"

"Yes and no," he said candidly. "Every instinct I have as a newsman is screaming I'm right. I also know the first rule in this business, Ann, and that's to get your facts straight. *Facts*. Of which I have distressingly little. Sure, I *know*. Maybe, that is. I know what Keith Johnson told me and what he's said about other pilots. But even Keith on a witness stand would have his story torn to shreds."

He drained his glass and placed both hands flat on the table. "That's what's so maddening about all this," he said, his face serious. "You're fighting shadows. Are millions of people off their bird? Because millions of people have seen things. I don't know. I don't believe in mass hallucination, but I've seen what suggestion can do. People will believe anything—and swear on a stack of Bibles they really saw an object when in fact they saw nothing more than a reflection of light or something of that sort. The trouble is these people are telling the truth—as they believe the truth to be. But there's a long way to go between what someone believes and what's really so." He looked at her and grimaced. "It's a can of worms, Ann."

Then a thought hit him. He came upright in his chair. "Ann, you said you'd be gone for a few days, didn't you?"

"Yes."

"All right, I'm starting this series—starting my interviews and research, I mean—tomorrow. I'm taking the company plane out to Ohio to get the ball rolling. Could you do something for me?"

"Of course. If I can," she amended.

"Would you start collecting the details of these airline incidents? You can get the stories. You know the stewardesses; I know how you share these things with each other. You can get for me what I as a reporter can't. Dates, names, places, just what happened, the . . ." His voice trailed off as he noticed the hard lines that had suddenly appeared on her face.

"What the hell's the matter?" he said. "Did I say a dirty word or something?"

"Names, Cliff?" She let the sentence hang.

"Of course I want names! I've got to document . . ." His expression showed realization for her sudden withdrawal. "Oh. I get it. *Names.*"

"That's right," she said.

He shook his head and gesticulated with a hand. "No sweat, beautiful. Same conditions I gave your boy Johnson."

"You don't know how these people have been smeared," she said, still protesting.

He didn't answer her right away. The intensity vanished as if he'd pulled a plug within his brain. He looked at her as if she were a stranger, and shrugged. "Forget it," he said slowly. "It didn't occur to me that my word isn't enough."

Her eyes flashed with anger. "You owe me an apology for that, Cliff. Of all the— Aren't you forgetting a few details, like Keith Johnson, and what I've already told you?"

"It's an old cliché," he said with a grin, "but you're even more beautiful when you get mad."

Her eyes stayed level with his. "Go to hell."

He stood and bowed slightly, mocking her. "Apologies are in order and are hereby extended to the beautiful young lady who is pissed off at me," he said loudly.

31

"Cliff! People are looking at us. Please!"

"Why shouldn't they? We're both beautiful. Oscar!" Heads turned.

"Cliff!"

"Apology accepted?"

"My God, yes, *yes!*"

Oscar stood by the table.

"The lady," Brady said with a deep bow, "would like to buy us a drink."

CHAPTER IV

"How do you want it, Mr. Brady? We can run you through this whole thing from any angle you like. We can start off with the reports we've discarded—sun dogs, airplanes, comets, meteors, stars and planets, birds, ice-crystal clouds, balloons, satellites, plasmoids and corona discharges, cloud reflections of searchlights, cloud formations, flares, fireworks, noctilucent clouds, contrails, rockets, skydivers: you name it, we've got it." Lt. Col. Jim Trapnell, USAF, director for Project Blue Book, swung his feet to his desk top and grinned at Cliff Brady.

Brady was at Wright-Patterson Air Force Base near Dayton, Ohio, headquarters for Project Blue Book, the Air Force investigation of UFO phenomena that extended back to the late summer of 1947. Brady had been assured before his departure from New York, the assurance stemming directly from the highest Pentagon levels, that the staff of Blue Book would open all their files for his perusal, and would, as well, respond to whatever questions he brought to them. But his experience at Barstow made him wary of Air Force brass.

He didn't return Trapnell's grin. "What else?"

"Hallucinations, delusions, illusions, hoaxes, pranks," the colonel rattled out quickly, ticking off each item one by one on his fingers. "Deliberate acts, misconceptions, autosuggestion, hypnotism—the whole ball of wax that has nothing to do with really seeing anything in the air. You can exclude from this the effects of mirages, inversion layers, refraction, reflection, and other similar effects."

Brady whistled. "You sound as if you've lived with this for a long time," he said at last. "Maybe I'd better find out right away if you've got any bona fide sightings."

The colonel waved a hand airily. "Oh, sure," he said easily. "Thousands of 'em." He gestured to an adjacent room filled from one end to the other with filing cabinets. "The master file, in there," he went on. "We break down reports into categories that enable us to dismiss many of them quickly. Saves time, and all that. After you've worked on this sort of thing as long as we have, you can do a run-through faster than you might think. At least ninety percent of everything we receive here gets into the 'immediately identified' files. That's the first group I gave you. Airplanes to balloons, planets to plasmoids. The lot. All quite ordinary, except"—he chuckled—"to the inexperienced onlooker. *He* can see anything."

Brady chewed his lip. He hadn't expected this breezy attitude to UFO investigations by the Air Force. Then he realized he didn't truly know what to expect. He'd heard the Air Force's Project Blue Book was a sinister plot kept under security cloaks so as to carry out a monstrous deception against the public. He'd heard, almost within the same breath, that the whole thing was a front, that the Pentagon assigned harebrained administrative clerks as a sop to public demands for UFO studies, and no one really gave a damn. Neither of the two extremes proved valid. What Brady found had him still off balance.

Lt. Col. James R. Trapnell, for example. A clean-cut, intelligent and alert officer who, by the ribbons on his chest, had managed to get in some violent, and successful, air combat. With his

34

own Korean air-combat experience behind him, Brady could recognize a pro when he ran into one. Trapnell was a pro. He was also, from what Brady had learned of him, a man with several degrees in engineering and science. If anyone were qualified to act as chief honcho for the Air Force's UFO shop, Trapnell was the right man. And that threw Brady. With all those attributes to his credit, Trapnell was unexpectedly open, calm, and quite objective about his job. Not very many people were paid the salary of a lieutenant colonel to look after errant UFO's.

"What about the unidentified files, Colonel?" Brady still didn't know how he was going to hack this thing.

"More than enough of those." Trapnell was all courtesy and cooperation. Brady pushed it.

"Are they . . . will they be open for my inspection?"

"Of course," Trapnell agreed quickly. "I know quite a bit about you, Mr. Brady, and I assure you complete cooperation is the order of the day."

That was overdoing it. "The Pentagon," Brady said, more in statement than in question. "They told me—"

"Forgive me," Trapnell interrupted. "Of course we've got the TWX from the funny farm. I wasn't referring to that."

Brady waited.

"You don't know my voice, Brady," Trapnell said. Brady didn't miss it. The colonel had dropped the "Mr."

"But I know yours," Trapnell went on. "Quite well, in fact." He laughed.

"Have we met?"

"Not face to face," Trapnell said. "I flew support missions in Korea. Thunderthuds." Brady grinned at the pilot slang for the old F-84 fighter-bomber. "And if I remember correctly, your call sign was 'Dingbat Seven-Two,' wasn't it?"

Brady stared. "I'll be damned."

"You flew one of those air-control jobbies," Trapnell continued. "We used to watch you going in." He shook his head in open

35

admiration. "It was bad enough getting down there in one of the iron birds. But in something with fabric on it; Jesus . . ."

No question about it, Brady knew. He *would* see everything the Air Force had on UFO's.

Project Blue Book occupied office space in the Air Force System Command's Foreign Technology Division. Instead of being shunted to some remote office as a sop to public outcries for official UFO investigations, as part of the Foreign Technology Division Blue Book had available the highest level of engineering and scientific intelligence. Rather than having to forage for themselves, Blue Book investigators could call upon the best scientific and engineering talent in the country. It was a priority effort with quality. Brady hadn't expected that. Trapnell convinced him, through the first minutes of their meeting, that the people assigned to Blue Book were of excellent qualifications. But that the UFO investigating staff had access to so much professional talent was new to him. It also confirmed his decision to utilize the results of more than twenty years of professional investigation. Brady never could have gained access to sightings from around the world, attended with the results of investigations, and specifically how those studies were carried out. Trapnell assured him he would also be given access to whatever the Air Force had available in the way of photographs and films.

Brady received Trapnell's words with growing hope he could dig through the morass of material to produce concrete results. But there was another bridge to cross.

"How much of your material is classified?" he asked Trapnell.

"You mean UFO's? None," the colonel replied. "However, certain files are classified, but that's got nothing to do with UFO reports." Trapnell noted the disbelieving look on Brady's face. "I know," he added quickly, "that sounds like a convenient cover-up. It isn't, believe me. The classification has to do with military equipment or facilities, and—"

"That's going to leave me with a couple of blank spaces," Brady said. He didn't like this part of it. Under the blanket of security you could hide anything, no matter how open he would find everything else.

"We anticipated that," Trapnell said. "Your name, as you know, carries weight in the Pentagon. Your record, plus the fact that you had top-secret clearance when you were in uniform, allowed us to do something that doesn't happen very often. Under the restriction—we'll have you sign some papers for this—under the restriction that you agree not to print material that's obviously classified, we can give you access to everything we've got."

"That can be a two-edged sword," Brady muttered.

Trapnell nodded. "Of course it can. We're not trying to lock you inside any—"

"Look," Brady broke in. "I appreciate the confidence. I mean that. But signing papers is out. I can't do that, Colonel. *You* are cooperative. Maloney in the Pentagon is cooperative. You may not be here next month and Maloney can get hit by a truck. That leaves a piece of paper with my signature on it. If someone then questions what I write, you've got me over a barrel. I don't mean you personally. Hell, man, you know the score. Signing papers on a subject this broad is idiotic. I'm sorry, because you're obviously trying to help. But I won't sign any documents."

Trapnell digested what Brady had said. Abruptly he leaned forward and made some notes on a pad. "All right," he said. "I see your point." He looked up at Brady. "I can't authorize your getting into our classified files on my own. You say you know General Maloney well?"

"Real well. We flew a couple of missions together in Korea."

"I'll put a call in to the general this afternoon and see what we can do. If Maloney's found your word good enough before, I can't see any reason why he'd change now."

Brady nodded. "That's fine." He looked around the office. "How's the coffee supply in this scientific nuthouse of yours?"

"Strong enough to curl your toes."

"I might need it," Brady said.

"You will." Trapnell laughed.

The first order of business, Brady learned, was to separate the wheat from the chaff. With the full-time help of Jim Trapnell, he went through the "obvious" rejections of UFO reports. "Obvious," in this instance, meant actual objects sighted in the sky that *seemed* to be anything but aircraft or balloons, but at the same time definitely were not unexplainable, no matter how bizarre. High-altitude balloons were one of the better examples. Balloons made of highly reflective material were sent to heights of more than 130,000 feet. During certain periods of the day, especially at dusk, when the sun's rays struck the balloon at a low angle, the balloon became a tremendous disc hurtling through the stratosphere. It picked up winds as great as 400 miles an hour. Put a few clouds between the observer and the balloon and the speed relative to the eye became several thousand miles an hour. Sometimes the balloon left in its wake a swirl of ice crystals and dust, and these, also caught by the sun, became the blazing exhaust of a great disc that just *had* to be a huge machine in the upper heavens—when it wasn't anything of the sort. Sometimes research balloons went out in clusters and accounted for reports of discs in formation.

There were other times when the balloons were responsible for reports of great disc craft hurtling with tremendous speed through the upper air and making right-angle turns at thousands of miles an hour. Temperature inversions in the air, Trapnell explained, gave the optical effect. To the naked eye, to a motion-picture camera, the disc *was* moving with tremendous speed and *did* make right-angle turns. Inversions, layers of air of different temperatures, distorted, bent, twisted, and otherwise affected light rays so as to create what could properly be termed a mirage.

The same inversion effects in the air, Trapnell went on, caused thousands of reports of every type of UFO. Venus setting near the horizon could change color rapidly, expand swiftly in size so that it seemed to be hurtling through the air, and became so bright it appeared to the eye as a dazzling searchlight.

"That's something that throws me," Brady said. "I've seen the planets plenty of times from the ground and when I've been flying. I just do *not* understand how you can take a planet for something whizzing through the air."

Trapnell listened with signs of growing amusement. "Brady, I felt the same way before I got in this business," he said. "Now I believe *anything* can happen in terms of what people see. You know that Venus is so bright, sometimes you can see it in broad daylight?"

"I've heard about that, but I've never been able to see it, and I've looked."

"Well, take my word for it. Sometimes Venus even throws a shadow after dark."

"I didn't know *that*."

"It's true. You get a combination of inversion layers, haze and mist, smoke, or whatever, and you've got a bona fide UFO on your hands. Especially where there's flat country, such as Florida, where Venus has been responsible for God knows how many UFO reports. Something else, too," Trapnell said as a thought came to him. "If someone stares for any length of time at Venus, or Jupiter, for that matter, and he doesn't have a balancing point of reference, *then* things get even wilder."

"You mean problems with the eyes?"

"Uh-huh. Most pilots know the dangers of staring without depth-perception reference. Other people don't. But when they don't have a balancing point of reference and they stare, you know what happens?"

Brady did. "Sure," he said. "You've got something wandering all around the sky."

39

"That's right. And it expands so swiftly because of inversion layers that it seems to be rushing back and forth and doing right-angle turns and all sorts of fancy maneuvers. All the time you're looking at plain old Venus."

Brady made some notes. "You mentioned mirages before. I know something about them, of course. How often do you figure mirages figure in your reports?"

Trapnell clasped his hands behind his head and leaned back in his chair. "More than is indicated in the files," he said finally. "That's because most people don't understand what makes up a mirage. They think it's got to be water in the desert or the effect of water on a straight road during the summer when it's hot. The fact of the matter is a mirage can happen just about anywhere."

Brady frowned. "That sort of screws up what you're trying to do, doesn't it?"

"Man, is that ever the truth," Trapnell said with a vigorous nod of his head. "Mirages, inversion layers, refraction, reflection, something we call reflectional dispersion—it's all there in one big grab bag. The problem is, the observer doesn't know what's in the air. Haze, ice crystals, industrial smoke particles, clouds, water droplets, sand, dust, all of them stirred up by the wind, all of them layered in different temperature strata—Jesus, Brady, it's a wonder we don't get more UFO reports from these effects. What you've got to understand is that all these things, the list I just gave you, form atmospheric lenses. *Lenses*," he repeated with emphasis, "just as much as if you've rigged a system of lenses and mirrors in the air." Trapnell leaned forward again. "Look, you've seen the reports of discs in formation? As many as twenty or thirty or more?"

"Right."

"You've seen how they move through the sky at different speeds? Sometimes at a few hundred miles an hour, sometimes at thousands of miles per hour. Okay?"

"Go on," Brady said.

40

"Do you believe there're discs moving in formation through the air? At thousands of miles an hour?"

Brady smiled. "No."

"Got any ideas as to what they might be?"

"Never mind the guessing games," Brady said, his irritation quick to show.

Trapnell laughed. "Forgive me," he said, "I don't often get an intelligent audience for this long, and I can't resist the tweaks every now and then. Okay. Would you believe automobile headlights?"

Brady made a face that spoke his thoughts for him.

Trapnell buzzed his secretary. "Set up the New Mexico films for Mr. Brady, will you? I'll want to see them in about ten or fifteen minutes."

"Right, Colonel."

Trapnell turned back to Brady. "We'll let that one lie for the moment and come back to it when you see the film. You want some more poop on mirages?"

"If it applies."

"It applies, all right. Let's take this one from the beginning. You understand how light rays travel through the air?"

Brady groaned. "Give me a quick run-through."

"It's simple enough. Normally light rays travel in a concave path that intersects with the horizon. 'Normal' means when temperature distribution through the air is normal. Often it's not. We get two conditions that set up a mirage."

Brady took notes steadily.

Trapnell waited for Brady's pen to stop moving. "Sometimes the air just above the ground becomes exceptionally warm," the colonel continued. "The air expands and it becomes less dense. Then, the convex path shortens. If it's really hot, the air itself becomes concave. Whap! Light starts playing tricks because it's everywhere it shouldn't be. And since all the human eye sees is reflected light, things start moving around or ending up where

41

they shouldn't be. Now, you also get the temperature inversion. In this case you get a layer of warm air over another layer of cold air. What happens is that the path of light rays lengthens. The light rays parallel the earth's surface at greater distance."

"And you get more optical . . . um . . . effects isn't the word I want," Brady mulled aloud.

"Mirage is as good as any," Trapnell offered. "Let me relate it to seeing things from the air. The distortion and the displacement can really be fantastic. Under the conditions I've described, for example, a city that's over the horizon will show up to a pilot as being in view, and sometimes a few hundred feet, or even a few thousand, above the horizon. Castles in the sky and all that. This is why we get reports sometimes of land areas distorted into unusual shapes that seem to float in the air. Now, if it's a lake that's being reflected, and you feed in the factors of the observer, the pilot in this case, also at altitude and moving, what you can end up with is—"

"A huge silvery shape rushing through the air," Brady finished for him.

"Affirmative," Trapnell said. "The next thing is that the speed of your great silvery shape changes rapidly. It can move slowly or with explosive bursts of speed. It can pick up lights from the ground, other aircraft in the sky, just about anything. We had someone report in that he'd seen a huge torpedo shape rushing through the air at night. He said there wasn't any question, that twenty people in the airliner confirmed the sighting. Said the torpedo shape had windows, that it left a wake behind it. The man was telling the truth."

Brady sighed. "I've learned a lesson from you," he said, "and that's not to lead your trick questions. So I won't ask what he saw."

Trapnell grinned at him. "Right. It was a mirage. Fortunately this observer—a pilot, by the way—had an exact recording of time, altitude, position, and course. We were able to backtrack on an occasion when the temperature inversion conditions were right. Know what he saw? A yacht."

"A *yacht*? Jesus, that's hard to believe."

"Sure it is," Trapnell said affably. "Nevertheless it's true. One of our investigators saw the same object a few nights later when he duplicated the flight path of the original observer. It turned out the yacht was thirty or forty miles away in a small harbor. Which, incidentally, was very well lit up. The yacht was moving slowly. The temperature inversion picked it up, projected it as an image in the sky. What the pilot, and his passengers, saw was the hull—they didn't see the superstructure or the masts. Just the hull, and the portholes, which were lit up. The wake the pilot saw was just that—the wake of the boat in the harbor. But when it was picked up by the particular optical conditions and transmitted as a mirage, the torpedo shape—the hull with the ports—seemed to be moving at thousands of miles an hour. Since the pilot was convinced he was seeing something in the air, he *knew*—he was interpreting with his eyes, of course—he *knew* that what was trailing his mystery ship just had to be exhaust of some kind."

Brady stared glumly at his notepad. What the hell did this do to the reports of Keith Johnson and the other pilots? Surely they would be able to distinguish between a mirage or something that really was in the air with them. Brady had flown enough formation so that he had experience with objects close by and at great distance. But according to what Trapnell was telling him, what the observer saw had nothing to do with his eyes playing tricks on him. A delusion was a mental condition. A mirage was something else. Optically the mirage was *real*. A camera's film recorded it. It had nothing to do with delusion.

What about that disc at Barstow Air Force Base? From what Trapnell was saying, it could have been a mirage or a similar optical effect. The eyewitnesses saw something. Their eyes didn't play tricks on them. But it could have been an optical eff——

Wait a moment, Brady thought. Mirages don't cut off radios sixty feet beneath the ground and knock out power stations!

"You got something special?"

Brady looked up at Trapnell. "Nothing for the moment," he said. "I'll come back to it later. That film of yours ready yet?"

The colonel glanced at his watch. "Should be. Let's take a look at it and then break for lunch."

"Good deal."

Brady ordered a double shrimp cocktail, steak rare, and a stiff martini. He went through the drink quickly, to the amusement of Jim Trapnell. "You look as if you needed that," the colonel observed.

"I did," Brady agreed, ordering a second. "That's a hell of a movie show you got there."

"Sure is," Trapnell said. "Straightens out a lot of enthusiasts." He hesitated a moment. "How about yourself?"

"I'm not a believer," Brady said cautiously, "in the sense that I've seen UFO's skittering through the air. But I've talked with . . ." He shook his head. "Never mind," he said. "Not yet, anyway. I want to save my questions for later. That film of yours was enough for lunch."

It had been all that. Perfect formations of discs hurtling through the night air. Sometimes four objects, sometimes as many as fifty or sixty. And every one of them, Trapnell said in a running commentary with the film, was simply a mirage. A reflected light, or lights. Auto headlights thirty miles away, shining into the air as cars drove along an incline. The lights flashed into the night sky, were bent, separated, and bounced against another inversion layer many miles distant. The observers looked up and saw discs in formation, ghostly, silent, but terribly real.

Was there proof they were optical effects? Proof enough. The Air Force scientists set up an experiment. When the inversion-layer effects were prominent, they drove cars up the same incline. This time they capped the auto headlights with transparent plastic. Presto: great formations of discs in yellow, red and blue sailing through the sky. End of case.

Trapnell had an even more interesting film to kick off the afternoon session. "We've put together in a sample film a group of sightings," he explained.

"You mean of actual sightings. UFO's?"

Trapnell shook his head. "Uh-uh. IFO's. Identified Flying Objects." He signaled the projectionist to start the picture. "I'll give you a running commentary as we go along."

Brady studied two DC-8 airliners flying through a hazy sky. Ordinarily DC-8's don't fly in formation. And certainly they don't fly in formation with one airplane holding a perfect *inverted* position over the other.

"This effect is common enough," Trapnell said. "Not ordinary, but not rare. There's only one airplane, of course, and it is miles away. You're not seeing the single DC-8, but its mirror image reflected from another part of the sky. Sometimes you get this double effect with the planes flying side by side and sometimes you see it like this—one airplane inverted."

The film clip ended and a new sequence began. Brady started from his chair. In the film, shown near the horizon, was a disc-shaped craft, absolutely clear in its outline, rushing through the air, the speed accented by clouds between the camera and the disc. What startled Brady was its color and the dazzling exhaust trail it left behind. Along the top of the disc the color showed as a bright blue. The bottom was a brilliant red, and a reddish-orange exhaust trailed behind. Suddenly the disc shot upward in a steep climb, hovered for several seconds, and plunged vertically.

"What the hell is *that!*" Brady exclaimed.

Trapnell's chuckle was the answer. "Hang on to your seat," he said. "You're seeing the planet Venus again. That's our old friend under a really wild temperature inversion. To save time, we kept the camera in place. See the clock on the side? Okay, this next scene was taken several minutes later."

The mixture of color was gone. A dazzling light in the sky replaced the multicolored disc. Now its shape was perfectly round.

"Keep watching," Trapnell urged.

Several minutes later Brady watched an ordinary picture of Venus sliding toward the horizon. He shook his head.

"Ready for the next one?" asked the colonel.

"Christ, I think I'm ready for anything," Brady said. "Let's have the works."

Two scenes showed in rapid sequence. The first appeared as a long broken streak in the sky, something glowing brilliantly, moving with tremendous speed. As it disappeared, it left a phantom glow in the night sky. The second sequence was much like the first, but the original light was more circular. As Brady watched, it broke up into a loose cluster that ripped across the screen.

"I recognize the second one," Brady said. "I've seen that myself. Fireball, wasn't it?"

"Right. Big meteor. When it heats up, it sometimes explodes into several chunks. They come in all colors. The ones that shake people the most are the green and yellow fireballs. People just won't believe they're meteors."

"What about that first scene?"

"Warhead reentry. It was taken from Ascension Island. You saw the entire sequence. Tracking camera stuff." In the gloom Brady saw Trapnell turn to him. "Now comes dessert."

By now Brady was ready to expect anything. He got more than he bargained for.

A huge disc showed on the screen. Sunlight reflected brilliantly from its curving upper dome. Between the top and bottom shell was a row of ports or windows. The disc, slicing at a steep angle toward the ground, rushed in and out of clouds, but tracked steadily by the camera. Brady saw the thin exhaust trail behind the disc.

Trapnell stopped the film. He turned again to face Brady. "Give up?"

Brady pointed to the screen. "Unless I've lost all my marbles, I saw a disc. A real, live, bona fide dyed-in-the-wool disc with ports and an exhaust trail and . . ." He glared at the colonel. "Are you going to tell me that goddamned thing is also an illusion?"

"We call this the Congressional Special," Trapnell said by way of reply. "It shakes up everybody."

"You're shaking *me*."

"You ready for the rest?"

"You mean there's more?"

"Sure. Lets you in on the secret."

Brady leaned back in his chair. "Christ, let's not stop now."

The film started again. The disc was still there, still rushing through the sky. Then something strange began to happen. The curving metal shape distorted, shimmering in the bright sunlight. Near the rear of the disc Brady watched a great tail begin to appear. As he studied the screen, his eyes wide, the curvature of the disc evaporated. Brady stared at a Boeing C-135 in a steep descent. The lights went on.

"That little gem," Trapnell said, "teaches us several things. One, cameras can be dangerous things. Two, never interpret with the eye—use the brain. Three, always have all the facts at hand. Four, always ask to see the full run of any film. Five, understand temperature inversions and meteorological phenomena. Six—"

"Hold it right there," Brady said. "Just tell me what was going on, will you?"

"The disc was a reality," Trapnell said, "but only in the optical sense. What you saw was part of a steep and rapid descent test

47

of the Charlie 135. The bird started down from forty-three thousand feet. On that particular day the temperature was minus eighty. That's Fahrenheit. The bird came down quickly and went through an inversion layer. Moist, warm air; that sort of thing. The metal was cold and the ship was near sonic velocity. With all these conditions put together, you get a condensation shock wave. Which, to the eye, or the camera," he added, "turns an ordinary airplane into a disc going hellbent for leather for the ground. A condensation shock wave also reflects light in the same manner that metal reflects light. When the plane went through the inversion layer . . . well, you saw for yourself."

"Does that sort of thing happen very often?"

Trapnell shrugged. "Hard to say. We've got one hundred and ninety-four intelligence people around the world, assigned to different bases—they pull double duty by investigating reports for us—but this is the only film I've seen that shows so clearly the upper and lower shock wave. Of course the shock wave itself is common enough. You've seen films of the B-70, haven't you?"

Brady nodded.

"Have you seen the shots where it's riding a visible shock wave?"

"No."

"Again it's a matter of understanding meteorological phenomena. You get shock contrails from wingtips, propeller tips, and when you're near Mach one. Not the same as the exhaust trails. It's not rare. But one like you saw on the film appears to be quite uncommon. If it happened more often, we'd be deluged in here with 'positive' sightings of discs."

Brady pondered what he'd heard and seen, and checked off a list on his notepad. "While we're on meteorological," he said, "give me a quick rundown on sun dogs, will you?"

"Make that sun dogs and moon dogs," Trapnell said.

"I didn't know there was a nighttime effect with that stuff," Brady admitted.

"There is. It's a reflection of the sun in a layer of flat ice crystals," Trapnell explained. "Technically, when that happens, you get what the scientists call a sub-sun. We've bastardized it into sun dog. The thing that shakes you when you get a good one is that the sun dog appears at a point adjacent to the real sun. What's important is that the apparition, so to speak, can be just as bright as the actual sun. It doesn't always appear as a single source point of light, either. It develops several sun dogs, so you have a cluster or a formation. The moon dog is the same thing at night. Except people get a lot more shook about something at night than they do during bright daylight."

"What do they look—I mean, how do they appear to a pilot?"

"Depends. Viewing angle, size of ice crystals. That sort of thing. But if conditions are right, it will take up formation with a plane. It may even chase the airplane. Remember, the pilot actually sees a source of light. It's real. Sometimes we get a fighter jock who's irritated and he goes to hot guns and turns toward the thing. He gets confused very quickly. The sun dog, or moon dog, will either speed up, slow down, hold a constant separation, or even seem to attack the airplane."

Brady felt overwhelmed. "How effective—or meaningful—are radar sightings?"

Trapnell shifted in his chair. "For tracking UFO's?"

"Yes."

"Unreliable, to sum it up in a word. Radar picks up ice crystals, birds individually and in formation, balloons, and all sorts of things. If it's near the ground but out of sight of the operator in the radar room, it will even show Ferris wheels as something moving through the sky. Then there's the effect of inversion layers when the radar beam is bent—"

"Wait a moment. I thought radar waves were strictly linear, always straight-line stuff."

"We thought so too for a long time," Trapnell admitted. "Now we know better. An inversion layer will bend a radar beam just as

49

it bends light. We've had UFO flaps where radar picked up things moving at tremendous speeds—and no one could see anything. It turned out the radar waves were bending and reflecting planes a few hundred miles away. In fact, we've even had UFO voices—ghost voices."

"How could that happen?"

"Same effect," Trapnell said. "VHF radio especially. Inversion layer bends the radio signal and we pick it up when nothing's in the air. Shook up a lot of communications people."

Brady shook his head. "I'll bet."

One more thing remained on his checklist. "Anything else that contributes heavily to your identification of UFO's? I mean as a major source of reports?"

"That would be electrical."

"Plasmoids?"

"You know about those?"

"Some," Brady said. "I've seen plenty of St. Elmo's fire and I've done research on plasmoids and corona discharges."

"How about ball lightning?"

"Uh-uh. Fill me in on that."

"Let me give you a quickie course on ball lightning and atmospheric plasma. It won't take long and it might straighten out a few points for you."

"Okay; shoot."

"Well, for starters, a plasma is essentially an electrified gas. Its electrons flow freely. But they do so in the middle of positively charged molecules without becoming attached to the molecules. This makes them electrically neutral. A plasma cloud has its own magnetic field. Still with me?"

"Yeah. I've almost but not quite got a headache. Don't quit now."

"All right. The magnetic field of the plasma, and surrounding magnetic fields that are always in the air, accelerate the electrons.

The electrons also collide with neutral molecules, those without electrical charges. The long and short of it is that energy is always being increased or released. And that energy is radiant—"

"Can it be seen?"

"Sure can," Trapnell said. "It oscillates, or vibrates, in the ultraviolet, the visible spectrum, and in the infrared. If it's in the visible blue or visible red part of the spectrum—that's electromagnetic, by the way—the plasma glows in blue or red colors to the human eye. And when people see glowing blue or red clouds, especially when they move erratically or travel in a long straight line, well, they get shook, and we've got a rash of UFO reports on our hands." Trapnell looked at Brady and grinned. "You ready for the ball lightning now?"

"I may not last much longer."

Trapnell guffawed. "I'll get Charlene to rub your fevered brow," he said. "Charlene's attended to more UFO headaches than any other living human. She's my secretary, by the way. I wasn't always this calm about things from somewhere out there. It took me months to quit growing gray hairs." The colonel lit a cigarette. "Okay, to the ball lightning. Short and sweet, it's simply a special kind of plasma. I really can't tell you too much about it—"

"Don't tell me it's classified, for Christ's sake."

"Your headache is showing."

"Sorry about that. Seriously. Go on."

"I can't tell you much about it because no one really knows much about ball lightning. It doesn't show as frequently as other phenomena. But when it does, wow! It comes in about every color, shape, and size you can imagine. Unless you're hep on the scientific end of things, you simply won't believe—"

"Never mind the rah-rah," Brady interjected. "I'm hep enough. And my headache *is* showing. Lemme apologize ahead of time."

Trapnell nodded in acceptance. "Okay. Size first. People have

51

seen ball lightning more than twenty feet in diameter. The most common colors change from orange to red and then they skip back over the spectrum to higher energies. That's the electromagnetic radiation, by the way. They go up into green, blue and violet."

"What about the shape?"

"You name it, we got it. Spherical, discoid, torpedo, wobbly, firm—the works."

"Any pictures?"

"Plenty. I'll show you some stills and movies. Sometimes they have edges that are . . . well . . . fuzzy is a good description. At other times they're sharply defined. And sometimes you see them surrounded by a glowing haze, or a blur. They also rotate when they feel like it. And they're not quiet."

Brady looked up at that last remark.

"Not all the time, I mean. They've been known to hum, whir, and pulsate. The sound sometimes is rasping, sometimes, well, it's a smooth keening cry. Some people have also reported it as sounding like a bass fiddle at its lowest pitch."

"That's great. It does everything but sing opera."

"Just about," Trapnell agreed. "I didn't mention that it hovers, or drifts slowly, or can go scooting across the countryside at hundreds of miles an hour. Maybe thousands, for all we know. It can also make right-angle turns, which upsets people rather easily. What shakes them up even more is when it tears down a road and then reverses direction faster than the eye can follow. *Without* turning, I should add."

". . . when it tears down a road," Brady said. "Could ball lightning be responsible for all those reports of UFO's following cars?"

"Uh-huh. That's our baby, all right. It can also knock out ignition systems or just screw up car radios and lights. It's happened many times."

Brady nodded. "Is that the course? Are you—"

Trapnell held up his hand. "One final item. That is, if you're still able to go on like this. You look like a man who's taking a beating, Cliff. You're getting in a few days what's taken me many months to absorb."

"Hell, the final straw can only break my back. Let's have at it."

"In a nutshell, it's auroras. The northern lights. Or, for that matter," Trapnell appended, "the southern lights as well. Are you familiar with—"

"I did a couple of stories on the subject," Brady said. "Give me the visual effects."

"Okay. You know, then, that auroras are created by intense electrical activity in the upper atmosphere—sometimes hundreds of miles high. I'll give you one shining example of what auroras can bring on. This incident was seen by many thousands of people across almost all of northwest Europe. The reports apparently were all accurate, that is, from different sources. What people saw was a huge and brilliant disc that showed up on the east-northeast horizon and then moved slowly across the sky. During its passage it changed shape from a disc into an elongated ellipse and then *back* to a disc before it went over the horizon. I should mention," Trapnell emphasized, "that many scientists tracked the disc. They were the one who confirmed the color as white, pearly-white, greenish-white, and yellow-white. You ready for the finale?"

"Don't spare me now."

"It was seventy miles long by ten miles in diameter when it assumed the elongated ellipse shape."

"My God. It must have been seen for hundreds of miles," Brady said.

"It was."

"Any photos?"

"Some. It was seen at night and they weren't too good."

"How about radar?"

Trapnell shook his head. "Nope. No radar tracking."

53

"But why? How could they miss something that big?"

"Oh, they didn't miss it. It's just that no one had any radar for tracking. You see, this particular disc was seen about eighty-five years ago."

CHAPTER V

BRADY SAW A LARGE RED BARN, A SILO NEARBY AND, SET OFF TO THE
side amid a stand of high trees, a neat farmhouse. It was a perfectly normal scene of a Midwest farm. "Look at the details,"
Trapnell advised him through the flickering gloom of the projection room. "Get them fixed in your mind." Brady made out
several trucks; a group of horses beyond a whitewashed fence.

"Anything special you want me to pick out?" Brady asked.

"Not yet," came the reply. "The action takes place in a few moments. I want you to get the scene clear in your mind so there
won't be any outside interference with what happens."

Brady concentrated on significant details, picked out a power
line in the distance, then saw several people and a dog enter the
scene from behind the farmhouse. But that was it. Impatient to
get with the heart of the matter, he realized he was losing his
cool. He was still in a funk about the previous day. Trapnell had
overwhelmed him with sheer weight of information on UFO's. Or,
to cut it closer, with IFO's—identified phenomena. If the man
had tried to conceal information, if he'd once been evasive,
Brady might have felt some measure of triumph. Even if it were
negative. But nothing of the sort had happened. Trapnell was

responsive in every way to Brady's pointed queries. Even General Maloney had come through from the Pentagon with the verbal okay for Brady's access to anything in Blue Book files.

Yet there was still hope. Agreeing to Brady's request, Trapnell concentrated first on the 90-odd percent of UFO reports, photographs, and films that fell into the identified category. Brady wanted as much grounding as possible before he entered the remaining 10 percent loosely regarded as "unknowns." Even there, Trapnell cautioned him, unknown could mean anything. It certainly did not mean, he emphasized, that an unknown could be equated conclusively as a mechanical object. It *might* be. Then again, it might also be certain phenomena wholly beyond comprehension of the scientists who attempted to categorize and identify every reliable UFO sighting report they received. Unknown, Trapnell stressed, was a literal identification. No one knew for certain what the phenomena, or "whatzit," might be.

Trapnell's voice cut into his thoughts. "Okay, here we go. This is going to be a beaut."

It began along the right side of the screen. Three white objects —no, gleaming white, Brady corrected himself—floated through the air. For a moment their movement prevented him from confirming their shape. Then he saw they were spherical. He tried to guess their size but knew it was impossible without depth references. The three gleaming spheres drifted slowly through the air above the farmhouse. Brady saw the people on the screen turn, hands pointing, gawking. Abruptly the spherical objects picked up speed. Brady couldn't tell the acceleration. One moment they moved slowly, almost lazily. In the next instant they streaked over the ground as if propelled from a gun. The photographer almost lost them.

Brady couldn't believe what his eyes saw. The three spheres took up a loose rotating and whirling formation as they raced over the ground. The camera showed them disappearing briefly behind several trees and a billboard along a road. *That's no illu-*

sion. Illusions or mirages don't disappear behind something and then show up on the other side!

As if reading his mind, Trapnell commented on the same point. "We've already run timing tests," the colonel said. "The speed maintained by the objects for a period before they reached the billboard checks out. In other words, there's no change in the speed between the time they go behind the billboard and when they emerge from the other side. Now watch what they do."

The spheres seemed to go crazy. Their motion of whirling one about the other became a frenzied spinning. Then they re-formed as a loose cluster, rotating vertically one about the other, the cluster itself racing low over the ground, dodging trees and other objects. Brady had never seen or even heard of anything resembling what he now saw on the screen.

"All right," Trapnell said. "Do you see the key? Those things are following the power lines."

Brady hadn't noticed that before, but this was his first viewing of the film and Trapnell had seen it many times. The other man confirmed his thoughts. "We weren't certain about the power lines until we sent some of our people to the area. They checked out everything on the ground, flew the route in a helicopter—the works. There's no question of it. The power line has something to do with those objects." By now the spherical shapes were receding in the distance. Brady blinked. They had vanished.

"What happened?" he fired at Trapnell.

"Just as you saw it," the colonel said. "They vanished." He motioned for the overhead lights and turned to Brady. "Want to see it again?" Brady nodded. The second time around he concentrated on the spherical white shapes. When the lights went on, he hadn't the faintest notion of what they might be.

"The science boys have pretty much ruled out a plasmoid or corona-discharge effect," Trapnell commented.

Brady shook his head slowly. "Any ideas?"

"Some. Mostly guesswork, however. One of our eggheads is holding forth a theory that the spheres represent a form of life."

"You're putting me on."

"Nope." Trapnell said it matter-of-factly. "We have other films of these things. High-altitude stuff, playing in and out of thunderstorms with strong electrical activity. That's a definite tie-in. They *always* associate with electrical force of one kind or another."

"But—Christ, you said they might be living creatures!"

"I know it sounds crazy," Trapnell admitted. "But look at it from an objective viewpoint. Have you ever compared a jellyfish like the Portuguese man-of-war with an elephant? What two more dissimilar forms of life could there be? Or take a shrimp or flounder that lives seven miles down at the bottom of the ocean, in the Marianas Deep. The pressure down there would squeeze a man into the shape of a thin wafer—yet sea creatures get along quite nicely, thank you. Or take the things that fly. Did you know the largest flying creature today weighs over a billion—that's *billion*—times more than the smallest? That's the ratio of the smallest gnat to the largest bird, the albatross."

"Man, you are asking a lot," Brady said with open disbelief, "when you ask me to accept those things as *alive*."

"Got any better ideas?"

"No, I don't. But that doesn't make me buy *your* answer."

"It's not a matter of buying it," Trapnell countered. "I said it was a theory. Which is growing in acceptance, by the way. That there are electrical life forms—based on electrical phenomena—that exist in the higher atmosphere and sometimes are attracted to lower levels. They're no more preposterous than the jellyfish and the elephant." The colonel smiled. "But like I say, we don't *know*. I just wanted you to be sure we weren't overlooking any possibilities."

Trapnell motioned for the projectionist to set up another film.

When he turned back to Brady, the colonel's face was deadpan. "I'm talking for the record now," he said. "Okay?"

"Yes."

"This next reel is classified."

Brady's interest quickened. "I was hoping we'd get around to the hard stuff," he said.

"Sure, sure," Trapnell replied, a slight irritation showing. "I want to caution you again not to leap to any hasty conclusions." A smile flickered and was gone. "Not that you won't, though."

"You seem pretty certain," Brady said.

"I am." Trapnell said it with the finality of long experience. "I've been here before, remember?"

Brady nodded. He'd come to pay close attention even to Trapnell's side remarks. "One other point," the colonel added. "No running commentary during the first run-through."

"Any reason for that?"

Trapnell shrugged. "There's a lot to see. Better for you to take it in without interference. I recommend you save your questions for later."

It was Brady's turn to shrug. "You're the conductor on this ride," he said. "Let's go."

The lights went out.

It took Brady several seconds to recognize the scene. He watched the camera panning across the high, sloping structure of an early-warning radar. No question that this lay somewhere north of the Arctic Circle; huge snowdrifts and ice-sheeted buildings testified to that. Several men crossed before the film, shuffling awkwardly in heavy clothing, bent over to avoid a wind evident by the snow it whipped before its passage. Brady wished the scene had more light. The sun low on the horizon confused him for a moment until he realized he was watching the Arctic sun. They had more than twenty hours of daylight out of every twenty-four. He'd ask Jim Trapnell later about the time the film was shot.

The camera crossed the small confines of the radar station and started panning back in the other direction. Along the left corner of the screen Brady saw a momentary flash. Apparently the cameraman had seen the same flash of light. The camera stopped, blurred in an awkward motion, then swung quickly back to place the light close to the center of the screen. At this point all that could be seen was the white snow foreground, an indistinct horizon, the sun off to the right side of the picture, and the object.

It appeared to move. Without buildings in the foreground and only a single ice-encrusted radio mast in the distance, the motion at first was difficult to detect. Brady watched the slightly changing reflection and expanding size of the object. He looked carefully for, and saw, its position change relative to the top of the radio mast. It was approaching the cameraman.

The motion ended. For several seconds, during which Brady caught himself holding his breath, the object remained still, hovering in one place. He didn't know specifically why, but somehow Brady was convinced the object wasn't an airplane or a balloon carried by the wind. Christ, of course he knew. Trapnell would never have screened a film with *Secret* emblazoned across the opening frames unless . . .

Suddenly the object began to glow. Brady corrected his first impression. He didn't know if the object glowed or the air around the shape had suddenly begun to glow. He couldn't tell. He saw the effect for only a second or two. Before he could adjust his eyes to the new scene, the object streaked off at a steep angle. The cameraman followed it briefly. In the changing angle Brady swore the shape became defined clearly as a disc. Until a few days ago he would have insisted he'd seen a disc. But after Trapnell's interrogation he knew he couldn't be certain of anything at first glance.

He heard the colonel's voice. "Stay where you are, Cliff. We'll run through it a second time in slow motion."

Brady didn't answer. All his attention riveted to the screen.

This time he *was* certain. Unless he was seeing an optical projection—and under those Arctic conditions he was convinced that wasn't the case—he had just watched a film of a disc in flight.

Brady let out a deep breath. "What the hell *was* that?" It was more demand than query.

The colonel held his gaze. "We don't know. We—"

"What do you mean you don't know!" Brady shouted. "You saw it big as life out there. You saw how it moved. That damned thing accelerated to a few thousand miles per hour before it went out of sight!"

Trapnell's bearing had stiffened. "I said we don't know. That's precisely what I mean. The official listing for the object you saw in this film is a 'good unknown.'" He rose to his feet and motioned for Brady to return to his office. As they walked along the hall, Brady pressed the colonel.

"I don't see how you can call that thing an unknown," he persisted. "It was damned obvious to me it was a machine and—"

"I'll grant it *looked* like a machine," Trapnell said.

"Looked, hell. Do you want it to come out of the screen and bite you?"

Trapnell laughed harshly. "Yes." Abruptly he stopped and turned to face Brady. "That is exactly what I would like to have it do. Bite me, or anyone else. Or knock down a building or shoot down an airplane or sink a boat or steal the Taj Mahal, or *something*."

"I don't get you."

"Jesus, we've got more film like the one you saw. Perhaps not as clear in terms of the UFO, the object," Trapnell corrected, "but we've got film up the ass. We've got movies taken over the Amazon River, over the North Pole, in Antarctica, over cities and deserts and oceans. But we're not able to make a positive identification of what we see on that film."

"Including that disc you showed me?" Brady was incredulous.

"Including that disc." He started walking again. "Let's get some coffee while we continue this, okay?"

"All right," Brady said with ill-concealed anger. "I'll take it your way. You'll agree it wasn't an airplane, a helicopter, a dirigible, a blimp, a balloon, a—"

"Save your breath, Cliff. I'll tote it up for you. Nothing we discussed fits the bill. Every possible condition of which we know was considered. We don't know what the object was. No," he said with his hand raised to ward off the interruption, "wait a moment and hear me out. I'll tell you what the film *didn't* show us. We've got nothing for size—only crude guesses. It might have been huge and a long ways off or fairly small and close in; you can't tell from the film. No reports of any sound. The men were wearing earmuffs and heavy head covers, and with the strong wind they didn't hear a thing. There wasn't any sign of external control surfaces, of a cabin, of an antenna. Nothing in the way of propulsion was evident. There—"

"Hold it right there. What about that glow I saw?"

"Just before it accelerated?"

"Yep. Right then."

Trapnell shrugged. "We don't know and you don't know," he threw at Brady. "It could be a camera fogging effect . . ."

"Bullshit."

". . . or it could have been, and probably was, some form of ionization in the air."

"It sure looked like that."

"As the madam said, 'In this business looks don't count.'" Trapnell grinned.

Brady sat back in his chair. "I don't get it," he said finally. "I don't get you or this outfit or the Air Force. What the hell. You've just given me a clear film of a disc, you have radar tracking, you have visual identification, you have . . ." He shook his head again and reached for the coffee. "You've got the whole thing locked up and all you tell me is a good unknown. That damned thing," Brady said angrily, spilling his coffee as he gesticulated, "was a machine just as much as you and I are sitting in this room together."

Trapnell laughed softly.

"What's so goddamned funny?"

"You know the film you saw yesterday? The one on the Charlie 135 in the dive tests?"

"So?"

"Run it through your mind again, will you?" Trapnell urged Brady. "But leave out the second part. Where you see the condensation shock wave dissipating. Okay?"

Brady thought it over. Before he could respond, Trapnell went on. "Just remember that film and what you saw. Perfect conditions of visibility. All meteorological, electrical, optical, and other factors well known. Broad daylight. Tracking cameras that are the best in the world. Radar tracking, with transponders in the big metal bird. Everything perfect, even better than the film we just saw at that radar station. So you see this disc coming lickety-split through the air, and you tie in all the other factors, and what have you got?" The colonel grinned hugely at the box into which he shoveled Brady. "We have, on the basis of your logic and common sense, absolute and unquestionable proof of a flying disc. A genuine, bona fide, caught-on-film disc.

"Which," the colonel added with a pointed finger, "was never there in the first place."

"Big deal," Brady sneered. "You don't twist me around that fast. From where I sit, you *refuse* to make a positive identification."

Trapnell studied him carefully. "You don't mean that," he said after a pause. "We don't refuse anything of the sort. We also don't go off half-cocked."

"That's a matter of opinion," Brady said rudely. "I think it's just as much your responsibility to make a positive finding on something like this as it is to bend over backwards not to, as you said, go off half-cocked."

Trapnell applauded lightly. "Bravo."

"Sorry for the sharp teeth," Brady apologized with an abashed look. "But I meant what I said, Jim."

"I know you did. Maybe you can answer something for me?"

Brady waited.

"We've got that film. We say it's not enough. We need more, much more," Trapnell emphasized. "Could you bring that disc back to us again so we could take more pictures?"

"I don't get you."

"We put cameras in every radar station in that part of the world," Trapnell said, "hoping for a repetition. We got a lot of lights and strange things in the air that glowed, glittered, shone, pulsated, quivered, danced, and did a great many other things, but never sat still long enough to get its picture taken. One sighting isn't enough. *Ergo*—a good unknown is the answer."

"Don't you have other reports," Brady pushed, "from other parts of the world?"

"Sure do. Thousands of them."

"I don't mean the whole barrel of fish," Brady said, again impatient. He felt he was always permitted to get almost within reach of what he sought and then it was snatched away from him. "Hard sightings. Stuff you would call a good unknown?"

"That covers a lot of territory. Do you know what shapes we've seen in our 'good unknown' files?"

Brady shook his head.

"Discs, torpedo or cigar shapes, doughnut rings, spheres, discoids, stars, wheels, glowing lights of every color and size, formless objects pulsating in different colors, diamonds, squares, rectangles, pie-shaped, in the form of kites, like ice-cream cones, like balloons of every shape and size; we've got them in the form of

64

huge ovals with sledlike runners, we've got spinning wheels, we've got central nuclei with blazing lights orbiting the center, we've got them like conventional aircraft but without wings or engines, we've got them in the form of rockets, delta-wing airplanes, submarines, scythes, eggs and ovals and boomerangs and ovoids and teardrops and crescent moons with bubbles in the center and God knows what else. And those are in the reliable and good unknown files. Any comment?"

"Yeah. You're a son of a bitch to deal with," Brady said.

"Thanks. I consider that a compliment in this job."

"I meant it to be," Brady came back. "All right, I'll lean on your experience. Out of all the material you've studied, if you had to pick the most reliable sightings—I mean the kind of shape —which way would you turn?" Brady motioned for Trapnell not to answer yet. "Let me add something to that. You've got things fixed in your mind from your side of the desk," Brady continued. "Try to take it from my side of the fence. Come into this thing cold, then consider everything. Not simply in the shape of the UFO, but the details of the sightings themselves. On that basis, what would you choose?"

Trapnell looked unhappy. "You're asking me to be two people at the same time, aren't you? Maybe I didn't make myself clear before." The colonel shifted in his chair. "I've lived with this thing"—he motioned to the offices about him—"for quite a while. I don't believe UFO's represent anything more than natural phenomena, no matter how weird or mechanical they may sometimes appear to be."

Brady nodded. "Okay, okay," he said, gesturing in impatience. "We'll come back to *that* in a little while. But stay with what I asked, will you? Make it theoretical or whatever else you want to."

Trapnell drummed his fingers on his desk. "You understand this has to be entirely unofficial?"

"Sure."

"Not so fast," the colonel admonished. "I've got to hear this said. No assumption. This conversation is strictly off the record. It's between two people. Officially it never happened."

"Agreed."

"All right, then. If I were to play Alice in Wonderland, there wouldn't be any question. The discs."

Brady snapped it out. "Why?"

Trapnell shrugged. "I'm playing by your rules. They fit best of all."

"Break it down for me, will you?"

"Everything else—elongated shapes, spheres, glowing lights, all of it—doesn't fit into a pattern. They've *got* to be some form of natural phenomena. A good many of the discs are the same, but in this business you learn that what someone describes as a disc can be a sphere seen without depth perception. That's just an example. If we go back to the old rule of separating the wheat from the chaff, then the discs emerge as the only likely possibility."

Brady slammed a fist into his palm. "Damn it, I *knew* it!"

"Now just hold on," Trapnell said loudly. "Let's not go off the deep end because of what I just said."

"Deep end?"

"Hell, yes," the colonel said with almost a glare. "I gave you an Alice in Wonderland simile. Don't go pasting 'authentic' labels on the discs so fast."

Brady almost whooped with laughter. "Jim, let me ask you another one from way out in left field. What would it take to convince you one of these things is real?"

"Real, shmeal. You're making the same mistake the nuts and kooks make. You're setting up artificial standards of proof and judging from *your* viewpoint." Trapnell shook his head. "It won't hold water."

"If I see something that looks like a duck, quacks like a duck and waddles like a duck, then I think I'm safe in assuming the goddamned thing is a duck."

"And you could easily be wrong!" Trapnell cracked the palm of his hand against the desk. "That's my whole point, man! If I saw my sainted grandmother go whizzing by in one of those things, I wouldn't believe it."

"I'll ask it again: What would it—"

"I heard you the first time," Trapnell said. "We would want to examine it. Kick the tires, work on it with a wrench and a hacksaw, take pictures, examine its teeth, the whole bit. We'd want to run lab tests, metallurgical samples, X rays, the lot. And *not* until then."

"Jesus," Brady said, "you people are hard to convince. That's my entry for the understatement of the year."

"Oh? Maybe you're missing the point of all this."

"I sure as hell am."

Trapnell nodded, his face serious. He rose from his seat to pace the room. "I think I screwed up," he said at last, and turned to look at Brady. "Do you know why this office is here?"

"Sure, to check out UFO reports and to—"

"Wrong."

"Wrong? Then what the hell is all this"—Brady swept his arm through the air to take in the Blue Book files and offices—"doing here?"

"Not to play nursemaid to UFO reports, as you—and everyone else, apparently—might think."

"I'm all ears."

"The long and short of it is that we're here to study and evaluate reports of UFO's only in the respect that they may constitute or pose a threat to the security of this country." Trapnell took a deep breath. "If that sounds like a speech, it is. But that's also on the level. We judge everything we see on the basis of an alien or a foreign or a whatzit being a danger to the United States. If it doesn't fall into that category, we're satisfied. I hope I've impressed that on you because it's our only justification for being here. Do things—objects, UFO's, whatever you call them—threaten air safety in terms of interfering with military, civil, or general aviation? Do they threaten people's lives, or installations? That sort of thing. If they don't pose a threat, we stick them in the files."

Brady didn't know what to say. Finally he knew what he wanted. "I'd like to lean on you for just a few more hours," he said to Trapnell.

"Sure," the colonel agreed. "I haven't had a good fight like this for a long time. Name your poison."

"Could you pull from the files, oh, say about two or three dozen of what you consider the most reliable sightings of discs?"

"No sweat. What else?"

"I'd like to study those and then ask you some questions."

Trapnell looked carefully at Brady. "You holding back on me?"

"Might be," Brady grinned. "We'll let it lie fallow for just a bit."

"Good enough," the colonel said. He glanced at his watch. "Just about closing time."

The next morning Brady buried himself behind a desk in Trapnell's office. The colonel personally had selected from the vast file of more than twenty thousand sightings two dozen of those he felt were disc observations that defied all possible explanation. Other, of course, than that they were machines and not natural phenomena. But as he cautioned Brady again, any conclusions to be drawn were not and could not be, in the view of the Air Force, any manner of proof that they *were* of an artificial nature. Bradly grumbled at Trapnell to go away and dug into the reports.

Several hours later he planted himself before Trapnell's desk. "You ready?" he growled.

The colonel looked up and grinned. "Don't you ever learn?"

"Nope."

Trapnell sighed. "Okay. Let's have at it."

Brady drew up a chair. He kept firing questions at the colonel, the latter doing his best to answer. Brady smiled grimly. The answers were less certain than they had been before, and there weren't so many ready explanations for certain situations raised in the reports.

"All right, then," Brady said, "what about this sighting? You've got a small passenger ship, I guess you'd call it a coastal steamer, that's been going up and down the African coast for years. British and Dutch crew, all well known, all with experience, all reliable, *and* they're familiar with every inch of the coastline. Are we agreed on that so far?"

"Sure."

"So these people, on a night without clouds, perfect visibility, see something huge moving toward the ship. Something moving through the air and descending. It takes up position between the ship and the shoreline that's less than a mile away. No question; these men—and there are nine of them—have been watching things at sea as far back as they can remember. Then a beam of light, a searchlight or something, comes from the bottom of this thing and plays straight down. Against the water. The light reflects back, it's bright, real bright. And in that light those nine ship's officers see a disc. They see it clear. No question. None," Brady said with emphasis. "It stays with them for several minutes. The light goes out and the thing—the disc they've seen clearly for several minutes under perfect seeing conditions—climbs away and disappears." Brady shoved the report before Trapnell. "How the hell do you explain that incident?"

"We don't," Trapnell said. He remained unruffled. "We don't because we don't *know* what that thing was, even assuming every aspect and detail of that sighting report is correct. Even as-

69

suming all that we don't know. All we do know is that nothing in that sighting shows any kind of threat to this country. It's not the only one of the sort, you know." Trapnell noticed Brady's surprise. "You can't go through all the reports without spending months here," the colonel explained. "I gave you a cross section. There are quite a few other sightings, some, no, most, less reliable than this one, but all of a disc that turned a searchlight downward." He returned the report to Brady. "Let me turn the tables a moment. Could you tell me what a disc, not of any known manufacture, is doing running around the ocean and playing searchlights on the water? What's the purpose, the reasoning, behind something like that?"

"How the hell would I know?"

"Then why ask me to come up with the answer?" Trapnell threw at him.

Brady didn't have a ready response. As he mulled over Trapnell's blank wall placed before him, the colonel caught him off balance. "Have you ever thought what all this signifies?" Trapnell asked. "If these discs are real, what the devil are they doing wandering around the Arctic and the Antarctic? Why do they show up over the oceans and the deserts and every kind of terrain imaginable? *Why* should there be such a vast expenditure of energy, and whatever it costs to keep such things going, without any rhyme or reason? What's it all about?"

Brady rubbed his chin as he thought. "There's one obvious reply to that," he said finally. "Only some of the disc reports are accurate. The others aren't."

"And there's no way of knowing which is which, is there?" Trapnell said immediately.

"I—Christ, I don't know," Brady admitted. "That's what's so exasperating about all this. *Some* of these things have *got* to be real. I'm absolutely convinced of that. But the authentic sightings are all mixed up in this hodgepodge of reports. What I'd like to do is separate the authentic sightings from this whole mess."

"When you do"—Trapnell laughed—"how about telling us? We could use the help."

It hit Brady suddenly. The notes he'd made a few days before. "Wait a minute," he said slowly, thinking as fast as he could, putting pieces together in his mind. "Wait just one ever-loving minute." He snapped his fingers. "Barstow!" he exclaimed. "There's one that's completely outside even your magic bag of tricky explanations."

Trapnell looked carefully at Brady. "You mean Barstow Air Force Base?"

"You bet your sweet ass I do," Brady said in triumph. "You've got that report, don't you? It's a recent one."

Trapnell showed little enthusiasm for continuing the matter. "Cliff, I don't want to sound evasive but—"

"—Barstow is under full security wraps, right?" Brady finished it for him.

"How did you know?"

"I went there. I talked with one of your missile-control people. Everything he *didn't* say made it obvious something screwy was going on."

"I can't give you any information on the . . . on Barstow," Trapnell said. He sounded stiff and formal.

Brady was astounded. "Why the hell not? You've let me crawl through everything else you've got here."

"I know, I know," Trapnell said, "but this one is out of my hands."

Brady sat back in his chair. "Better explain that to me."

"The security classification—and it's way up on top—is from Strategic Air Command," Trapnell explained. "That's out of our jurisdiction."

"That stinks."

"Maybe," Trapnell said, "but it obviously involves SAC weapons in one way or the other."

"It sure as hell does," Brady said grimly. "Like blanking out all communications of a Minuteman complex command post sixty feet beneath the ground."

He saw Trapnell start suddenly. It was the first time Brady had seen the other man caught off guard. "Found a sensitive nerve, didn't I?" Brady chuckled.

"Where did you get that information?" Trapnell said. It was a demand.

"Uh-uh," Brady replied. "Sanctity of sources and all that. It doesn't matter. What—"

"It matters," Trapnell barked.

"I'll take that up with you some other time," Brady quipped. "Let's stay with the subject, huh?"

"I can't discuss it with you."

"Why not?"

"I told you. It's SAC, and it's got top security on it."

"To hell with SAC. I'm not interested in the missiles. I'm interested in something you've been telling me for days isn't real, can't be real, and you don't care about it because it doesn't pose any threat to national security. Them's your words, Jim, not mine. But this thing, this disc, or whatever it was, *did* interfere with the untouchable SAC, didn't it? Don't answer. I *know* it did."

Brady shoved aside the reports he had been studying. "I think I'm getting warm," he said. "The disc, the UFO, fits too many categories, doesn't it?" Trapnell didn't answer, and Brady rushed on. "If it's a plasma, what the hell was it doing at a hundred thousand feet before it came down to ground level and went back up again?" He noticed the frozen face of Trapnell and laughed. "You're trying too hard not to show any reaction," he said. "The eyewitnesses who saw it *all* reported a clearly defined object. Experienced pilots among the eyewitnesses, by the way. So we have something that went from a hundred thousand feet down to the deck and back up. It disappeared from sight for a while. It was seen visually, it was tracked on radar. It generated enough of an electrical field, or electromagnetic, or *something*, to knock out automobile radios and engines, to screw up a five-thousand-watt commercial broadcasting station. It even fouled up a main power station. And it cut off all communications with a superbly shielded, fail-safe command post sixty feet below the ground."

Brady watched Trapnell for several moments. "Any comments?"

"I know this doesn't sound good," Trapnell said, "but you've got to believe me. We can't cut across the lines of a security rating by SAC."

"Look," Brady said, doing his best to sound earnest. "You've been great with me, Jim. I mean that. But I've got to be honest with you. What you've just told me stinks to high heaven. It's censorship. You've impressed upon me for several days that censorship is the last thing you people want. Now you build a great big wall of censorship and you hide behind it."

"We're not hiding behind anything." Trapnell glowered.

"No? What would you call it, then?"

"I *told* you! It's out of our hands."

"My, my. How convenient."

Trapnell sat back in his chair. His voice was cold. "Do you think I'm lying to you?"

"Christ, of course not," Brady said. "If I've even given you that inference I apologize. No, *you* are not lying. But SAC is sure as hell covering up something. By *your* own ground rules, something mucked up an ICBM complex. And *that* constitutes interference with the security of the country, doesn't it?"

"I can't make any comments on the matter."

"Orders?"

Trapnell shrugged. "You've been in the business a long time and you wore the blue suit yourself," he answered.

"So there's an official blanket over the case, huh?"

"I can't even comment on that," Trapnell said, obviously unhappy with his defensive role. "All I can tell you is that like any other case, when we break this one down, it goes into the open files."

"From what I know of this case"—Brady grinned—"we could both have long white hair by that time."

"I told you: no comment."

"I guess we've wrapped it up, then, haven't we?"

"I wish," Trapnell said, "you weren't leaving here with a sour note about all this."

"Sour? By no means," Brady said. He was almost chortling. "You've just proved to me what I've wanted to know. Not in any details, perhaps, but enough."

"Which is?"

"You know the answer to that one. *Something* is out there. You don't know what it is. You can't do anything about it. You— I mean the Air Force, of course—is in a flap about it. Otherwise SAC wouldn't have its heavy hand in the middle of it all."

"Cliff, you can't prove a thing, and you know it."

"Why'd you say that? I didn't say I could *prove* anything."

Trapnell recognized the slip. Brady held up a hand. "No sweat. This conversation never happened."

The colonel nodded. "Thanks."

Brady rose to his feet. "I'll be in touch with you," he said. "If I have any questions about certain sightings, can you give me answers by phone?"

"Sure. Everything—except Barstow—is open to you."

"Thanks. What about those reports? Can you make copies for me?"

"Will do. You want to wait for them, or have me mail them to you?"

"Mail will be fine."

Trapnell drove Brady to the flight line where his Aztec waited. The newsman was jubilant.

He *knew* he had been right all along.

CHAPTER VI

BRADY CUPPED HIS HAND OVER THE PHONE AND SHOUTED TO ANN. "Whaddya' want? Corned beef or pastrami?"

"Pastrami."

"Rye or roll?"

She looked at him from across the room and shrugged. "Hell, I'll order for you," he muttered. He spoke again into the phone. "Make that one corned beef and one pastrami. Both on rye. What? Sure, mustard, catsup, relish on the side. So I like relish on my corned beef! Yeah, two orders of French-fried. Hey, wait one. Stick two six-packs of Budweiser in the bag. Got it cold? Great. Uh-huh. Apartment nineteen-B. Right, thanks." He dropped the phone onto the cradle and walked back to Ann. "I'm starved," he complained. "Forgot all about the time. Didn't you have anything to eat?"

Ann sat on a high barstool, her hands clasped about her knees. She'd removed her uniform and slipped on a Japanese lounging robe from Brady's closet. She moved her toes back and forth and sighed.

"Nope," she said. "I wonder sometimes if I'm in an airliner or a restaurant. God, we were full. Not a seat open. By the time we got through serving dinners and cleaning up the mess . . ."

"Bumpy flight?"

"Not too bad. Couple of urpers in the crowd, but it could have been worse. Anyway, we were letting down by the time we got everything ready." She wrinkled her nose and made a face. "After you get through cleaning up somebody's dinner, when they've thrown up all over themselves, it sort of ruins your appetite."

Brady laughed.

"But I'm hungry enough now," Ann added.

"It'll be here in a few minutes." He gestured at the papers strewn across his worktable. "C'mere," he said gruffly. "I want to show you how this is working out."

Ann slipped from the stool to join Brady and kissed him lightly on the cheek. "What's the delivery boy going to say when he sees me lounging around in your bathrobe? I'll ruin your reputation."

Brady smiled. "That's not a bathrobe. It's a happy coat."

"Happy coat?"

"Sure. That's what the Japanese call it. Got lots of happy memories. I wore that at a hotel spa in Japan when I went there on leave for a month."

She ignored the robe. "What happy memories?" she prodded.

"Ummm, you know."

She moved her thigh against his. "Don't know," she murmured. "Tell me."

"You're not old enough."

She giggled. "That's what you think." She leaned forward to tickle his ear with her tongue. "You can tell me," she whispered. "I'll never tell."

"Knock it off," he growled with mock anger. "My former love life isn't for publication."

She blew in his ear. "Get laid much?"

"Enough."

"How much?"

76

"Enough, goddamn it."

"How many times?"

"Jesus Christ," he exclaimed, "I didn't keep score."

"Was she good?"

"Who?"

"Your Japanese lover."

He couldn't resist the dig. "Which one?"

"Oh, any one of them. All of them. Tell me."

He glared at her.

"Did you make love to one at a time or did you have a gang bang? That's what they call it, isn't it?"

"Will you knock it off?"

"Tell me then."

"That's none of your business."

"Oh." She pouted. "Now you'll ruin my survey."

"*What* survey?"

"A study of your sex life."

"Who's it for?"

She pointed a finger at herself. "Me," she said brightly. "I was wondering when you were going to make a pass."

"I don't make passes," he retorted.

She stuck out her tongue. The doorbell rang as he lunged for her.

"Saved by the bell." She laughed. "Food?"

"Guess so," he said as he crossed the room to the door. He handed Ann the package and paid the delivery boy. They spread out their sandwiches and beer on the bar. Ann bit into her sandwich and nudged Brady with her foot. "You want to be serious for a while?"

"No. You've got me all excited. Let's get laid."

She chewed lustily. "Sorry about that," she murmured through her food. "Out of the mood now. Besides, I'm too hungry."

He grabbed his sandwich, bit in and shouted with pain.

77

"What happened?"

"Miserable goddamn— I bit my tongue," he rasped. "Son of a bitch, that hurts."

She laughed quietly. "Serves you right," she said. "Here. Soak it in some cold beer."

"Fat help you are."

"So I'm a lousy nurse." She shrugged.

"Shut up and eat," he admonished her. "We got work to do."

He assembled the reports into neat piles and tapped the large chart spread before them. "There it is," he said after a long pause. "The pattern. It's beginning to show."

Ann looked over his shoulder. "Only discs?"

"Uh-huh. Everything else is eliminated." He pointed to the reports. "Not only that, but I'm using only disc sightings I feel are reliable. No lights in the sky or that sort of stuff. Every one of these," he emphasized, "refers to a confirmed disc. If there's any doubt at all, the report gets thrown out."

"How many reports do you have?"

"With what you brought back, over three hundred and eighty."

"That should be enough," she said.

"Maybe. I hope so." He turned to her. "You were a big help with these, Ann. More than you know."

She kissed his nose. "Thank you, kind sir."

"No, I mean that. I could never have gotten those people to loosen up for me."

"What's the next step?" she asked.

He climbed from the table. "I'm still trying to pin something down," he complained, starting to pace the floor. "I need more than I've got. Somewhere in all this"—he jabbed his thumb at the papers covering the table—"there's a key. I haven't quite got my finger on it."

"Shall we fight about it?" she asked.

He stopped in mid-stride. "Fight?"

"I mean it," she said, nodding. "Whenever my dad got into a real hassle with a story, when he couldn't get it all together smoothly, we'd have a rip-roaring argument about it." She laughed. "People who heard us thought we were really angry. Dad shouted and cussed and I gave it right back to him. Sometimes he'd cut the fight short in the middle of a sentence and rush off to the typewriter. He'd usually solved the problem."

Brady walked up to her and kissed her on the forehead. "Sweetheart, I'm not writing a story," he said. "I'm trying to find the missing piece, or pieces, to a puzzle."

"Same thing," she insisted.

"I don't feel much like fighting."

"I don't mind," she said. "A good fight always clears the air."

"Sure. And sometimes makes for bloody noses."

"So what makes you so special?" she demanded.

"What?"

"You heard me, Cliff Brady. If it worked for my old man, it'll work for you."

"Oh, Christ." He reached for his cigarettes.

"Do you believe there's a government plot behind UFO's?" She threw the question at him as a challenge.

"A plot? No."

"Why not?"

"Couple of good reasons. That captain at Barstow was frightened. The Air Force doesn't go around scaring its own people. Not when they're in critical positions like playing nursemaid to a brace of citybuster missiles. Besides, SAC takes a dim view of anyone screwing up their ICBM sites." Brady rubbed his chin while he thought. "The open-house attitude of Blue Book *could* be a blind. You know, let the yokels in to gawk at the pretty things and they go away thinking they've seen it all. But Trapnell isn't that good an actor. He leveled with me. The discs have been reported from all over the world. Some of the best reports are from Brazil and Russia. That lets out the discs being something we've put together. If it's that good, we wouldn't dare risk the loss of such a machine by letting it wander all over the planet. So that's out. Besides, it can't be ours."

"Why are you so positive about that?"

"I've already told you. Not only that, but the propulsion system . . ." His voice trailed off. Ann watched, silent, knowing he was buried in thought. Brady could have been her father in that same position and with the same facial expression.

"That could be the lead," he said. She could barely hear him.

"The drive," he mumbled.

"The drive, Cliff?"

"Oh." He emerged from his fog of concentration. "What makes those things go. It sure as hell isn't any kind of push I know about." He returned to the table and the sighting reports. "Ann!" he called over his shoulder.

He pushed a stack of papers to one side of the table. "Go through these, will you? Look for anything that refers to propulsion. Engines, jets, exhausts, a glow . . ."

"Glow?"

"Uh-huh. Ionization field. It's been reported a few times. A glow or a haze around the disc."

"What's it from?"

"Later, later," he said impatiently. "Just go through these, will you?"

She sighed to herself. Here she was half undressed in the apartment of the man who interested her more than anyone she'd ever known, whose maleness aroused her, and now they were burying themselves in reports of UFO's.

She stood to his side and studied his profile. She wondered if she was falling in love with the big ape.

Relish on corned beef? My God.

"It's *got* to be some form of electrical propulsion!"

Brady slammed a powerful fist into his palm again and again

80

as if to pound reality into his convictions. He spun around and jabbed a finger at Ann. "There's nothing else, *nothing*, that could account for such performance!" The words poured from him with a breathless rush.

She laughed and threw up her arms in mock fright. "I'll agree to anything," she cried. "Just don't beat me any more!"

He grinned self-consciously. "Sorry about that," he mumbled. "I didn't mean to get carried away."

"Think nothing of it," she said with a wave of her hand. "Whatever it is you were shouting about, that is."

"The drive for the discs," he snapped.

"What makes them go," she said.

"What the hell do you think I've been talking about?"

"You're raising your voice again. Do you always get so carried away when you have relish on your corned beef?"

"Will you listen, damn it?"

She threw herself into his arms, forcing him to hold her tightly or they would both have tumbled to the floor. "Ann, for Christ's sake, will you . . . mmmm . . . will . . . I mean . . . mmm."

Brady's head swam as she embraced him. Ann stepped back, her eyes dark and wide. A little more of that and Brady would never be able to control himself. She'd felt that. Good Lord . . .

"I think you'd better tell me about how those things go," she said, still breathing hard.

He didn't move. She knew that kiss had banished everything from his mind except her and the bed in the next room.

Silence. "Cliff, answer me!"

"Oh. What?"

"Tell me about the engines."

"The engines. You want me to tell you about the engines."

"Stop mumbling."

"What engines?"

"The—oh, stop it. You know very well."

"I don't want to talk about the goddamned engines." His

hands were clenched tightly and he looked as if he were standing on eggshells.

"I told you I don't make passes, Ann. I want very badly to make love with you, but I won't play games."

She looked at his face and thought of the pain that had carved those lines and scars. She wanted nothing more in the world at that moment than to cradle that scarred head and face in her hands. But she didn't move.

"Cliff, will you listen to me?"

He swayed slightly, his hands still balled into fists. "I'm listening."

"I want to tell you something. I know how you feel, that you want me. I hoped that you would." She motioned for him not to interrupt. "Hear me out, please. I want you, Cliff. I want to make love with you." She shook her head and he watched her hair and the light changing across her face, and he knew he was falling in love with her. What the hell was she saying?

"But not now, Cliff. Not yet."

He didn't answer her immediately. "Any good reasons?"

"Not for anyone else but me," she said slowly. "It's just too soon."

He let out a long breath and she saw him start to relax. He shrugged. "I always figure a door works both ways," he said.

Instantly she stiffened. "Are you asking me to leave?"

"No, no," he said, careful to be gentle with her. "You're reading me wrong, baby." He saw her confusion. "You know what I want with you," he went on. "That's only a part of it, but it's an important part." He sighed audibly. "But you're an equal partner and I told you I don't push. I can't figure why you want to wait but that's up to you." He moved closer to her and took her hands.

"It's out in the open and I'm glad of that." She nodded. "You know how I feel," he said. "Now it's up to you to come to me."

"Yes." Her voice was a whisper.

"You're something, Ann," he said gruffly. "You get to me, and you do it good. I don't understand it all and I'm not going to try. I know I want you and I'm mixed up about you. I'll let it ride right there for the moment."

She kissed him lightly. "You're marvelous. Do you know that?"

CHAPTER VII

Strange, he thought, just how the feel of her against me can be so important. Ann slept soundly, her hair silk-soft against his arm, the pressure of her body warm and satisfying. The jet-liner rocked gently in turbulence and Ann murmured in her sleep. Brady smiled and turned his head to look through the window. Except for cumulus build-ups over distant mountains, the sky was a clear, deep blue. He glanced at his watch. Another hour and they'd start letting down for Phoenix.

Ann's presence was the result of a last-minute decision to take advantage of Brady's trip to Arizona and Colorado. He told her he'd be spending several days out west.

"Where?" she asked.

"Fly commercial to Phoenix," he said. "I'll rent a plane there and take it up to Flagstaff. Be there for one day, I guess. Then I'll go on up to Denver. I want to spend some time with Walton."

"And who is Mr. Walton?"

"Not 'Mister.' Professor. He's the mucky-muck running the UFO investigation for the University of Colorado. Under contract to the Air Force."

She looked up at him. "Why Phoenix and Flagstaff if you're going to Denver?"

"Denver's last in line. I've got a meeting first in Flagstaff with Dr. Taggert. He's supposed to be pure genius with electrical-propulsion systems."

"Oh."

"Oh, what?"

"Isn't Flagstaff near the Painted Desert?"

"Uh-huh. Why?"

"And Monument Valley?"

"You on a scenic kick?"

She was suddenly excited. "Cliff, I've always wanted to see those places," she said. "Why don't I go along with you? Will you have enough time to . . ."

"Sure," he said in anticipation of her question. "By plane it's only a few hours out of the way." He looked at her and grinned. "Unless you're planning to go by horse."

"Silly. Seriously, Cliff, I'd love to go with you."

He didn't waste any time on the matter. "Great," he said. "What about your job?"

She waved her hand to dismiss any problems. "I've got plenty of time coming to me, and there are more than enough girls to handle the flights, and besides, I'd love to be with you, and—"

"Hold it, hold it!" He laughed. "I get the message." He smiled warmly. "It would be great to have you."

She kissed him. "What flight are you on?"

Five minutes later she was gone, rushing to her hotel to prepare for the trip. The next morning he picked her up by cab and they drove together to the airport.

He shifted carefully in his seat so as not to disturb her. For the first two hours of their flight she'd prattled gaily, as happy as a young girl starting a summer vacation. Then, tired from the heavy workload she'd had for the previous week, up late the night before, she fell asleep.

It gave him the opportunity to think, to run through his mind what he might accomplish with his appointment in Flagstaff.

Taggert—Dr. Kenneth Taggert—was a long shot. Brady had no way of telling what were the odds, but it was the kind of bet he couldn't pass up. Taggert was supposed to be the kingpin of electrical-propulsion research. If anyone might answer the questions Brady found so frustrating, Taggert was the man. But it would help if he came to the scientist with a solid grounding on the subject.

If the discs were real, then they used a propulsion the likes of which the world had never seen. What made them go?

Everything pointed to electrical propulsion. It was anybody's guess as to what type. It could be electromagnetic, electrogravitic, something to do with static electricity or—Brady shook his head. He was out of his depth. It could be just about anything and probably was a type of which he had no knowledge. Something revolutionary in concept and in practice.

Once again. What could be the propulsion, the drive? He reviewed again in his mind the many reports of the ionization in the air, the dimly glowing corona that confirmed an electrical energy disturbance of some kind. Most sighting reports made it clear the discs could move at thousands of miles per hour, and they moved that fast within the atmosphere.

Brady stiffened as a new thought came to him. They could move at thousands of miles per hour *within* the atmosphere. *But no one had ever reported a sonic boom.* Here was another piece to the puzzle. It tied in with a program underway by the Federal Aviation Administration. The FAA was gung-ho to solve the problem of sonic booms. When the supersonic transports showed up, all hell would be breaking loose on the ground beneath the SST's flight path. The boom would break windows and crack walls and have many thousands of people up in arms. The most promising research into eliminating the boom was electrical. A sonic boom was the result of a pressure wave. The air piled up like the forward wake of a speeding ship. The air moved with the speed of sound, but the SST went faster. It left behind it a continuous shock wave that traveled to the ground and woke up people and disturbed chickens and smashed windows. The trick, the science boys had figured out, was to break up the air so that the shock wave couldn't form. They were testing electrical fields. They were *ionizing the air*. It worked in tests. If it worked for supersonic planes . . . and no one had ever reported a sonic boom for a disc . . . They've *got* to fit, Brady thought grimly. And Taggert would know how.

With minimum movement Brady reached for the briefcase at his feet. He glanced at Ann. The shifting of his body stirred her, but only for a moment. Her eyes opened sleepily, she smiled and was almost immediately fast asleep again. Brady opened the briefcase and withdrew his notes on the scientist.

Dr. Kenneth Taggert was unusually young to have earned the prominence he enjoyed in research circles. His background and experience belied his thirty-eight years. Taggert had been through Cal Tech and MIT . . . Brady wasn't surprised to see he had performed advanced rocket-engine research in the Santa Susana laboratories—and, yes; there it was. After two years he left Rocketdyne to get into electrical-propulsion systems with Republic Aviation in Farmingdale, New York. The notes triggered Brady's memory. Taggert, he recalled, had worked on a plasma pinch engine, leaving Republic when the National Aeronautics and Space Administration moved the research program into one of NASA's own laboratories. Taggert followed wherever the most advanced research beckoned; he smacked of the scientist who insisted on going his own way. That made him a rarity in today's world of "scientist teams" within which individuality faded and "group genius" was the goal. Group genius, my ass, Brady thought—a bunch of pencil pushers hot after job security.

Taggert lasted only a year with NASA and then answered the call of Lockheed's nuclear-propulsion program for the AEC. Brady saw the word "Nerva" penciled in his notes, and without going further he knew that Taggert had left *that* program as well.

Nerva had become a funds-depleted foot-dragger that would make a mind like Taggert's ache for release.

For the last two years Taggert had been the director of research for Blackburn Aero, a division of the huge Blackburn industrial empire. Brady searched his memory. Blackburn Aero had invested heavily in the production of huge commercial air freighters, intended primarily for cargo hauling on international routes. Brady recalled they were especially interested in South America where, Frazer W. Blackburn was convinced, the movement of heavy cargo by air had tremendous promise. According to Brady's files, Taggert was directing an engine research program for the great air freighters.

Blackburn constituted one of the true industrial empires, and Blackburn Aero was only one in a family of divisions that ran the gamut from locomotives to huge tankers, from concrete to a massive plastic industry. And power. Everything else old man Blackburn considered transitory. Shipbuilding empires came and went and so did the others. Except one. Commercial power, in any form, was Frazer Blackburn's key to industrial might. Steam plants, electric generating plants, and more lately nuclear-power plants. Blackburn investigated everything in the way of power, from tapping volcanic fires to nuclear coil heating of enclosed bodies of water.

Brady couldn't be certain, but he'd give odds that Blackburn had snatched up Taggert with the one offer no scientist of Taggert's ilk could possibly refuse: open-ended research in his chosen field—electrical propulsion. With unlimited funds, facilities, and personnel. If Taggert was really into something that revolutionary in the power field, then whatever Blackburn spent would be a pittance against the potential return.

"My, you're all wrapped up, aren't you." Ann squeezed his arm gently as she smiled at him.

"I thought you were asleep."

She nodded and yawned. "Was." She stretched and snuggled

against him. "One thing always wakes me up when I'm flying."

Brady glanced out the window and noticed they were in a steady descent. "Built-in alarm clock, huh?"

"Never fails," Ann said. "Just let an airplane start down and I'm Miss Alert. How much longer?"

Brady studied his watch. "Less than thirty minutes."

She disengaged her arm and sat up, reaching for her purse. "Time to powder my nose."

He studied her walk down the aisle. That girl, he thought fondly, has just got to have the most beautiful ass in the world.

"Cliff! Just *look* at it!" Ann pulled at Brady's arm. The horizon swung through a sharp arc as the sudden movement jerked Brady's hand on the control yoke. He righted the Aztec and glared with mock anger at her.

"You wanna fly this thing?" he growled.

She muffled her laughter. "Sorry about that."

"What's got you so fired up?" he asked.

"Over there." She pointed toward the fiery patterns of the Painted Desert. "Aren't we going to fly over it? You said we could . . ."

"On the way out," Brady replied. "I don't want to be late for Taggert."

"Nuts to Taggert. I thought you were giving me the grand tour." She pressed her face to the window. "I've always wanted to see this from up close. Cliff, isn't that a volcano? It is! Look!"

Brady laughed at her excitement. "The whole country is lousy with volcanoes. You'll see plenty more of them," he promised. "We'll take it all in when we leave here."

Brady swung toward the airport in Flagstaff and the cindered wasteland exploded into lush forest. Brady fought increasing turbulence as he descended through his traffic pattern. The runway was seven thousand feet above sea level. He didn't like the field. He couldn't remember a single time when the air was calm.

89

The Aztec protested the bumpy ride, and Brady surprised himself when the tires squealed satisfactorily in a letter-perfect touchdown.

Twenty minutes later they were in a cab on the way to Taggert's office in Blackburn Aero. It wasn't until then that Ann thought of her presence with Brady.

She linked her arm in his and leaned against him. "Who am I, Cliff?"

"What kind of nutty game are you playing now?"

"The man who thinks of everything," Ann said, shaking her head. "Am I your wife, sister, broad, secretary, friend—"

"Secretary."

Ann looked doubtful. "Are you sure you want me along? I should think I'd only be in the way."

"Anything but," he reassured her. He opened his briefcase and withdrew a small folder. "Pad and pen in there," he said. "I want you to sit and listen. If you hear anything that strikes you as odd, or different, or important, anything at all, jot it down."

"But—"

"I don't know what it'll be or even if there'll be anything," he said quickly. Blackburn Aero appeared at the end of the road. "But you've been around this stuff enough to know it almost as well as I do. Play it by ear, will you?"

She nodded. "You're the boss."

"And don't forget it," he quipped.

It didn't go well at all.

Dr. Kenneth Taggert was brilliant, cooperative, friendly, and bland. Brady was almost convinced the scientist patronized him, but there remained a shadowy doubt that kept Brady off balance. The newsman had a surgical skill in eliciting information from those he interviewed, but the knife scraped ineffectually against the urbanity of the man who had received them. Taggert was not an imposing man in the sense one expected of a scientist with his reputation. He was meticulous in every aspect of his appearance. Right down to the manicured fingernails which, Brady knew, damned few scientists ever permitted. There wasn't a visible trace of scientist in Taggert who, even after twenty minutes, seemed almost a carefully packaged nonentity. Brady couldn't find a flaw or a major distinction about the man. That he was a loner Brady had already discerned from his research on the man; he confirmed this opinion within the first few minutes of conversation.

Usually Brady could connect with some form of rapport. He couldn't make it with Taggert and from growing signs of impatience Brady knew he'd better cut the mustard and not continue with pleasantries. Brady shrugged to himself and went to the point. He had already told Taggert of the series he was preparing; in that conversation Brady made certain not to include his personal involvement or convictions. He knew how necessary it was for him, Brady, to appear the objective outsider.

"One of the safety directors of the airlines," Brady was explaining, "and his business involves anything to do with passenger and aircraft safety, is concerned about interference with electrical and electronic systems. He doesn't give a fig about UFO's one way or the other. He sees everything in the light of its effect on safety."

Taggert nodded for Brady to continue.

"In certain disc sightings, pilots have reported some manner of interference. Ignition systems, navigation equipment, communications; that sort of thing."

Taggert moved his hand and Brady waited. "Discs?"

"That's right, Dr. Taggert."

"Or disc-shaped plasmoids?" Taggert smiled.

"The pilots were emphatic about the disc shape," Brady said.

"I'm sure they were," Taggert said. And that was all. Brady couldn't figure the question ending right there. He had no choice but to continue.

"I'm familiar with plasmoids, corona discharges, and similar effects," Brady said. "I thought I'd save your time by simply stating that as a fact. My point is that with complete descriptions of such effects, including St. Elmo's fire, the pilots insist a clearly defined disc has been involved."

"Interesting." Again only the brief murmur from Taggert.

"To review," Brady said, "when holding formation with the aircraft—this includes commercial, military, and private—the discs have shorted out systems, blanked out radios, and made hash of VHF radio navigation equipment. Some radios have even been burned out completely."

"What do you make of all this, Mr. Brady?"

I'll be damned, Brady thought. He's tossed the ball right back to me, and I came to him for help. "From everything I've researched," Brady said with a shrug, determined to remain casual in his approach, "the discs, if they are some sort of machine, utilize a form of propulsion that's electrical in nature. What kind, I have no idea. But whatever it is, it gives off a tremendous electrical field that's picked up by the electrical and electronic systems of the aircraft involved." Brady gestured to indicate he wasn't yet through. "I'm not that well up on electromagnetic systems, *if* that's involved." He forced a grin. "But if anyone is, you're the man. I don't think anyone is more qualified than you are to—"

"Mr. Brady."

The newsman stopped in midsentence. Brady wasn't sure if he'd been rebuked.

"Mr. Brady," Taggert repeated, "I do not wish to appear unkind, but aren't you carrying a process of elimination for rather a long distance?"

"I'm not carrying anything anywhere," Brady said quickly, "except something that's baffling a great many people. If I'm doing any carrying, it's bringing this to you in the hope you can shed some light on the matter. Of course," he added as a thought came to him, "I'm perfectly willing to consider this as wholly conjectural."

Taggert nodded slowly. "I do think that's wisest. You see, you're starting off with a premise that in itself is doubtful. I don't know very much about your UFO's, Mr. Brady, but to have interference with the high-capacity systems of a modern aircraft, from an outside source such as you have described, calls for an intense force field."

Taggert shifted in his seat and smiled at Ann, then turned his gaze back to Brady. "What you're talking about could easily mean an electromagnetic field, although, to be strictly accurate, all force fields, no matter of what appearance, are electromagnetic in nature."

"All?"

"Most certainly," Taggert said. "They must be, of course, since they all function with the same subnuclear energies. What we see as variations in energy dispersion or direction, Mr. Brady, are only the results of our inadequacies in judging correctly the forces that are involved."

Brady glanced at Ann. She was sinking fast. Who the hell ever expected Taggert to get into elemental basics? Goddamn it, he couldn't pin the man down!

"Well, no matter what the system—I'll buy the electromagnetic force field, of course, since you're the one who knows best—but no matter what the system, could there be some sort of leakage from the propulsion unit? Whatever drives the discs?"

This time Taggert's smile could only be, and was, patronizing. "Once again, Mr. Brady," he said in that soft voice, "you're starting off with a premise, and then asking me to build upon that. I suppose, if you wish to continue this as strictly theoretical, that *if* you did build an electromagnetic drive, and *if* you did place it within a disc-shaped machine—although for the life of me I don't know why, since aerodynamically you're introducing a host of problems; but, to stay with your premise, if you did all this,

93

in your disc—it is possible there could be some, umm, leakage would be an acceptable term, I would imagine."

Brady felt a headache coming on. "Would that leakage interfere with aircraft systems?" he asked.

"If all your ifs work out," Taggert said, "which is accepting a great deal on faith, why, yes, it's possible."

"Dr. Taggert, do you feel an electromagnetic drive of some sort is feasible?"

"Anything, given proper knowledge, is feasible. There are certain limiting factors, of course, which—"

"Forgive me, but I mean feasible in the contemporary sense."

Taggert, Brady swore, almost laughed aloud. "Mr. Brady, we have electromagnetic drives right now." He did laugh at the expression on Brady's face. "In fact, we've had them for years. So, for that matter, have the Soviets. We have both carried out extensive testing of plasma-pinch, photon, and magnetohydrodynamics-propulsion systems." Without even a pause, he turned again to Ann. "Did you get that all right, my dear?"

Ann looked up with a vacant expression on her face and nodded.

"Not only that," Taggert went on, "but we have flown several of these in different spacecraft. The Russians as well, I repeat."

Suspicion nibbled at the edge of Brady's mind. Taggert's next words brought confirmation. "Of course, the energy distribution of these systems leaves much to be desired," the scientist continued. "The truth of the matter is that the thrust developed by even the most successful drive flown—they have been orbited, you understand, as part of certain satellite experiments—well, the greatest thrust achieved to date has been exactly a tenth of a pound, and the maximum duration is somewhere on the order of eight days."

Shot down in flames, Brady cursed to himself. Shit, I knew all that before I got here. Time to change the routine.

"Dr. Taggert, are you involved in any research in this area?"

Taggert was openly condescending. "Company research is hardly a matter of public discussion, Mr. Brady." The scientist held up his hand to forestall Brady's expected apology. "However, I understand the manner of your question and I can answer it for you. It would be, ah, more convenient for me if no direct attribution were made."

"Of course," Brady said.

"Your reputation is sufficient assurance," Taggert said with unexpected praise. "But to the point. Every major firm in the nation is engaged in a maximum effort to produce a new system of power. Mr. Blackburn's emphasis on this matter hardly needs to be examined; it's too well known. As I say, all of us in the field are engaged actively in the search for new power systems, for drives, as you have put it."

"Including yourself?"

"Of course," Taggert said.

"Are you into any antigravity programs, Dr. Taggert?"

"We are *all* interested—intensely—in such a matter. I know of at least twenty corporations in the country, each of which spends a small fortune every year trying to find *that* holy grail. However"—Taggert chuckled—"there is a slight problem. We're all of us no closer to the heart of the problem than we were twenty years ago. We've eliminated some blind alleys and we all feel we're smarter than we were, but really . . ." He shook his head and smiled again.

"Could you identify, well, as you might put it, the major problem?"

"Oh, to be sure. We don't even know, you see, what *is* gravity. Really, we have no idea in terms of indisputable fact. We wrestle with Einstein's Special and General Theory of Relativity and we go tramping through the woods of his Unified Field Theory, and we dabble with Lorentz and wonder if quasars will shed some light on the matter; but really, we simply don't know."

Brady noticed that Ann had given up completely.

"I'll sum it up for you, Mr. Brady. If you can bring to me an unquestioned solution as to what constitutes gravity, I can assure you," Taggert said, "you will, overnight, become wealthy beyond your fondest dreams."

Brady made a final stab at it. "What about electromagnetic systems?"

"Mr. Brady, gravitation and electromagnetic forces, or energies, as you will, are separate and distinct. They are also inseparable. We are wrestling with philosophical as well as elemental mysteries. I assure you they are all quite profound."

Before Brady could reply, Taggert rose to his feet. "This is most interesting," the scientist said, "and I would like to continue our discussion. However, time presses." He pushed a desk button and a secretary appeared through a side door.

"Good day, Mr. Brady. It's been a pleasure, Miss Dallas." Taggert was gone before Brady could say another word.

"Well, how did you figure him?" Brady demanded.

Ann slumped in the cab. "My head's splitting," she complained.

"Never mind the skull bumps," Brady snapped. He was irritable and it showed. "Something was goddamned well wrong in there and I still can't figure it."

Ann lifted her hand, then dropped it. "Oh, it was wrong, all right. It has nothing to do with what happened. That old devil, woman's intuition, however."

"Well, go on."

"For a while"—Ann sighed, kneading her forehead with her fingers—"I felt as if your brainboy was patronizing us." Brady nodded. "Then it occurred to me—the intuition bit, I mean—that he wasn't."

"Patronizing us?"

"Uh-huh."

"So?"

She turned to look at Brady. "Cliff, I've never felt smaller in

96

my life." She grasped his hand. "He just didn't *care* whether we were there or not," she went on. "He had to see you because of your reputation, I suppose. Or someone in the front office felt he should see you."

Brady nodded slowly.

"Do you know what he did? Taggert, I mean. The whole interview was like brushing a fly off his sleeve. That's what you and I were. Two flies. He brushed us and went about his business. That's all we meant to him."

Ann hit it smack on the head. The Blackburn outfit spent millions every year to build their public image. So why would they brush off one of the top reporters from the second-largest wire service in the world? It didn't fit, it didn't add up. It felt *wrong*.

What the hell was Taggert hiding?

Maybe, a small voice said to Brady, he just thinks UFO's are so much crap, and anybody who pushes the subject has got to be a nut. Are you a nut on UFO's, Mr. Brady?

He couldn't turn off the pip-squeak dancing around in the back of his head. The unhappy fact of the matter was that Brady had yet to find a single scientist who believed the UFO's—no, he corrected himself, the discs—were even worth bothering about. And they all smiled politely at those who pursued the matter.

Like Cliff Brady.

CHAPTER VIII

BRADY LOOKED AT HIS WATCH AND CURSED. WHO DID THIS SON OF a bitch Walton think he was? Despite his scheduled appointment, Brady had been cooling his heels for an hour in Walton's outer office. Brady couldn't figure what would keep a college professor closeted in his office while he had a visitor from two thousand miles away sitting on his hands. I'll give him another twenty minutes, Brady thought. Then he can go fuck himself.

The previous day's events had already soured Brady. First there had been that infuriatingly nonproductive interview with Taggert. Ann did her best to get the supercilious scientist off his mind, but it didn't take. They left Flagstaff in the rented Aztec, and Brady kept his promise to Ann with several hours of dazzling scenic flight. He circled Meteor Crater, did the Painted Desert from six thousand down to only ten feet above the ground, keeping Ann breathless until he hauled the plane up in a soaring climb. Monument Valley overwhelmed her as Brady approached the vast arena of carved buttresses and sculptured formations from two miles above the ground. Then he took the plane down to a hundred feet, twisting and turning amidst the great stone monuments that gave the valley its name. Finally he eased into a climb and turned for Denver. He'd never felt closer to Ann. He felt as if the final barriers had been dissipated, that this night Ann would give herself completely. They landed in Denver and everything fell apart. Brady cursed Ann's sense of responsibility. If only she hadn't checked with her airlines' operation office. Damn it. But she had, and there was an urgent request for all stewardesses on leave to report in. Something to do with crews on the East Coast being down with food poisoning. Brady didn't know and he didn't care. There'd been an apologetic look in Ann's eyes when she kissed him good-bye. There wasn't time for anything else as she ran for a waiting plane.

Brady cursed and went to bed alone. Early the next morning, still exasperated with Taggert and irritated because of Ann's absence, he showed up at the University of Colorado. His appointment was for nine sharp, and here it was a quarter after ten, and that son of a bitch Walton was playing games. Well, maybe it would be worth it. Brady hoped so, for this trip had so far turned out to be about as useful as teats on a boar.

Five minutes before Brady's imposed limit of telling Walton to go screw, the professor's secretary ushered him into Walton's office. It took Brady no more than sixty seconds to realize he had again come a cropper. The white-haired scientist with whom he sat would have been better off mating rabbits or guinea pigs. Brady fumed as Walton tut-tutted the newsman's sense of urgency in establishing the discs as controlled machines.

"Utter nonsense," Walton said heavily. He made deprecating gestures with his hands and motioned Brady to silence. "The notion that these things, what everyone has popularized as UFO's, might be mechanical contrivances is preposterous. Even the term UFO is ridiculous. It represents an unidentified flying object. The only phrase with any accuracy, young man, is when we say 'unidentified.'"

Brady clamped a tight rein on his temper. The frosty old bastard. He'd rehearsed this goddamned speech of his so many times, it came out of him like water from a tap. Brady pressed his lips together and forced himself to continue writing down notes. Notes, shit, he told himself. I want to quote this mother word for word. I don't want to leave out a thing. The pompous old—

"Are you listening, Mr. Brady? My time, really, is quite valuable."

It should be, Brady thought. The taxpayer is shelling out six hundred grand for your line of crap. "I'm all ears, Professor," Brady said aloud.

"As I said before, the very phrase UFO is responsible for much of the confusion attending this phenomenon. Certainly what people are seeing is unidentified. Much of it exists only above their eyebrows. Hah, hah, it's a cranial sighting, that's what it is. All in the mind. Take the rest of UFO. Flying, eh? Most of these things don't *fly*, Mr. Brady. How can they fly? How can sun dogs fly? Or mirages, or—"

"Colonel Trapnell filled me in pretty thoroughly on the atmospheric effects," Brady broke in.

"Umph. Very good. But to finish, eh? The last word. Objects. Come now, Mr. Brady. If the good colonel provided you with a thorough interrogation, then you of all people should know these are not objects. Not in the sense we regard solid, substantial matter. How could they possibly be objects? We are referring to what I already mentioned briefly. Mirages, reflectional dispersion; that sort of thing. UFO, indeed!" A finger wagged annoyingly at Brady. "I'm afraid it's people like yourself, Mr. Brady, who are responsible for much of the mess in which we now find ourselves. Yes, yes. The newspapers." He says newspapers, Brady grimaced, as if a squirrel had just shit in his mouth. Maybe it did. Brady did his best to ignore Walton's stigma of irresponsibility.

"Professor Walton, I wonder if you would hear me out for a few minutes?"

"Eh? Oh. What on earth about?"

"Discs. Not UFO's. Discs," Brady repeated with emphasis. He

100

didn't wait for Walton's acquiescence but plunged into his research study of UFO sightings. He detailed the extensive pilot reports. He described the film taken at the radar station which even the Air Force could not explain. He went through the discs from beginning to end. He emphasized what had happened at Barstow Air Force Base. He didn't leave out a thing. He hammered home to Walton that he had gone through every possible precaution in retaining only the authenticated, reliable sightings. When he had finished, he sat back in his chair and waited for the reactions of the other man.

He didn't get what he expected. No scientific defense of the Air Force position or even that adopted by the University of Colorado. Walton smiled benignly, as if Brady were a congenital idiot. Brady had expected anything but derision from a man who was this deep into a serious study of reliable sightings of UFO's. No man with an ounce of common sense, Brady knew, could have studied the reports and the photographs and the films, could have judged the radar sightings confirmed by visual observation; no man could have done all these things and emerge from such an effort without acknowledging that, if nothing else, at least the matter demanded impartial evaluation.

Walton acknowledged nothing of the sort, and he took little pains to conceal his reaction to Brady's presentation. The scientist fairly twittered with amusement. He made a steeple of his fingertips and peered owlishly over them at Brady.

"My. Oh, my, but you *do* sound like one of those, hah, hah, one of those enthusiasts we get here so often." Walton snuffled with quiet laughter. "You know what I mean, of course. They frequent those UFO conventions or séances or whatever they call their nonsense, where they have all manner of visitors from Venus and other worlds. Including," Walton said drily, changing his facial expression, "the astral. I'm surprised that someone in your position would—"

"Just hold it right there," Brady said. He knew he was now

101

snarling at the professor, but he no longer cared. "That's enough, Professor. I didn't say a word about visitors from anywhere. I came here hoping to get an objective scientific viewpoint regarding those UFO sightings that appear to have merit to them. I didn't expect a canned speech from you."

"Canned speech?"

"You'll forgive my seeming lack of respect in such august surroundings," Brady said with open sarcasm, "but you've just recited your stock speech number four, or whatever you call your little talk."

Walton was no longer amused. "Your insults are quite unnecessary, Mr. Brady." He spoke in icy tones. "My position toward aerial phenomena is quite scientific and requires no defense from me. I find it quite interesting, however, that your tirade and your lack of good manners is precisely what we encounter with all the other rabid enthusiasts—and I'm being kind—who come flocking to our doors. They *all* have revelations, Mr. Brady. All of them, I repeat. They come in—no, I advise you to listen. Don't interrupt me. You came here for an evaluation, and that is exactly what you are getting. You may quote me if you like—"

"I'll do that, Professor."

"By all means, Mr. Brady, and I would be most interested to read that you are honest enough to include yourself amongst those I am describing to you. To repeat, those like you who come here are always burdened with some deep and dark secret that purports to let us in on solving the mystery of UFO's. There is no end, it would seem, to their ingenuity. If you have indeed spent time with Colonel Trapnell at Blue Book, then you are aware of those poor souls who know, who absolutely *know*, Mr. Brady, that they are in the right, and we deluded folk of science are all obstinate, thickheaded, muddled, and God knows what else because we don't agree with them." Walton leaned forward over his desk. "That description, I am sorry to say, Mr. Brady, is one that applies to you."

102

Brady had regained his composure. He stood up and closed his briefcase. "You remind me of Trapnell," Brady said slowly. "Not that you're in his league, Professor, but you both have the same party line."

"You've lost your amusement value, Mr. Brady," Walton said coldly. "Be good enough to leave."

"Oh, I'm going, all—"

"Professor Walton, Mr. Brady, I'm sorry to disturb you like this . . . ." Brady turned to see Walton's secretary in the doorway.

"Yes, yes, what is it?" Walton wasn't exactly sweetness and light to his own employees, Brady noticed.

"It's Mr. Brady's office," the woman said. "A Mr. Parrish, I believe. They say it's extremely urgent."

Brady looked at the telephone on Walton's desk. "May I?"

Walton frowned, then nodded. "Of course."

Brady picked up the telephone and waited for the operator to connect him with his office in New York. In a moment he heard Parrish's voice. It had been a long time since he'd heard it with such excitement.

"You listening, Cliff?"

"Go ahead, Milt. What is it?"

"Better sit down, boy."

"Get with it, will you?"

He heard Milt Parrish chuckle. "Okay. Hang on to your hat, fella . . ."

Several minutes later Brady replaced the telephone on its cradle. Professor Walton studied his face. "I hope, Mr. Brady, it's not bad news?"

Brady turned to the scientist. "Thanks for your concern, Professor." He said it simply and meant it. At least the old bastard *could* be decent. "No, it's not bad news. Not for me, anyway. I think even you would find it interesting."

"Mr. Brady, I am really very busy, and there are other people waiting to—"

"That was my editor in New York, Professor Walton. He's just had a report from Cape Kennedy." Brady paused deliberately. "It seems that a Minuteman missile was fired a short time ago from the Cape."

"Now, really, Mr. Brady, I don't wish to be unkind, but—"

Brady looked down at him and smiled. "It was a failure, Professor. Not a normal failure. Do you follow me?"

"I do not. I wish you would go."

"In just a moment. I'm almost through. I said it wasn't a normal failure. Parrish said the missile was about three thousand feet up, just beneath a cloud deck, when it exploded." Brady picked up his briefcase and remained silent.

"Missiles have exploded before," Walton said, his exasperation evident.

"They also got some tracking film," Brady said. He smiled again. "But that comes later. Apparently there were a number of newsmen on the press site at the Cape. They were watching the launch. Very carefully, I'm glad to say." He placed the briefcase on the floor and rested both hands on Walton's desk. He looked directly into the eyes of the other man.

"At least a dozen people saw it, Professor Walton."

"Saw what?" Walton shouted. "Will you either get to the point or get out of here?"

Brady relished the moment.

"A disc," he said slowly. "They saw a disc. They saw it emerge briefly from the clouds. The reporters saw it through binoculars. Quite clear, too. They saw some sort of light flash from the disc. At the missile. *At* the missile, Professor. The Minuteman exploded, but you know what? It didn't explode until after that light beam had cut the missile in half."

Brady laughed harshly. "Any comment, Professor Walton? For the record, of course."

The elderly scientist looked back at Brady. A long moment of silence passed. Brady could hardly believe his ears when Walton chuckled and gave Brady a look of pity.

"Do you truly"—Walton sighed—"believe that rubbish?"

"Rubbish, my ass! I told you we had confirmation from—"

"I know, I know." Walton made a lazy gesture with his hand. "Mr. Brady, I *do* wish you would listen. That report you received just now . . ." Walton shook his head and smiled. "If I have heard one such report, I have heard a thousand. You'll see, Mr. Brady. Once the initial excitement dies down, what you heard will most certainly be altered drastically. Discs coming out of the clouds and firing ray beams at missiles. Pah! Rubbish, I say, and rubbish it is!"

Brady grunted to himself. "I should have known," he said. "What if I told you there was film confirmation of what happened? Tracking cameras were—"

"Did your editor in New York see the film, Mr. Brady?"

"No. He—"

"Has *anyone* seen the film?"

"I don't know, of course, but—"

"Yes, yes, I've heard it all before," Walton said in his final dismissal of his visitor. "In due time you'll learn, Mr. Brady. Will you have the courtesy to leave *now*?"

Goddamn all scientists, Brady thought acidly. He left without another word.

CHAPTER IX

"GODDAM IT, THAT'S *great.*"

Brady slammed the newsreel cameraman violently on the back. "Phil, that's tremendous. You don't know what that's going to do for me." Hendricks gasped for breath as Brady poured drinks for himself and the three newsmen crowded into their motel room at Cape Canaveral. Brady waved the bottle at arm's length. "Run that son of a bitch through for me again, will you?"

Hendricks grinned at Brady, "Man, you've already seen it three times."

"And we'll see it three times again, if necessary," Brady cracked. He almost chortled with glee. All the bile he'd accumulated during the past several days had spilled out of him.

Fats McCabe from the *Washington Chronicle* made a rude sound. "Screw him," he said. "I know what I saw. You should have been there. It was clear as a bell. You tell this Professor What's-his-name *I* said he should go play with himself. Maybe"—McCabe smirked—"that's his trouble."

"I'll bet." Someone snickered.

"Phil, how come you got this film, anyway?" Brady asked of Hendricks. "You don't usually cover the Minuteman launches. I didn't think anyone came out for that bird anymore."

Hendricks shrugged. "Usually we don't," he said. "But I had a long lens I wanted to try out for the next Saturn in a couple of weeks. This was the only shot between now and then." Hendricks showed a toothy smile. "Jesus, I never thought it would turn out like *this*."

Brady threw his next question to the group. "Anybody see the tracking film?"

Hendricks, McCabe, and the third man, Ben Rogers, exchanged glances. "What's the mystery?" Brady demanded.

McCabe tapped the projector. "Good thing Phil got this," he said, his demeanor serious. "The Air Force classified their film."

"What?"

"Yeah. Real cute, ain't they?"

"But the Minuteman . . . that goddamned thing's been wide open for years!"

"Sure," Rogers said. "But suddenly it ain't so wide open anymore."

Brady lit a cigarette and dragged deeply. "What's their story?"

"What you'd expect," Rogers replied. "Some crap about a new warhead on top of the bird."

"It's all baloney," McCabe assured Brady. "They had that warhead on display for a week before the shot. No one cared enough about it to take a look."

Brady buried himself in thought. He looked up at Hendricks. "Phil, who else knows about this film?"

"Five people," Hendricks said immediately. "The four of us and Parrish. It's World Press film." He nodded at McCabe and Rogers. "What they know is strictly off the record."

Brady glanced at the others. "Keep it that way, will you? At least until we think it's ripe to break this."

"Sure."

"Of course."

"What about copies?" Brady asked the cameraman.

"Haven't had a chance yet," Hendricks replied. "Jay said he'd let me use the NBC lab soon as they clear some rush work out of the way. I don't want to take this to a commercial house," the photographer emphasized. "I want this baby right in my own sweet little hands."

They laughed with him. "Good deal," Brady said. "Can you make up some stills at the same time?"

"No sweat. How many?"

"Um, maybe six of each. Pick out a few of the best shots, okay? Hey, what about copy negs?"

Hendricks nodded. "Same time I print the film."

"Fine."

"You want to see this now?"

"Let's go. Douse the lights, will you, Fats?"

For the fourth time within an hour Brady devoted his full interest to the screen. The film was short. It would be, of course, with a cloud layer only three thousand feet up. The Minuteman came out of its silo so fast, the whole launch sequence would be over in seconds. Brady watched the Minuteman pad expand in size as Hendricks played around with his telephoto lens. The camera zeroed in on the pad and Brady noticed the red flasher lights warning of a hot bird in the silo. Hendricks panned back so he wouldn't lose the missile when it erupted from the ground. The fire came. A searing burst of flame, clouds of boiling smoke and a giant smoke ring leaped upward. Through the flame Brady saw the Minuteman already pitching over in flight. It ripped away from the ground.

"Phil, slow motion."

Hendricks slowed the projector and the screen flickered as events took place at half speed. Brady wished the damn thing were clearer, but with an overcast sky they were fortunate to have even this much. Before the missile started into the clouds, a disc appeared to one side. Brady strained his eyes to catch every detail. There wasn't much, but something suddenly appeared on the film. A glow, not quite a clear beam, flashed between the disc and the missile. Just as the Minuteman was swallowed up by the clouds, it appeared to break in two.

That was all to be seen for the first sequence. The only sound in the room came from the projector and the heavy breathing of the four men. A faint glow appeared in the clouds.

"That's the blast," Rogers said. "We checked the timing. Range safety officer set off the destruct charges just about then."

Moments later blazing chunks fell from the cloud layer. Several huge pieces plowed into the Cape to throw up sandy geysers. The film flickered, then ended. Someone turned on the lights.

Brady grunted as he made a decision. He grabbed for the phone and dialed the motel switchboard. "Operator, this is Mr. Brady in two eighteen. I want to make a person-to-person call to New York. Right, code two one two. I want to speak with Miss Ann Dallas at the Hotel Lexington. No. Call the information operator in New York for me, will you? Thanks. Right, I'll wait here for you to call back." Brady hung up the phone and looked at the others. "There's a certain young lady who'll be very interested in this film. *Very* interested."

He stood up and stretched, grinning hugely. "Who wants a drink?"

Every World Press office had been instructed to teletype to New York all reports of UFO's. No sooner had the story broken that a disc might have been responsible for the loss of a Minuteman ICBM at Cape Kennedy than the UFO floodgates burst wide open. Overnight Brady came to appreciate, as he hadn't before, the frustrations of someone like Jim Trapnell at Blue Book. The deluge included virtually the complete spectrum of sightings Trapnell had described to Brady. People were seeing UFO's everywhere, and the usual rash of strange visitations plagued the news media. Milt Parrish assigned three secretaries to Brady, who in turn put them to work weeding from the mass of incoming material the reports he wanted. He stuck with his original plan. Disc reports only. Everything else to be discarded. All other shapes, lights, objects, or phenomena were tossed aside. The girls then broke down the disc reports into more detailed categories for Brady to study.

An oddball curve had shown up in the pattern and he couldn't figure it. Reports of discs from South America had increased tenfold. Normally that would have meant little. Brazil gloried in its reports of flying discs and had done so for years. The Brazilians saw discs scooting along harbors, dashing over mountains, landing in the jungle. The Brazilians muttered darkly of secret liaisons with the mysterious occupants of discs that landed in high plateaus. They even had a few juicy murders on their hands that thrilled every lover of suspense in the South American country. Several men with strange radio equipment and crude lead face masks had been found dead nine thousand feet along a plateau. Their grief-stricken families told police of secret meetings at night, of trips to fog-shrouded valleys. The stories assumed the proportions of mass contact between a secret organization and the disc occupants. Brady laughed aloud. When it came to direct contact with disc occupants, he wanted the same terms as Jim Trapnell from Blue Book. He'd want to kick the tires, cut off a piece for lab study, and take a ride in the thing. Until then? Just some more good stories to tell on a dark night.

But the news reports from South America—and Central America as well, he noted—had nothing to do with secret conclaves. These were within the reliable-sighting category, discs reported by airline crews, military pilots of local governments, and even by the crews of American military aircraft in that part of the hemisphere. The discs had all been sighted along the West Coast or over the Pacific. Nothing over the interior or to the east. He shrugged and stacked the reports. He could worry that one for weeks and still come up with a blank.

One report among all the others gnawed at his professional

curiosity. He wished he had more information. He withdrew the teletype from the file and read the cryptic sheet again.

INFORMATION ONLY. STORY FOLLOWS. MACDILL AIR FORCE BASE NEAR TAMPA, WEST COAST OF FLORIDA, SCENE EARLIER TODAY OF FIRE DISASTER. BASE CLOSED OFF, SECURITY. BEST REPORTS INDICATE SEVERAL BAKER FIVE TWO BOMBERS ON COMBAT READINESS FLIGHT LINE DESTROYED DURING SEVERE ELECTRICAL STORM. UNABLE CONFIRM BUT APPARENTLY BOMBERS LOADED WITH HYDROGEN BOMBS. VIOLENT SQUALL LINE HIT MACDILL BEFORE DAWN HEAVY RAIN STRONG WINDS. POSSIBLE TORNADO FUNNEL NO CONFIRMATION. CIVILIANS OUTSIDE BASE OPEN VIEW FLIGHT LINE INSIST CIRCULAR SHAPE SIGHTED IN GLARE LIGHTNING IMMEDIATELY PRIOR FIRE AND EXPLOSIONS. NO COMMENT RADAR TRACKING. CIVILIANS WHO SAW CIRCULAR SHAPE CLAIM VERY BRIGHT BEAM THEN FIRE AND EXPLOSIONS. FLAMES SET OFF FUEL TANKS. ESTIMATE LOSS EIGHT BAKER FIVE TWO BOMBERS. AIR FORCE STATES NO DANGER NUCLEAR WEAPONS INVOLVED. MORE FOLLOWS.

Within an hour from the World Press initial report, the Air Force issued official statements that a tornado had struck the flight line and destroyed a number of B-52 bombers. Brady didn't believe it. Civilians along the fenced perimeter of MacDill had seen a circular—or disc, Brady thought—shape, and then the same sequence of events that had taken place at Cape Kennedy. The disc appeared briefly beneath the clouds, there was a light or energy beam of some kind, and then all hell broke loose. Everything matched too closely to be sheer coincidence. Brady wondered how the civilians could have seen the disc and the fires along the flight line, but never see the thundering tornado the Air Force claimed was responsible for the loss of the bombers.

There was something else. . . . *If* the MacDill report turned out to be true, then, tied in with what had happened to that Minuteman at Cape Kennedy, the discs *had* to be machines, constructed through techniques far beyond anything with which Brady was familiar. Their propulsion, what appeared to be an energy beam of some form, their performance . . .

But that smacked of something from *beyond* the Earth! Try as he might, Brady couldn't accept this solution. And that left . . . A big nothing squeezed itself between Brady's ears. He was ready to start his series on UFO's and still he couldn't come up with the final answers he needed. Russia, England, France, China, West Germany, Japan . . . every one of them had the means of creating the discs. They were in the same technological league with the United States. Well, cross China off the list. The Red Chinese had produced the hydrogen bomb and they were working on long-range missiles, but everything they did, and Brady judged this without deprecating their accomplishments, rested on the pioneering and established results of others. Originality in concept, design, manufacture, and operations lay, especially at this time, beyond the ken of the Red Chinese.

If the Russians had produced the discs; well, goddamn it, they wouldn't be stupid enough to wander all over the United States, tearing up real estate and weaponry in the bargain. The Russians may have been crazy but they weren't stupid, and the arguments against the Soviet discs were so apparent that Brady wasted no further time on *that* subject. Unfortunately, the same arguments applied to the other countries on his list. Each one had the technological acumen, but nothing else fit. Why would they perform in a manner that would be utterly stupid for the United States or the Soviet Union?

They wouldn't, of course. That knocked them out of the box.

So who had the answers? There wasn't a doubt in Brady's mind the Air Force said as little as possible about the disc sightings that had *them* buffaloed. Oh, sure, Trapnell did a convincing song-and-dance routine. He could afford to because everything he said about the discs, lumping them in with the rest of the UFO's, was true enough. It was what the Air Force *wouldn't* say that fouled things up so badly. Maybe, Brady thought, they're just as messed up over all this as I am, only they won't admit it.

There lay the backbone of his series. The discs were real as far as he was concerned. He couldn't pass the Trapnell Test by dragging one into a laboratory, but he could come pretty damned close. His series would lay it on the line, tell the facts in a logical, sober, and yet dramatic manner. He didn't have to hoke up what had happened. One of the beautiful things about putting together a series like this, Brady knew, was that you didn't need to act like a pitchman selling a cure-all snake oil. He would lay it on the line as he saw it, and—

His office buzzer snapped him out of deep thought. Brady pushed the switch. "Yeah?"

"Milt here. We got troubles."

Brady straightened in his seat. "What's up?"

"Rather tell you face to face."

"Be right there." He cut the switch and started for Parrish's office.

Parish hit him in the belly with it. Nice and clean.

"Phil Hendricks just called. He lost the film from the Cape."

Brady's face spoke for him. Parrish couldn't remember the last time he'd seen Brady gape.

"Maybe 'lost' is the wrong way to say it. Phil said the film was stolen."

"But . . . Jesus, I mean . . . what about the copies?"

Parrish shrugged. "Gone."

"How? Where? What the hell happened?"

"Don't know. Hendricks is beside himself. They were stolen from his apartment sometime last night." Parrish looked up at Brady. "You ready for the rest?"

"There's more?"

"The Air Force released the tracking film of that Minuteman launch."

"Christ, that's something. At least that'll show—"

"There's no sign of a disc. Randall just called from Washington. He saw the film. The Air Force ran it three times for him. Nothing showed."

"But what about the goddamned missile?" Brady shouted.

"It's there. Also the failure. But no disc. Randall was positive about it."

"Milt, that fucking disc was on that fucking film!"

"So you told me. But it's not on the Air Force film."

"Do you think I'm—"

"Don't bother saying it. I know better. Besides, even if I wanted to question you, there's Hendricks and McCabe. And Rogers. Do you think the Air Force doctored their film?"

"What else?" Brady said through clenched teeth. "The sons of bitches. It wouldn't be hard to—"

A copyboy came into Parrish's office with a Teletype sheet. "Sorry to bust in, Mr. Parrish, but you told me to—"

"Thanks, Jimmy." Parrish scanned the sheet. "Well." He sighed. "Here it is." He looked up at Brady with sympathy on his face. "Read this," he said. "You're being shot down in flames."

Brady read quickly. Parrish watched the newsman's face whiten with renewed anger.

LATEST ADD. WP SPECIAL. PENTAGON. THE DEPARTMENT OF THE AIR FORCE STATED OFFICIALLY TODAY THAT AN EXHAUSTIVE EXAMINATION OF THE TRACKING FILM OF THE MINUTEMAN MISSILE THAT EXPLODED IN A RECENT TEST AT CAPE KENNEDY SHOWS ABSOLUTELY NO SIGN OF A UFO AS HAS BEEN CLAIMED BY CERTAIN NEWS SOURCES. THE FILM WAS EXAMINED BY PROFESSOR DAVID A. WALTON OF THE UNIVERSITY OF COLORADO, BY MISSILE SCIENTISTS FROM THE EASTERN TEST RANGE, AND BY

114

OTHER SCIENTISTS WHO SPECIALIZE IN AERIAL PHENOMENA. THE AIR FORCE ADMITTED THAT THE SEQUENCE OF EVENTS OF THE MINUTEMAN EXPLOSION COULD HAVE BEEN MISTAKEN BY INEXPERIENCED OBSERVERS AS INDICATING ANOTHER OBJECT IN THE AIR. IMMEDIATELY BEFORE THE MISSILE ENTERED THE CLOUD LAYER ABOVE CAPE KENNEDY THERE WAS A PREMATURE IGNITION OF THE SECOND-STAGE MOTOR. A JET OF FLAME ISSUED AT A RIGHT ANGLE TO THE BODY OF THE MISSILE. THIS SUDDEN LIGHT WAS REFLECTED FROM A NEARBY CLOUD, GIVING THE IMPRESSION OF A CIRCULAR OR DISC-SHAPED OBJECT NEAR THE MISSILE. SEVERAL NEWSMEN CLAIMED THIS OBJECT, IN REALITY THE CLOUD THAT WAS REFLECTING LIGHT, SENT AN ENERGY BEAM OF SOME MANNER AT THE MINUTEMAN. THE AIR FORCE HAS NO KNOWLEDGE OF ENERGY BEAMS. HOWEVER, A LINE OF LIGHT DOES APPEAR ON THE FILM. THIS HAS BEEN IDENTIFIED AS THE FLAME JET THAT ISSUED FROM THE MISSILE WHEN THE SECOND-STAGE ENGINE IGNITED PREMATURELY. POOR VISIBILITY AND LOW CLOUDS, STATED THE AIR FORCE, COULD PRESENT TO AN EXCITED OBSERVER AT A DISTANCE THE OPTICAL ILLUSION OF A PHYSICAL OBJECT AND A LIGHT RAY. THE AIR FORCE NOTED THAT THE PRESS SITE ON CAPE KENNEDY USED FOR OBSERVING THE MINUTEMAN LAUNCH IS A MINIMUM TWO THOUSAND FOUR HUNDRED YARDS, OR APPROXIMATELY ONE AND A HALF MILES, FROM THE MINUTEMAN PAD. UNDER CONDITIONS OF POOR VISIBILITY, THE VIEWING DISTANCE, THE FLAME AND SMOKE FROM THE MISSILE SILO, AND THE SPEED OF THE LAUNCH, MIS-IMPRESSIONS AND OPTICAL ILLUSIONS ARE QUITE COMMON. THE REPORT THAT THE MINUTEMAN WAS CUT IN HALF BY THE ENERGY BEAM IS OF COURSE ERRONEOUS, STATES THE AIR FORCE. THE PREMATURE IGNITION OF THE SECOND-STAGE ENGINE INITIATED THE STAGE SEPARATION SEQUENCE AT THE SAME TIME, BRINGING ABOUT A NORMAL BUT PREMATURE SEPARA-TION OF THE FIRST AND SECOND STAGES. THIS EFFECT AP-PARENTLY WAS ALSO MISINTERPRETED BY PRESS MEDIA PRESENT

AT THE CAPE. PROFESSOR DAVID A. WALTON COMMENTED THAT SUCH MISINTERPRETATIONS ARE COMMON. THE PROFESSOR. . . .

Brady felt sick. There wasn't any use in reading further. He could anticipate well enough what Walton would have said. Brady tossed the sheet back to the desk.

"What's next, lover boy?" Parrish quipped.

"What the hell are they so scared of they've got to steal films from—"

"You don't know *they*, and I assume you mean Air Force," Parrish broke in, "stole the film."

"Who else could have done it?" Brady snapped. "Only the Air Force knew about it."

"You're too mad to see straight," Parrish said, not unkindly. "I believe like you do. The blue-suiters had something to do with copping the film. But you can't prove it and I can't prove it. However," Parrish said with a tight smile, "it does involve me a bit more than it did before."

"How so?"

"I don't like my film being stolen."

"How do you think Hendricks feels?" Brady asked.

"Lousy. But I wasn't finished. We were scheduling the series to start a week from Monday, right?"

"You changing things around?"

"Sure am. You're going to have a busy weekend. This is Friday. I want to start the series *this* Monday. We're pushing it up a week."

Brady hesitated. "But that means—"

"I know what it means," Parrish said quickly. "It means you don't sleep this weekend and you don't get laid and what you will be doing is to write your fingers to the bone. I want the copy in here no later than ten Sunday night. We start sending at two A.M. Monday to make the morning papers. Anything else?"

Brady shook his head.

116

"You don't look happy," Parrish observed.

"Like you said, I don't sleep or get laid. I just write. Hell of a weekend."

"Yeah, my heart bleeds. This is your baby and I'm letting you run with the ball. Any complaints?"

Brady grinned at his editor. "None."

"Take off."

Brady held up his middle finger and went back to his office.

Ann Dallas pulled the covers gently over the sleeping form of Cliff Brady. She slipped into the pajamas she'd brought to his apartment and eased into bed next to him. I could blow a bugle, she thought, and it wouldn't bother him. Brady slept with complete exhaustion. He'd worked all Friday night and through into Saturday without rest. Ann found his urgent message waiting at flight operations when she landed from a West Coast trip. She called him to learn of his marathon stint at the typewriter.

"You know how to make coffee?" he barked into the phone.

"Y-yes," she stammered, taken aback with his brusqueness. "Why?"

"Get your beautiful ass over here fast as you can," he said. "I need you, baby, and not for the sack. You can make me coffee and cook for me and keep me awake." He told her he must deliver his first four articles no later than Sunday evening. If he could do it, he added, he wanted to complete the series by then.

"I'll be there," she said, sighing audibly into the telephone. "Although I have had better invitations—"

"I think I love you," he said gruffly. "Hurry up. Bye." The phone went dead.

She made drinks for him, cooked, rubbed his aching shoulder and neck muscles, and was kissed fervently as the result of sudden inspirations on his part. He gulped down Benzedrine capsules to stay awake and attacked the typewriter with almost religious fervor. She studied him with growing admiration. He

117

never slowed his pace except to stretch and groan with complaining muscles, which brought her hurrying to him with soothing fingers.

By four o'clock Sunday morning he couldn't work anymore. The words were there, but he couldn't get them straight. His fingers stumbled on the typewriter keys. He knew it was time to break. He stood up, clothes rumpled, his face bearded. His eyes were hollow. "I need six hours' sleep," he said hoarsely. "Get me up no later than ten. I've got two more articles to do and then I want to edit the stuff." He blinked several times as if to confirm she was really there.

"Did I tell you I love you?" he asked.

She nodded, a smile on her lips.

"Christ, I think I do." He went into the bedroom and collapsed.

She moved closer to snuggle with him. He mumbled in his sleep and turned, his arm resting across her breasts. In the darkness she smiled to herself.

CHAPTER X

"I THOUGHT *you* WERE THE FUCKING EDITOR AROUND HERE!" CLIFF Brady gestured with open contempt. "Ass kisser is more like it."

Despite himself Parrish whitened. His voice came out like a hiss. "If I were you, Cliff, I'd—"

"Thank Christ you're not," Brady snapped. "At least I can look in the mirror without throwing up. The first time, the very first goddamned time you've got to stand up and be counted, you fink out." Brady stabbed a finger at Parrish. "Well, you fooled me. That's a hell of an act you've been putting on all this time. Where's your fucking skirt?" Brady sneered. "Because you sure ain't got any balls to fill those pants."

Parrish eased himself slowly into his chair, never taking his eyes off Brady. My God, he had no idea Brady would flip this way. They'd killed the UFO series after the first three installments, and Brady acted as if it were the end of the world. Parrish forced himself not to lose his temper. One madman in the office was enough.

"Will you let me get in a word?" Parrish said it with a thin smile in an attempt to regain the warmth that usually existed between them. It didn't take. Brady was too far gone to bring this back to a gentleman's level.

"Get in a word? You unholy son of a bitch. Bad enough you

killed the series. *You!* Not anyone else!" Brady shouted. "So long as that fucking sign on your desk says 'Managing Editor,' you run the show. At least that's what you've told me all these years." Brady gesticulated wildly. "But the first time they put on the pressure, you crack like an eggshell. Get in a word, huh? Where the hell were your words when you killed the series? The least you could have done was to pick up the goddamned phone and—"

"I tried to reach you!"

"I just bet you did. For ten years you've always been able to get hold of me no matter where the hell I was. Now I'm in the same goddamned city and all of a sudden nothing works." Brady was close to becoming physical. Parrish didn't want that. If Brady blew his cool completely, there'd be a breach so wide neither man would ever be able to close it.

Parrish put all the sincerity he could manage into his voice. "Cliff, I told you I did everything possible to get you," the editor said. "There wasn't that much time. I was told to kill the series immediately." He shook his head. "Jesus, I know how you feel. I'm sorry as hell about—"

Abruptly, Brady calmed down. Where before he had exploded with anger he was now cold. "All right," he said with a release of pent-up breath. "We'll hear you out. Who ordered you to kill the series?"

"It came from the top."

"Don't play games with me, Milt. I asked you *who.*"

Parrish shrugged. No use hiding it. "Wilkinson."

The name stopped Brady, as Parrish knew it would. Wilkinson *was* the top, the president of World Press.

"I've been trying to explain," Parrish continued. "It was Wilkinson personally. Himself. No secretaries or flunkies. He called me directly and said he would confirm it in writing." Parrish made a face. "He didn't ask or recommend. He *told* me to kill the series effective immediately."

120

"And you just took it lying down?" Brady was incredulous. "You're supposed to be the big goddamned lion of Editors' Row, and you get a lousy phone call and just like that"—Brady snapped his fingers—"you blow everything I've done for all these weeks? Either I don't know you very well or you're lying."

The words hung ominously between them. Parrish preferred not to hear that Brady had called him a liar.

"No, I didn't just take it lying down."

Brady made an obscene gesture. "It looks like it. You killed the series just like the good little boy you were told to be, and you tell me you didn't take it lying down. What kind of shit is that?"

Parrish flared. "You asked me what happened and I told you!"

"Like hell you did." Brady smiled coldly at the other man. "You told me you got a phone call and you went to see the man. *Now* tell me what happened in your little tête-à-tête."

"Wilkinson said it was a matter of policy," Parrish said. He knew it was lame but it was the truth.

"Policy!"

"That's what the man said."

"Since when have you let someone tell you how to run your shop?"

"It's not the same. This is the first time that—"

"Don't crap me," Brady said. His voice was quiet. "I've known you too long, Milt. Just don't shit me."

"I told you straight."

Brady's disbelief mirrored in his eyes. "Just like that, huh? You didn't say anything. You just took your castor oil and crawled back under your desk. You—"

"I've had it," Parrish burst out, his own anger pouring over his self-control. He came to his feet and shoved a finger against Brady's chest. "Have you stopped to think *why* Wilkinson killed the series?"

Brady knocked aside Parrish's hand with an easy blow that

sent pain stabbing up the editor's arm. He tried not to wince. Brady didn't know his own strength and . . .

"You're asking *me* why?" Brady asked. "I've been trying to find out from *you*. Quit the games and lay it out, will you?"

"You're way out in left field."

"Did Wilkinson say that?" Brady demanded.

"Not in quotes but in so many words. He—"

"Did he say why I was out in left field?"

"No, but—"

"Did you *ask* him?"

"I talked about it for a while."

Brady's quiet was ominous. "You talked about it for a while," he mimicked Parrish. "Did you tell him *you* were the editor here and that if he didn't like it he knows what he can do?"

"You're awfully free with *my* job, aren't you?"

"Did you tell him even that?" Brady was almost pleading for Parrish to tell him he'd stood up to Wilkinson.

Parrish paled. "No."

"You going to tell me why?"

"I don't have to tell you *anything*," Parrish said coldly. "Not a damn thing."

"No, you don't," Brady agreed. "You haven't got any balls either."

"All right, damn you. As far as Wilkinson is concerned, you sound like a nut." He saw Brady stiffen but plunged on. "Some of your stuff *is* way out. I've told you a hundred times it's not enough to feel you're right or even be positive about it unless you can *back up* what you're saying. The—"

"And I can't back it up, huh?"

"That's the way it is," Parrish snapped. "You can't back up what—"

"Even with the eyewitnesses to what really happened at Cape Kennedy. Funny," Brady said, "you were awfully willing to accept what I saw in the film because it was supported by Hendricks and McCabe and Rogers. You made me pretty speeches about getting involved because of stolen film. You—"

"You wait right there," Parrish broke in. "I called your eyewitnesses. I spoke with all three of them. They admitted that if it came down to the kind of questions you've got to answer from a witness stand, they couldn't be positive about a disc. They said maybe the Air Force was right. They think they're right, but they couldn't swear to it."

"That's not what they told me."

"It's what they're saying now!"

Brady didn't answer for a while. He took a deep breath. "All right. I won't interrupt. Let's hear the rest of your fairy tale about Wilkinson."

"You just won't believe you might be wrong about this whole scene, will you?" Brady refused to answer. "Okay, okay," Parrish said, "we'll lay it all out nice and neat. The way your copy reads it sounds as if you're accusing someone of carrying out a monstrous scheme against the country. Or the world. It's hard to tell," he said, sticking it in deeper. "But you don't know *what* kind of plot. Or *who's* carrying it out. *If* anyone is carrying it out. Whether it sits well with you or not, you *do* sound like a nut. If you . . ."

Brady lifted his hand and Parrish lapsed into silence. "Maybe," Brady said softly, "I'd better get something clear. Do you think I'm a nut?" He held up his hand again. "No speeches. Just a plain yes or no."

Parrish sighed. "Of course not. No." He emphasized the word.

"Thanks for the towering vote of confidence," Brady said. He was ungracious about it and he didn't care. "If you don't think I'm some kind of nut, then you must have confidence in my work."

"You know I do," Parrish said, hoping the thaw had started. "We've worked together for a long time, haven't we?"

"Yeah, we sure have," Brady agreed. It was the most pleasant tone of voice Parrish had heard from him since the fracas started. "And you've always backed me up all that time," Brady continued. "We've made a hell of a team."

Christ, Parrish thought with overwhelming relief, the storm's over. "Damn right we have," he said.

"That's why I'm asking you to tell Wilkinson to go shit in his hat."

Parrish stared.

"And run the series."

Parrish didn't believe what he was hearing. "Are you out of your mind?" he shouted. He knew his voice was shrill but he couldn't help himself. Here it seemed everything was back to an even keel and now . . . now *this*! "You know I can't run the series if Wilkinson refuses!"

To his astonishment, Brady remained calm. "You ought to take lessons in lying, Milt." Brady smiled at him. "I could buy your argument about the series, about my being off base," he said, "except for one little mistake you made. Sunday night, just four days ago, you read this series. It didn't bother you then. It bothered you so little, you committed the full nine articles. Now that Wilkinson has made his little speech, suddenly you don't like the series. Not until now. Quite a switch, wouldn't you say?"

Parrish fought for the words.

"You got no balls and you're a liar to boot," Brady said. "Shove your job up your ass."

Ann tried for hours to reach him. The World Press operator said he had left the office and she had no idea when he would be back. Ann's flight left in only two hours. But she *had* to reach Brady. Thirty minutes before flight time, she talked another girl into standing in for her. Every twenty minutes Ann dialed Brady's number. At ten thirty that night he finally answered the phone. Ann could hardly understand him.

"Darling, will you listen? *Please*. I must talk with you."

"Shure. Wanna talk with *you*. Ever tell you I'm in love, in love wish you?"

My God. Of all the times . . . "Cliff, I'm *serious*."

"So'm I. Where the hell are you?"

"At the field. Will you wait there for me?"

"I'll wait anywhere for you. Till hell freezes over. Even till it melts. Howzat? Pretty good, eh? Till hell melts over. I'll be waiting for youuuuu."

She had never heard a hairy laugh before. She looked at the telephone as if it had turned into a snake. "Cliff. Cliff? *Listen* to me."

"Shure. I'm . . ."

"Never mind," she said firmly. "Take a cold shower. Do you hear me? Take a cold shower. Drink coffee. Lots of hot coffee. All right?"

"Thas' silly. Why should I take a hot shower and drink cold coffee? Never heard' anything so silly in m'life."

Ann groaned. "I'll be right there. Just wait for me." She hung up the telephone and took a deep breath. Well, it didn't matter if he *was* smashed. What she had to say would sober him. And fast. She hurried through the terminal to get a cab.

She pushed open the door to his apartment and heard the shower. Thank God for small favors. She glanced at the table in the living room. She couldn't tell if he had spilled more coffee than he managed to get into him. But at least he'd tried. The bathroom door was open. She stood outside and called him. "Cliff?"

"That you, honey?"

"Are you all right, Cliff?"

A waterlogged head peered around the edge of the shower curtain. At the rim of the bathtub. The head grinned sheepishly at her.

"What on earth are you doing down there?"

"Trying to drown myself. Gimme a kiss."

"You're getting me all wet!" she exclaimed.

"Good for what ails you."

"Me? You're the one who needs—"

He kissed her again.

"Cliff, you idiot. Let go."

He grinned at her. "You're beautiful and I love you and I'm glad you're here and what's so all-fired important?"

"Later," she said. She straightened her skirt.

"What's wrong with now?" he asked.

"Later," she repeated. "Hurry up out of there. I'll put up some fresh coffee. By the way, what were you doing in there before? Drinking coffee or washing the table with it?"

"Can't remember."

"I'm not surprised. Head hurt?"

"Just minor agony."

"Want an Alka-Seltzer?"

"Gaagh. Yes."

"I'll bring it to you."

Fifteen minutes later he came into the living room and grabbed for the coffee. They didn't say a word until he had downed the second cup. He leaned over and kissed her gently. "All right," he said. "I'll probably last through the next few hours. Where are my cigarettes?" She lit one and placed it between his lips. He dragged deeply and leaned back on the couch.

"Okay. Let's have it," he said.

"I don't know where to begin."

"Punch hard. It's easiest that way."

She placed her hand on his arm. "We received the word just this afternoon."

"Ann, stop playing games." He showed his annoyance. "*What* word?"

"We're forbidden to talk with you."

He stared at her. "You mean the crews?"

"That's right."

"Spell it out, will you, hon?" She tried to read his expression but couldn't get through. She sighed. "It's simple, I suppose. Your articles are having a tremendous impact. Someone found out—you've been seen with me and several of the crews, of course, so it wouldn't be difficult—anyway, the company found out you'd been talking with some of the crews, and"—she shrugged—"everyone has been told not to speak with you. Any inquiries on your part, about anything," she emphasized, "are to be directed to the front office, blah, blah. That's about the size of it, Cliff." She squeezed his arm. "I'm sorry."

"Sorry? What for?"

"Isn't it obvious?" His poker face and the question flustered her. "I mean, here we're all being told to have nothing to do with you, as if, as if"—she groped for the words—"you're something terrible who would contaminate us. Cliff, that's a terrible thing to do to someone!"

He smiled at her. "No, it's not." He drew deeply on the cigarette and blew out a long plume of smoke. His face had a lopsided grin. "Besides, you haven't heard *my* news."

She gestured toward the half-empty bottle of Scotch. "Were you celebrating?"

He snorted sarcastically. "I suppose you could say that."

"I must say you don't seem very disturbed over what I told you," she said. She felt exasperated, as if Cliff should have reacted more strongly to the news she had brought him. If something like that had happened to her . . .

"Shit, I'm not disturbed."

She noticed a sudden change, as if a cloud had passed over his face. "What were you going to tell me?" she prompted.

He was buried in thought and she waited for him to respond. "By God, it might just fit." She was annoyed. Cliff was talking to empty air and not to her.

"Will you tell me—"

127

"Sorry. Didn't mean to be rude," he said. His apology surprised her as much as his fleeting moods and the rapidity with which he changed. "Pour me another coffee? I want to get something straight in my own mind."

The cup was almost empty when he came to a decision. "Ann, I started to tell you before." A rueful grin appeared on his face. "Yeah, I've got some news all right. First WP canceled the UFO series."

"Oh, Cliff . . ."

He held up his hand. "That's only for starters."

"But *why*? The series is wonderful! Everyone who's been reading about it is . . . why," she almost spluttered in indignation, "even the passengers are talking to us about—"

"Wait, wait a minute, baby. Hear the rest of it first."

"Well, it can't be any worse."

"Hah. I quit today."

She didn't have any immediate response to his announcement. He grunted in reflection. "I told Parrish to shove it."

Finally she found her voice. "Was it because . . ."

He patted her hand. "What else? I couldn't do anything else. You've either got balls in this game or you don't. And one of the things you *never* do to a byliner is pull the rug out from under his feet. Especially when you don't notify him first, and, most especially, when you haven't got more than a pisspoor excuse about policy for creaming the guy."

"Policy?"

"That's what they told me." He reviewed the episode with Parrish. "It's a blind. It's *got* to be a blind. Policy, my foot. They were putting the screws to me, Ann. Bearing down with the pressure."

He turned and held her eyes. "Someone is trying to shut me up."

"But who, Cliff? And why would they want to do such a thing?" She tried desperately to stay with his thoughts.

"The only 'who' I know is the bastard who gave the orders. Wilkinson. He's top dog for WP. But what puzzles me is that Wilkinson has never stepped into anything before. Jesus, even when we did that series on trying to look at communism from *their* side of things. We practically had mobs stoning the office. But no one interfered with us. But *now*," he shook his head, "now the roof caves in. And because of what I've been saying about the discs."

He reached for another cigarette. "I didn't have any leads until you showed up here," he said. "I mean, I couldn't figure Wilkinson. And I still can't figure Parrish sucking eggs the way he did. But what you told me begins to put some light on this whole thing. First Wilkinson steps into the picture. That's all wrong. I've never even *seen* the man. Did you know that?" She shook her head. "I don't even know what the mother looks like. Then right out of the blue he sticks his heavy hand into things. Parrish walks the plank and cancels the series."

He turned again, his face grim. "Do you know what they did today? They boxed me in. They *knew* I'd quit because they knew I'd *have* to quit."

He scratched his chin, lost again for the moment in thought. "They're squeezing me. Get rid of the one weapon I've got—my column. If they fire me it's too obvious. So they squeeze me into a corner and they force me to quit. Neat. Oh, baby, it's neat. I did just what they wanted me to do."

"But—but, who is 'they'?"

"I don't know," he confessed. "Maybe Wilkinson, or maybe someone who got to Wilkinson. I don't know. But they're out to get me, to turn me off. Look, I've talked to pilots and crews only from your airline, right?"

"I—I guess so, Cliff."

"Sorry. You couldn't have known one way or the other. But that's what I did. Most of my airlines sightings have come from your outfit. I never identified the pilots or anyone else. I never identified the airline. I made sure *not* to do that. Yet the very same day the series is killed and I'm boxed into quitting, it's *your* airline that sends out notice I'm poison. That's a damned convenient coincidence. Want to take odds no other airline got the word like yours did?" She started to speak, but he motioned for her to wait. "There's something else I want you to consider. How'd they know I was talking with you and the others? I never told anyone. I never even told Parrish what outfit you worked for."

He stubbed out his cigarette with an angry gesture. "Someone's been watching just about everything I've done. That means organization of some kind."

"Don't you have any idea of who they might be?"

"Uh-uh. Not yet, anyway. Maybe Wilkinson is tied in or maybe he's doing someone a favor. I don't know. From the way it looks, Wilkinson figures to be a part of the picture. Parrish I can't figure. Maybe he's getting old and he's scared that good jobs are hard to get. I wasn't able to latch onto the size of the effort that's going into this. Not until you showed up."

She felt her body relax. At least she knew she'd done right, that what she had to say was important to him.

He brought the telephone to the table. "Ann, call someone you know at one of the other lines, will you? Stewardess, pilot; doesn't matter. Just so long as they're crew. Ask them if they got any word like you people did."

She called stewardesses of three separate airlines. None of them knew anything about company orders not to discuss UFO's. Only one of the girls knew Cliff's name.

"See?" he said when she completed the calls. "There's a direct tie-in all right. I never mentioned your company and yet they're in a sweat about me. They got the word from someone, Ann. Someone who's got a hell of a lot of influence with the line."

She tried to be practical about matters. "What happens next, Cliff? What will you do?"

130

He dragged the Scotch to the table and poured for both of them. "Do? First things first. Try to figure this out." He took a stiff drink and sighed. He put his feet up on the table and wriggled his toes. She wanted to hold him. The import of what he'd been saying was beginning to sink in. The series canceled, he'd lost his job, he . . .

"So first they label me as a nut," he was saying. "A lunatic who's gone ape over UFO's. No one makes any distinction about the matter. I'm just a nut who's scrambled his marbles. It's easy to do. There are plenty of kooks around who come from Venus or screwed Miss Mars of 1969, or God knows what. I'm lumped with the rest of them. Ready-made character assassination. The more I protest, the worse it gets. Instant shithead, that's me. They don't have to say a word. Anyone with an ounce of common sense," he said sarcastically, "*knows* that UFO's aren't real. They're not even there. If you say publicly they *are* real, then you're one of the lunatics. It's perfect, almost as if the whole thing were set up in . . ." His voice trailed away and he stiffened visibly as a wild thought came to him. He put it aside, not rejecting it, but filing it mentally for attention later.

"Okay," he said, "we'll take this piece by piece. For some reason, someone's decided I've got to be turned off. Nothing drastic like a concrete bath. Just turned off. Made to look like a jerk who's gone off half-cocked about UFO's. Next question," he said, holding up two fingers, "is why."

"That's what I'd like to know," Ann murmured.

"It's obvious. I'm on to something. I've gotten home. Why else would they steal that film from Hendricks, unless I'm under their skin? They're not worried about my saying that UFO's are real. Entire organizations devoted to UFO research, like NICAP, have been saying just that for years. But in my own way I've been sorting out the nonsense from what's real. I'm on to something and I've got—I *had*—a column with millions of readers every day. So the next question is, Whose cage have I been rattling?

The whole idea sounds so wild I don't even want to say it out loud." He looked at Ann. "Am I making any sense?"

"I'm not sure," she said.

"I don't blame you," he replied. "Stick with me. Maybe the pieces will start to fall into place. We'll assume I hit the right nerve with someone. I'm agitating them. They're upset. Whoever they are, they've got influence. That much is obvious or I wouldn't be out of a job. But I don't know *who* it is. This thing with Parrish isn't kosher, Ann. Milt wouldn't balk at a story if I told him I turned into a werewolf every time the moon was full. Two guys have worked together as long as we have . . ." He shook his head. "So it can't be Parrish. Someone got to him, all right."

"How do you mean that?"

"They played him like a fish on a line. He backed me up, but he never really bought the 'UFO's are real' bit. They didn't ask too much of him. Just get Brady off his kick with UFO's and little green men from Mars. They tell him there's opposition, people are complaining, and they don't ask him to go out and break my back. From his viewpoint he's supporting me as a matter of faith. He'd rather have me doing something else, anyway. So he passes on the word and—I forgot his canceling the series the way he did. I don't know, honey, maybe they told him to do it that way or maybe he felt a nice clean cut was the best answer. It really doesn't matter, I suppose."

He leaned forward to rest his face in his hands. Ann knew he was talking aloud to himself as much as to her. She didn't mind. Cliff would share it with her when he had his mental affairs in order.

". . . worry about myself except for a couple of other items. First, the film. Unless the film proved something that this . . . this group, whoever or whatever they are, didn't want before the public, why the devil would anyone want the film? But the biggest mystery of all is Wilkinson."

"Maybe," Ann smiled, "he just doesn't like UFO's."

"Christ, that's about as valid as anything I've come up with," Brady muttered. "But seriously, Wilkinson shouldn't give a damn one way or the other—hell, I've already gone through that with you. He's the chairman of the board of World Press, but he's also on the board of a dozen corporations. He's not a newsman, he's a financier. He's a shrewd money handler. Brilliant, for that matter. Wilkinson's not the kind of individual to get involved in policy matters with news. He's—hey, maybe that's it!" Brady's sudden shout made Ann jump.

"W-what's—"

"Hold it," he barked at her. "Goddamn it, if I'm right . . ." He dialed his office. "Ralph? Brady here. Yeah, I know. Thanks. Later, will you? I need something. Pull the file on Wilkinson, huh? Right. Wilkinson, Drew David. Sure, I'll hang on."

He cupped his hand over the telephone. "Cross your fingers or pray or something, baby," he told her. He wouldn't say another word but waited with mounting impatience.

"Yeah, I'm here. Got it? Good. Okay. Read me the list of corporations he's involved with." Brady's face was a mask as he listened to the other man. Suddenly he came alive.

"Give me that again," he ordered. "I'll be damned. Are you sure? Jesus. Ralph, thanks. And keep it close to the vest, will you? Sure thing. S'long."

Brady's face showed triumph when he hung up the phone and turned to Ann.

"My hunch was dead on," he said.

"Cliff, I haven't the faintest idea of—"

"I know, I know," he said. He burst into a roar of laughter.

"It turns out that Mr. Mucky-Muck himself—Wilkinson—is a member of the board of directors of Blackburn Aero."

He waited to let it sink in.

"And that ain't all, baby." He grabbed her by the arms and kissed her roughly.

133

"Umm, I ought to do that more often," he said gleefully.

"Will you tell me what—"

"Our friend Wilkinson, it just so happens," Brady said, serious again, "*also* is a member of the board of directors of a certain airline. You should recognize the name. You fly for them."

CHAPTER XI.

BRADY WATCHED THE SALT RIVER SLIDING THROUGH THE PEAKS OF the Superstition Mountains. Beyond the upcoming range Phoenix sprawled across its valley. The jet banked steeply as the crew took the airplane down in a heady descent. Brady leaned back in his seat, judging he had time enough for one more cigarette before they'd be on final approach.

His face remained passive, his attention seemingly on the terrain drifting beneath the jet.

Ann . . . She had been with him for hours before he became aware of the change in her. The aftereffects of drinking and his preoccupation with being pushed out of his job crowded almost everything else from his mind. Not until midnight did he realize he hadn't eaten and, for all he knew, neither had Ann. He asked if she'd like to go out for a midnight breakfast when, for the first time, he noticed her bags in the foyer.

"Didn't you check into the hotel?"

She shook her head.

"I'd better call for you," he said.

Again she shook her head.

He was struck by the look on her face. It hit him then. Without another word.

Ann started for the kitchen. "We'll eat here," she said. "How's the refrigerator?"

"Huh? Oh. Christ, I don't know. There should be a couple things in there."

He sat on a stool, leaning his elbows on the bar that doubled as a breakfast table. For several minutes they didn't speak. He was content to watch as she explored the kitchen. Finally she stood quietly. "This place is a gastronomical horror."

He shrugged.

"Well." She sighed. "There's enough for a Western omelette. Daddy Dallas style."

"One of your old man's creations?"

She nodded. "Very exclusive."

"What's in it?"

"Tell you later. With what you have here, I'm going to experiment a bit."

"Blargh," he said.

"Even before you taste it?"

It went like that for the next hour. Comfortable small talk. A feeling of being contented.

Brady wondered about it. With his wife it had been a whirlwind. Moonlight and nights out on the town and mixing with friends and being social as hell. The right perfume and the dresses that appealed and tantalized just enough, everything fitting within the accepted boundaries of courtship, modern style. Almost as if the whole damned thing had been ordained.

There'd been none of this with Ann. He didn't poke around in his mind to pluck his emotions like a violin string, hoping for the right chords of understanding to come back to him. He'd been that route and ended up with a marriage that went to hell in a wheelbarrow. He didn't know if he loved Ann, but he didn't care. Not that it wasn't important; he just didn't care if all the factors were right. He followed the way he felt. He wanted her with him, he missed her when she wasn't around.

When they ate they sat around and talked for another hour. It wasn't as if we were hesitating, he thought, as if there were some inner delay in sharing the bed. We were just plain enjoying being with one another.

Finally Ann kissed him. "Go to bed," she said. That was all. He slipped between the sheets and heard her turn on the shower. In the soft darkness of the room he saw the outline of her body. Then she was with him and their lips met.

Afterward, they lay together, warm and close. He felt marvelous, the knot of tension gone completely. He wondered if he loved her, if she, like him, had yet to resolve her emotions.

When you were off to a start like this, things took care of themselves. Just stay loose, he told himself. They slept together like children.

There was still the crying immediacy of the events that had shattered his professional life. Brady intended to patch up the pieces. Fast.

Discovering Wilkinson in a web that included World Press, TWA, and Blackburn Aero was the first solid break in the wall that had so thoroughly baffled him. He didn't know yet what the breach signified. Somehow the discs were involved. They *had* to be . . .

He was making someone damned uncomfortable with the needle he had threaded through the overwhelming mass of UFO material. Now he was getting the backlash of his effective stinging. Someone was out to shut him up.

Brady kept returning to the thought that the discs *were* real and they were connected somehow with the group he had angered with his series. Angered? If they were of Wilkinson's class and they were linked somehow with the discs, "angered" might be self-praise. "Annoyed" might be more realistic, Brady thought wryly.

Whatever the extent of his irritation, it had certainly provoked

137

a reaction. The unknown group was turning him off. Within a few hours of his storming out of Parrish's office the word was being passed among the major news services. And the papers. *Cliff Brady's a leper. Don't touch him.*

Officially he was poison, but he had good friends in the right places. Even those who couldn't work with him in their professional capacity would do almost anything he asked as a personal favor. Those favors included some immediate research.

If he had suspected before that Dr. Kenneth Taggert's position with Blackburn was a blind, he was almost convinced of it now. Brady had kicked himself for missing what should have been obvious to him. Blackburn Aero was supposed to be developing huge transports to wrap up the entire air-cargo market of Central and South America.

Once he took a deep look into the claims of Blackburn Aero, the pitch of giant new air-cargo transports rang hollow. To develop giant cargo planes involved astronomical costs. Not even Blackburn could easily absorb that staggering dollar drain.

The Blackburn air-cargo program was a sham. Blackburn Aero's research center was in Flagstaff, Arizona. Okay so far. But where was their facility for flight-testing their giant airplanes? Into what manufacturing complex would flow the machinery and matériel, the skilled workers, and all the other demands of a huge industrial effort?

The flight-test center for Blackburn was an isolated area within the Colorado Plateau, east-northeast of Flagstaff and just south of the Arizona Mountains. But that was madness. The country was unspeakably desolate and forbidding. There weren't any major roads leading into the area. No rail lines of any kind. That part of the United States was as savage as the worst of the Gobi Desert. It was insane to move a vast facility into such a Godforsaken part of the country None of it added up. Brady had flown through that general area with Ann in the Aztec and there hadn't been the least indication of something big. Of course he could have missed it in so vast and desolate an area. Brady intended to cover it all this trip. He would rent a plane and fly over the Colorado Plateau and look for that damned airstrip himself.

CHAPTER XII

"GOOD MORNING, MR. BRADY."

Brady stared at the tall brunette behind the receptionist's desk. The brunette favored him with a radiant smile. "It's a pleasure to see you again, sir."

"Uh, sure. Good morning."

Brady felt like an idiot. He knew Blackburn Aero, or whoever was involved with Wilkinson, might be keeping tabs on him. Obviously they were, to some extent. But when it worked so well down the line that secretaries recognized him on first sight . . . Christ, what had he gotten into? He knew his whereabouts were simple enough to trace and that a TV monitor could have picked him up as he climbed from the cab in front of the building. Someone else who recognized him on sight could pass the word to the girl behind the desk. That didn't bother him. He could figure out plenty of ways to carry out this routine. Why they'd go to the trouble was something else.

Even as he stood before the reception desk he was contemplating the "why." If nothing else, it confirmed that he'd affected the group involved with Wilkinson to such an extent they would keep tabs on him. It was more than that, he realized. They were

140

anticipating his moves. He didn't like that. He liked it less the more he thought of it. It smacked of organization and control well beyond anything an outfit like Blackburn Aero should require.

Brady rallied. "I haven't got an appointment," he said, "but I would like to see Dr. Taggert. He, uh, we've met before, and—"

The girl nodded. "I'm so sorry, Mr. Brady, but Dr. Taggert is unavailable."

Brady thought of the long trip to reach Flagstaff. "I know he's busy," Brady said, "and I'm barging in. I can wait or come back later in the day."

"I'm sorry, sir, but that won't be possible."

"Is Dr. Taggart out of town? Perhaps you could tell me when he'll be back."

The brunette tossed her hair aside. Brady studied her and knew this girl had been selected carefully and trained down to the last detail. She was beautiful, crisp, efficient, poised and . . . he spotted it then. Even her speech. Letter-perfect. Receptionist, hell. Whatever she was, it smacked of a professional handling difficult visitors. For all he knew, they'd yanked the regular girl the moment they had confirmed his arrival at Flagstaff.

"I'm sorry, sir," the girl repeated, again with that dazzling smile.

"Sorry about what?" Brady snapped. "I just asked if he was out of town and when he'd be back."

He didn't ruffle a single hair. "Dr. Taggert is unavailable, Mr. Brady," she said, her tone unchanged. "Is there anything else I can do for you?"

Brady wanted to go right over her desk and through the doors beyond. What that would accomplish he didn't know, but he damned well wasn't going to be stopped here.

What did he do now? The girl led him by the nose. "Is there anyone else who might help you, Mr. Brady?"

He hadn't expected that. Who could there be? Should he try

141

to beard Frazer Blackburn in his den? He didn't believe the industrialist would even be here. Who else that he knew was involved in one way or another with this mess? Drew Wilkinson? What he might be doing in Arizona was something Brady couldn't figure and didn't expect.

"No," he said, trying to keep the anger from his voice. "But I'd like to find out when Taggert will be back so that I—"

"Mr. Brady."

The voice came from behind him. Brady turned. He stared at a woman who was the most physically perfect female he had ever seen in his life. He had never seen her, and yet, again, he was being addressed by his name.

"I'm Dianne Sims. Perhaps I can help you."

"What? I mean . . ."

She bailed him out of his flustered reaction. "Would you come this way, please?" She turned and walked through a doorway Brady hadn't seen before. Then he realized it wasn't a doorway; a wall panel had slid open.

"Dianne?"

The blonde stopped and returned to the desk. "Of course. How careless of me." She picked up a security identification badge extended by the receptionist. "If you would, Mr. Brady?" The newsman took the badge. He blinked as he clipped it to his jacket. *The badge had his name and his photograph sealed in plastic.*

Dianne Sims brushed by him as she returned to the open panel. Brady caught the scent of a fresh breeze. Her physical presence was overwhelming. He shook his head and walked after her. As he stepped through the doorway, the panel closed behind him. He turned and looked at a blank wall. Not a trace of a sliding panel.

"Very neat," he observed.

She nodded and flashed a smile for answer. Brady walked with her along a pale-green corridor, through a structure unlike anything he knew. The floor appeared steel-hard yet accepted his steps with the resiliency of soft carpeting, absorbing the sound of their shoes. It took him several seconds to notice the absence of lights. Yet the walls and ceiling glowed in a softly pervasive illumination. He did find what he expected: the concealed lenses of closed-circuit TV scanners. Had he not sought them out he would have missed them in the pattern of ceiling panels. What was this building that demanded such security?

Dianne Sims stopped before an elevator for which there were no buttons. After a brief interval, a door slid aside noiselessly and she motioned for Brady to precede her within. He couldn't tell whether they rose or descended. They left the elevator and walked another corridor identical to the first. At the far end they stopped before a blank wall. Brady spun around as a soft hiss sounded and steel bars barricaded the way behind him. Before he could question the girl, another panel opened at the corridor end.

"Mr. Brady?" Dianne Sims waited with her arm extended. Brady stepped forward into a large office paneled in dark wood. Soft light glowed from ceiling and walls.

Standing behind a large desk was a giant of a man. Brady recognized him at once.

"Ah, Mr. Brady." The voice was low but filled the room with its power. The giant smiled warmly.

Brady shook the outstretched hand of Vadim Mendelov.

Of all the men who were listed among the great scientists of the world, none looked less the part than Dr. Vadim Mendelov. The sheer physical bulk of the man was overwhelming. He stood six feet four inches tall with a frame of huge girth. Yet this physical mass detracted nothing from the tremendous impact of presence the man radiated. His green eyes were startlingly clear and penetrating. Some big men were cursed with voices disproportionately high or weak. Not Mendelov, who commanded attention with a subdued tone in a closed room. And Brady discerned in the scientist the rare example of a huge man who moves with swift reflexes and unusual agility. If he ever decided to quit the brain business, Brady mused, he'd be a natural in the wrestling ring.

A socioscientist of the first order, Mendelov was equally famed as an anthropologist and a doctor of medicine, and he was an expert in many allied sciences and technologies. One of Mendelov's gifts was photographic memory. Being able to correlate what he imprinted in memory, he had the astounding capacity to cross-reference in his own mind the disciplines of the many sciences in which he delved. At Princeton University, where Mendelov was on the faculty as a professor in the humanities, his colleagues considered him a socioscientist who taught the applied science of constructive planning for the social structure of man.

Within a limited circle of intimates, Mendelov was as famed for his personal life as for his extraordinary mind and his physical bulk. The Russian-born scientist lived with his sister off the Princeton campus. Fortunately for the tastes of the scientist, Rachel, his sister and housekeeper, professed an objective outlook of her brother's equally huge capacities for philosophy, food and wine, and a discreet but unnumbered flow of women tempted by association with the great man. Never married, Mendelov preferred such fleeting relationships, some lasting no more than an evening, others enduring for weeks or even months. Beautiful women moved, bag and baggage, into his capacious home, where they were tagged with the status of "research assistant."

And yet, reviewing in his mind the background of the scientist, Brady wondered if Mendelov ever slept. The scientist was an established writer whose works were brilliant. His textbooks, translated into dozens of languages, brought him a steady and sizable income.

In those few seconds of meeting Mendelov, Brady reviewed in his mind all that he knew of the scientist. He knew instinctively

144

that this strange association of Mendelov, Taggert, Wilkinson, and Blackburn contained the solution to the enigma of recent weeks. But the presence of the scientist who now greeted him with such open warmth raised an obvious question.

What was an evolutionist doing in the midst of a scientific and technological empire?

Brady took the seat before Mendelov's desk, noticing as he did so that Dianne Sims had left the room. He looked directly at Mendelov. "The receptionist made it obvious I was expected," he said carefully.

"Of course. We didn't question your return here." Mendelov's voice rumbled from his huge chest. He sat behind the desk with the poise of a granite mountain.

Brady reached for a cigarette and lit up slowly. Now that he was here and had more than he'd bargained for, he didn't want to blow the whole thing with stupid questions. Had he encountered Taggert, he would have been crisply efficient from the outset. Mendelov was something else, and the newsman wasn't sure of his ground.

"You were that certain?" Brady said, his words as much a statement as a query.

"We were." Mendelov nodded and clasped his hands across his stomach. By his expressions and movements he made it clear to his visitor that an equal exchange was under way.

"You're aware of my professional, ah, fields?" Mendelov smiled as he saw Brady's nod. "Well, then, you know that among other things I am a psychologist. Let me assure you that your actions have been wholly predictable. Ah, that appears to cause you some distress. It shouldn't," Mendelov said with a slow movement of his head. "You function within a human skin, and it would have been remarkable had you acted other than you did. Any intelligent man would do his best to run down the names of those individuals who have been responsible, or even who appear to be

145

responsible, for the upheaval in his affairs. So"—the giant shrugged—"there is no magic involved. You had no choice, really, except to seek answers to your questions. You are here."

"You make it sound as if someone is pulling strings and I'm dancing to your tune." Brady didn't disguise the anger in his voice.

"Not at all!" Mendelov boomed, his eyes twinkling. "No one guided your destiny but yourself."

"It doesn't sound like it," Brady grumbled.

Mendelov unfolded his hands and swung the chair around. "Mr. Brady, you are a man of strong will. Your past record makes that evident. No, please, if you will," Mendelov said with a motion to avoid interruption from his visitor. "I am not playing games with you. I have no need to fabricate." The scientist chuckled deep in his throat. "You're also a creature of curiosity," he said with a brief smile. "That established the pattern you'd follow. It's quite simple, Mr. Brady. The only person who pushed you was yourself."

"Okay. I'm curious," said Brady. "Then maybe you can answer some questions I'm here to ask?"

"Perhaps I can," the big man said amiably.

"For starters, I'd like to know how *you're* mixed up in all this," Brady demanded. "What the hell is going on around here?"

"What am I doing here?" Mendelov had the smile of a hungry cat. "If you came here to question Dr. Taggert, then surely I don't interest you. Didn't you wish to question Dr. Taggert about, um, I wish to use the very words you yourself have employed; would flying discs be correct?"

"That's almost right," Brady said coldly. "Almost, but not quite. I came here before to ask Taggert about electrical propulsion systems. He did a fancy song-and-dance routine and the neatest disappearing act I've ever seen. I didn't come this time for a repeat. As far as I'm concerned, Dr. Mendelov, there's a direct tie-in between Taggert and Wilkinson *and* Blackburn and certain disc sightings, and—"

"And yourself, of course," Mendelov interjected.

"And myself," Brady snapped. "I won't pull out the crying towel. But one way or the other, today or tomorrow or the day after that, I'm damned well going to find out *why* someone's put the screws to me."

"And I can help?" Mendelov asked. *Too* innocently, Brady thought angrily.

"Maybe," Brady answered. "Since I don't know how you fit in, you can answer that better than I."

"Ask away, then," Mendelov said with a wave of his hand.

"All right," Brady said, his mood grim. "As far as I'm concerned, the discs—not *all* discs, but those I've been singling out—are real. Somehow there's a link between Wilkinson and this place. Wilkinson made sure I was squeezed out of my job. That's the way it goes, sometimes. But not this time. It's too pat. Wilkinson is tied in with Frazer Blackburn and that's too much coincidence. I don't know how you figure in all this, but—"

Mendelov had motioned to Brady and the newsman interrupted himself. "Please, Mr. Brady. I apologize for breaking in like this. But I have nothing to do with Wilkinson's association with you. That's between the two of you. But this matter of discs—"

Brady broke in. "That's right," he said. "Discs. Discs that fly, discs that—"

"You're referring to mechanical objects?"

"I am."

"Of a disc shape?"

"I made myself clear, Dr. Mendelov."

"So you did, so you did."

An uncomfortable silence rose between them.

Finally Mendelov sighed audibly. "Normally, Mr. Brady, I

wouldn't even entertain a conversation that has as its basis a pre-conclusion that UFO's are mechanical."

"I didn't say UFO's. I said discs."

"Yes. Forgive me. Being specific, then, *I* do not believe discs, or any other object embraced within the broad description of UFO's, represent anything even remotely artificial in nature." Mendelov leaned forward. "I don't wish to have an exchange with you on the subject. I know your attitude toward this, and—"

"Do you really?"

"Yes, I do," Mendelov said, showing the first sign of pique since Brady had met him. "I read your articles. Perhaps"—Mendelov smiled warmly—"I should mention that I have read your work for some years. You're outstanding in the field. Which is why"—the smile vanished as Mendelov went on—"your preoccupation with the subject is somewhat distressing."

Brady studied the other man and waited.

"You didn't come here for an exchange of views on the subject, did you?"

"No," Brady admitted. "But if the damned things aren't real, why's Wilkinson so hot and bothered over it all?"

"I must repeat that's between you and—"

"So hot and bothered he's gone to the trouble of getting me out of my job," Brady said, ignoring Mendelov's interruption. "That's a hell of a lot of *non*concerned action. And now I find *you* tied in with everything else. You'll forgive me, Doctor, but I don't believe you."

"Specifically what don't you believe?"

"I don't believe you know nothing about the discs," Brady shot back. "And I believe even less you're not aware of Wilkinson's involvement. And to top it all off, somehow *this* outfit is involved."

Mendelov drummed his fingers on the desk. "I'm not going to respond to your, um, allegations, Mr. Brady. Not point by point. Discussing UFO's is like arguing the validity of God in a physical sense. It would lead us nowhere. However"—Mendelov

148

leaned back in his chair with a creaking of springs—"I don't wish to be uncooperative. What *can* I tell you that will set your mind at ease?"

"Well," said Brady, "let's begin again. What's *your* place in all this? You're a psychologist and an anthropologist. I didn't know Blackburn Aero had gone into the head-shrinking business."

"Oh, but they've been in the head-shrinking business, as you put it"—Mendelov laughed—"for some years. The psychological approach to machine design, to controls, to any system where there is a man-machine relationship . . . well, the better the psychological preparation, the more efficient the final product in its use. But to answer your question directly, in reference to my being here with Blackburn . . ."

The scientist appeared to reach a decision. "I'm not at liberty to discuss details of our project here," Mendelov said. "I believe I have the discretion, however, to discuss it briefly under certain conditions."

"Which are?"

"Nothing is for publication, Mr. Brady."

Brady shifted uncomfortably in his seat.

"Your word is necessary," Mendelov pressed.

"All right," Brady said, giving in. He really didn't have much choice. Maybe what Mendelov had to say would fit a few of the pieces together.

"How familiar with nuclear propulsion are you?"

Brady's heart leaped. Finally . . . !

"I'm fairly well up on it." He didn't want to say another word, delay Mendelov even a second.

"Including Nerva?"

Brady knew the nuclear-rocket program well enough; he'd written several articles on the project. He nodded.

"Do you know of Draco?"

Brady's expression answered for him. "No, I don't," he said, confirming the look on his face.

Mendelov nodded. "Of course not. I didn't expect you would. Draco—the dragon—is an unexpected derivative of Nerva. I must repeat your promise of silence is critical. I have, ah, well, let's say I have breached a security code. Draco is a nuclear drive, Mr. Brady, that at present has the highest national priority for its development. You can understand the stress I have given to security when I explain that Draco is not simply an engineering study. Every emphasis is on producing Draco as an operational machine."

Brady felt elation. "Is Draco flying now?"

"It has been for some time," Mendelov said. "The name comes from the distinctive sound of the nuclear-thrust unit. Forty thousand pounds thrust through a nozzle throat of narrow diameter is, ah, rather spectacular. Someone likened it to the cry of a dragon"—Mendelov smiled—"and the name stuck. It's appropriate."

"What kind of ship—I mean, how's Draco being used?"

Mendelov read the double meaning of Brady's question. "Oh. I think I see what you mean. I'm sorry, Mr. Brady, but there is no disc form involved. The test aircraft are of delta planform."

Brady didn't reply. Mendelov showed the barest hint of a shrug and went on. "In all fairness to you," he said, "I must say that many UFO—discs, in this instance—reports are attributable to the Draco flight tests. The machines fly at very high altitude and the delta form, seen at a great distance and moving in the supersonic regime . . ."

Mendelov paused. "Well, those are the details. But if you will understand the need for security, you can see how you've been misled. I have taken a risk and I don't mind saying so, in even discussing Draco with you. Obviously, Dr. Taggert could not do so and—"

"Is that his tie-in here?"

"Of course. Taggert spent some time on the Nerva program with Lockheed and the AEC."

Jesus Christ, Brady groaned to himself.

"I believe," Mendelov continued, "this should explain his presence."

Brady nodded. He felt crushed. He'd never thought of any of this. The nuclear-propulsion project of the Air Force had been dropped years ago, after more than a billion dollars had vanished into the maw of inefficiency and corruption. It had been stupid of him to think the Air Force would have left it there. And Blackburn Aero. Sure, the air-cargo story was a farce. It was a cover for the Draco program, and he had turned it into a monstrous scheme. . . . No wonder Taggert had seen him out as quickly as he had. But there was still . . .

"Dr. Mendelov." Brady faltered for a moment. "You're a psychologist. I don't see how you fit into—"

"Of course." Mendelov nodded. "Draco has a flight endurance of twelve days." The scientist smiled in sympathy with Brady's discomfort. "Keeping flight crews efficient for that period of time, even with double crews, when they're working immediately adjacent to a nuclear furnace, well, the problems are obvious. The solutions are more psychological than mechanical."

Brady felt numb. He rose to his feet. All he wanted was to get out of there. He'd made enough of an ass of himself without compounding his stupidity with more questions. "Thank you," he said to Mendelov. "You've been generous with your time. If you'll have someone take me back to . . ." Mendelov nodded and as if by magic Dianne Sims appeared in the room.

"Good-bye, Mr. Brady," Mendelov said, offering his hand. "Perhaps I'll see you sometime at Princeton." He chuckled. "We can discuss anthropology, if you'd like."

"Sure. Thanks again."

Behind him the sliding door opened and Brady turned to leave.

"One more thing, Mr. Brady."

He turned back to the scientist. A strange smile played across Mendelov's face.

"To save you time and disappointment," Mendelov said, "you'll

151

find your tape recorder won't have worked very well. But you'll have an excellent recording of an electronic interference signal. It's been a pleasure, Mr. Brady." Mendelov grinned his hungry-cat grin. "Good luck with your, ah, discs."

CHAPTER XIII

STILL SMARTING FROM THE HUMILIATION OF HIS INTERVIEW WITH Vadim Mendelov, Brady took a taxi to the Flagstaff airport. He wanted to get up in a plane again. To clear his mind, if nothing else.

Thirty minutes later he was in the grip of renewed vexation. He couldn't find the Blackburn flight strip on the Arizona charts. He checked the dates and confirmed the charts were the latest issued. Brady cornered the airport operator, asked him if he knew where he could find the strip.

"Nope. Don't know a thing about it," was the reply.

"How can that be?" Brady persisted. "It's supposed to be a ten-thousand-foot strip. It's got to be on a chart somewhere."

The other man studied Brady carefully. "You got business there?"

What the hell was this? Brady thought. "All I'm asking you is: Do you know where the strip is?" Brady said patiently.

The airport operator shook his head slowly. "Don't know a thing about it. Anything else I can do for you?"

Brady took off, pointing the nose of the Debonair away from Flagstaff along a course of seventy degrees. Every time he found something else connected with Blackburn Aero, he was jarred off balance. A strip two miles long and nothing showing on the flight charts? Brady would have given a hundred to one that any flight-testing facility would also have its own VOR homing and communications facility, but he couldn't find out a thing about that, either. Interesting, he mused. Someone's got a finger in with the FAA and the Coast and Geodetic Survey offices. They'd need a strong contact somewhere to keep a strip that big off the charts.

Brady was well aware of the difficulties in locating even a two-mile strip in the vast area of the Colorado Plateau. But he could cut down the area of search. He was almost positive the strip would lie generally east of the Little Colorado River that cut in a diagonal line across the northeastern quarter of the state. There stretched the Colorado Plateau and its deep gorges, washes, canyons, and desolate terrain. To find the airstrip Brady decided *not* to search it out. He wanted no part of looking for the needle in the haystack. If Blackburn Aero had any sizable facility in the remote plateau, it needed power, and power meant long lines marching across the ground. Power lines that stood out far better than did any airstrip. Brady figured, as well, that the power lines would be new and they wouldn't be on the chart. If he was right, it would cut down greatly the search pattern he needed to fly.

It took him just under two hours. He was crossing the Oraibi Wash, six thousand feet above the rock-strewn terrain, when he saw the power lines. He studied the chart. Nothing. *Goddamn!* he exulted. He swung the Debonair around in a steep turn to follow the power lines he knew would take him straight to the field he sought.

Straight as an arrow the lines led him to the Blackburn airstrip. What he saw bothered him. There was enough power feeding through those lines to fill the needs of a small city. Brady circled the strip from six thousand feet, looking for any trace of industrial or research facilities. Nothing. Why all the power then? Nothing he saw gave even a hint for all that inflow of energy. Brady took several pictures of the strip and the surrounding countryside. The sun was low on the horizon and he got some excellent shadow effect. But he wanted more than he could capture on film from this height. He pulled the power and dumped the airplane in a swift, steep spiral.

As details enlarged with his descent, he made out several four-engined transports and a half dozen small jets and executive planes. Several hangars were aligned neatly near the airstrip, but there wasn't anything even remotely large enough to accept a giant cargo plane the size of the C-5A or the 747. Nothing. Down to five hundred feet he made out the power substation into which the lines flowed, and again he was struck with the enormous energy available to the limited facilities. Something else tugged at him—no roads! Not a single road leading to the strip. A few dirt paths, but that was all. Flight-test facility, my ass! Whatever's going on down there hasn't got a thing to do with any cargo planes, that's for sure!

He readied his camera and took a series of photographs. A group of people by a truck flashed a red blinker light at him to climb away. Brady thumbed his nose and laughed. The laughter died when red flares hissed into the air, several of them streaking close to the plane. Brady lost his temper. Everything that had happened during the day boiled over. He shoved the prop control to flat pitch and pushed the throttle against the panel. When he came around out of his diving turn, he was flat on the deck, the Debonair wide open at nearly 230 miles an hour. He whooped loudly when he saw people diving wildly for the ground as he ripped scant feet overhead, pulling away in a high climbing turn.

He was at nine thousand feet, climbing slowly as he homed

in to Flagstaff. The sun had sunk below the horizon and the eastern sky was dark and showing its early stars. Ahead of Brady showed the faint light lingering after the desert sunset. Brady looked about him, drinking in the scene and enjoying the moment of relaxation the flight gave him. He saw a light high above and to his left, descending slowly. Brady twisted in his seat for a better look, believing he was watching one of the lower and brighter satellites traversing the early night sky.

He knew it couldn't be a satellite when it continued to expand in brightness and size. At the same moment he knew it was rushing directly toward him, he saw the circular shape. Brady tensed on the controls, his limbs reacting automatically in case it was necessary to hurl the plane away from the onrushing shape. At the instant he was about to haul the Debonair into a climb, the disc slowed.

Brady stared with his mouth agape. Holding formation off his left wing was a huge disc. It held position, unmistakable, absolutely clear, unbelievably real. Brady saw the rounded dome above the disc, a wide-bellied protrusion beneath. He judged it at more than a hundred feet in diameter. Instantly he searched for every detail of which he had heard during all these weeks of studying disc reports. The rounded windows, the ionized flow before the disc, a lesser glow behind. He remembered a warning: Never believe what you see through glass. That was stupid; what the hell did pilots do when they took off and landed? Despite the thought he pulled open the narrow vent window to his left. A small explosion of air sounded through the cabin. Brady hunched down in the seat to look through the opening. He sat up straight as the air about the disc glowed suddenly. The disc accelerated with blinding speed. As fast as it moved forward it burst upward, faster than Brady could react. Cursing, he hauled back on the yoke to lift the nose. In those few seconds the disc became a faint light that in the next moment winked out of sight.

156

Brady felt the pounding of his heart and he took deep breaths, forcing himself to calm down.

The thought rose with absolute clarity in his mind: What the hell do I do *now*? For instantly, completely, he knew that no one would believe what he had seen.

He wasn't sure he believed it himself. He was right. The discs were real. And Vadim Mendelov was a goddamned liar.

CHAPTER XIV

Brady studied his drink. Wunnerful drink. Wunnerful bartender. Made margaritas *exactly* right. Perfect. Thas' what they were. Perfect drinks. Brady wanted heavy on the salt and he got heavy on the salt. Marvelous bartender. Splendid fellow, he. This was the fifth drink and it was perfect. Fifth? Maybe it was the sixth. He couldn't care less.

When Brady had landed at Flagstaff, he felt numb. He rented a car and drove to the hotel downtown. He wanted to run down the middle of the street waving his arms and shouting about the disc. But since he knew he would end up spending the night in jail or in a padded cell or laced tightly into a straitjacket, he kept his mouth shut. He signed in for his room and sent the bellboy hustling for a drink. He had to tell *someone*. But who would believe him? Of course; he had grabbed for the phone and put in a person-to-person call to Ann. No dice. She was on a flight and wouldn't be in for several hours. The operator found out she would be landing in San Francisco. Brady sent a telegram that would be waiting for her on arrival. He asked her to call him. He even used the word "urgent."

But Ann was hours away. Brady took a shower, shaved, and

slipped into fresh clothes. He went to the lounge and climbed onto a barstool. It took three drinks to shake the feeling of numbness. He drank another quickly and felt it coming back. Oh, Christ, he thought, I should have remembered. He had spent several hours at high altitude during the day. And Flagstaff was about seven thousand feet above sea level. And alcohol always hit you harder at altitude where there was less oxygen . . . Jesus, but I am getting *stoned*. A sloppy grin appeared on his face because he didn't care. He wanted to get stoned. He was tired of thinking, tired of trying to unravel the spaghetti of contradictory information, all the hints and the shadows, and chasing ghosts, and after what he had seen today, knowing that everything he had done had been right . . . And he couldn't tell a single goddamn human being because Ann was mixing drinks for someone thirty thousand feet up. . . .

Piss on it. He tipped the glass, licking the salt from the rim and draining the drink. He motioned to the bartender for another. Wunnerful. He felt the warm glow spread through his body and he accepted it greedily. "Just right for what ails you," he announced to himself. He lifted the glass again and sipped slowly. His hand froze as he looked into the mirror behind the bar.

Dianne Sims. She stood just within the entrance, looking around, obviously missing someone. Brady slid from the barstool, steadied himself, and made his way toward her. He tried not to sound too much like an idiot and asked her to have dinner with him. No, she didn't have a date. Yes, she'd love to join him for dinner. Right here in the hotel, the finest steaks in Flagstaff. Brady sat across from her at the dinner table and he marveled at her beauty. She was breathtaking and he told her so. She smiled and thanked him, and in the way she responded to his compliments she was more beautiful than ever.

He leaned forward and rested his hand on hers. "Would you believe me if I told you," he said with deliberate slowness, "that today I saw a giant purple elephant flying through the sky and towing a bright-orange barge with sixteen naked broads on it? And they were all throwing flowers at me as we flew alongside each other?"

She laughed. Brady noticed she didn't remove her hand from beneath his. Well, he thought smugly, goddamned evening may not be a complete bust after all.

"Well, d'you believe me?"

"I don't think so." She tasted her drink.

"How about a, um, an ahh, how about a whale in an oxygen mask? At nine thousand feet. Wouldja believe *that*?"

"No, Mr. Brady, I wouldn't." She frowned with mock seriousness.

"No?"

She laughed and said "No," again.

"Well, then, how about a great big flying disc a hunnert' feet across with round windows and a blue glow that goes *Zap!* through the sky? How about that, huh?"

"Purple or orange?" she said lightly.

"Forgot to ask," he mumbled.

"If it was bright orange, I might believe it," she said.

"Oh." He pouted and provoked more laughter from her. "Then you'll never believe me because this disc was white with turquoise stripes."

"Oh, my."

"'S' fact," he said.

"It must have been very pretty."

"Beautiful, beautiful." He looked at his glass. "Whaddya know. 'S empty. Wanna drink another one, or would you like to eat?"

"I'm starved, Mr.—"

"Cliff."

"Cliff." She smiled, squeezing his hand.

Dinner was a hazy memory. The steak didn't slow down the tequila. Brady tried to remember what Dianne had said about why she was at the hotel, but he couldn't remember—and what the hell, it didn't matter. He ignored it and concentrated on her. God, but she was beautiful. He pictured himself with her on cool sheets and he knew he could make love to her through an entire night. Goddamn, she—he shook his head. The evening blurred and he remembered leaving the restaurant, driving in her car, going to her apartment. She pushed him gently onto a wide couch and removed his shoes. "Make yourself at home," she said, brushing her lips against his. Moments later a drink was in his hand, and she was gone again. He removed his jacket and tie and took her at her word, relaxing completely. He watched her and marveled at her body and felt the heat rising within him. He wondered if he was too drunk to make love. The hell I am. He grinned idiotically. Dianne turned on a gas fireplace, started a tape with soft music, and dimmed the overhead lights. Brady felt as if he were watching a scene from a movie. Things just didn't happen like this. But it was happening, all right. Even to the point where she reappeared in a filmy negligee and sat next to him on the couch. He took a stiff drink from his glass and stared at her. He had never seen a woman so beautiful and . . .

Brady felt a compulsion to talk. He wanted to talk. He wanted to throw away his clothes and strip the negligee from her and bury his face in her breasts and crush her lips and love her and at the same time he wanted to talk, to let the words run free from him. He couldn't understand himself. What the hell was the matter with him? "Make love to her, you fool," he shouted to himself. But he couldn't stop. The compulsion to talk overwhelmed him.

He talked about the discs, about everything that had happened to him, even about Ann, to his astonishment. He told her Mendelov was a liar and he knew it and until a few hours ago he hadn't known why, but *now*, by God, he did. He told her about the disc, he repeated every detail his eye had captured. He told her he had fitted the pieces together, that Taggert was tied in somehow with the propulsion system of the disc. He felt—he didn't know, but somehow he was positive—Vadim Mendelov was the mastermind of whatever was going on. He knew now why Wilkinson had acted as he did, how and why he was involved.

"But how could Dr. Mendelov be involved?" she protested mildly. "You said he was the mastermind, Cliff. About what?"

"I don't know," he said, raising his voice. "But I'm sure ash hell going to find out. You can bet on *that*," he concluded in drunken assurance.

She pressed the point gently. "But what good will it do? You said no one will listen to what you have to say, Cliff. If you do find out what he's doing with the discs, you can't do anything about it."

Brady grinned. "Ho ho ho," he said slowly. "Ho ho."

"You must have someone very special in mind, Cliff."

"Do," Brady said in a conspiratorial whisper. "I sure do."

"And he'll really listen to what you have to say?"

"Whaddya' mean, *lissen*? He'sh in a position to do sumpin'."

Dianne waited. Brady couldn't remain silent if he wanted to.

"Know who he ish, I mean, is?"

She shook her head.

"Old Felix, thash who."

"I don't know him, do I?"

"Doubt it."

Again she waited.

"Felix ish m'Russian buddy. He'll lissen t'me. Don't you think the Russians wanna know what happened? Don't you think they'd like t'know what wash over Moscow when they fired all their missiles? When they tried to shoot down those pretty lights? When alla time they were discs, huh?" Brady waggled a finger at her. "Oh, they'll lissen, all right. Y'don't know Felix Zigel, do you? Hah, I'll bet y'don't. Old Felix ish Doctor of Science at the Russian Aviation Institute. How y'like them apples? Pretty good, huh? Not only that," Brady ran on, "but he'sh in charge of UFO inveshti . . . invesh . . . UFO studies of th' whole Russian

162

guv'mint." Brady threw his arms open in an expansive gesture. "Whole Russian guv'mint! How 'bout that?"

Brady's eyes narrowed and he leaned closer to the beautiful woman on the couch with him. "Wanna know sumpin' else? Felix, he'sh a believer. That'sh right." Brady's head bobbed up and down vigorously. "Believer, all right. And I know him and he knows me and he trusts me and he'll lissen to me and we'll by God do sumpin' about all thish. Howzat, huh?"

He thought Dianne had a strange, sad expression on her face. "I'm sorry to hear that, Cliff," she said, so quietly he could barely hear her words. There was a blur. He would remember her holding a small aerosol can. He thought she turned it to him. He couldn't remember the spray coming at him, but he remembered the can. It didn't matter. The aerosol spray enveloped him and the lights went out with a crash.

CHAPTER XV

Brady awoke with a cottony mouth and a skull fragile as a Ming vase. He made certain not to move. He opened his eyes slowly. He was seated in a wide, comfortable chair, arms relaxed, his body cushioned pleasantly.

Slowly focus returned to him as he stared directly ahead. He blinked several times and blurred images contracted into clear definitions.

The huge form of Dr. Vadim Mendelov took shape. Mendelov was also seated, watching him silently. Brady turned his head slowly, scanning. He was in an enclosure of some kind. The room was small, and was filled with these wide, thick chairs, which were luxuriously upholstered in leather. He pressed down with his feet and felt soft carpeting. He looked higher along the walls and saw steel plates.

"You may remove the seat belt, Mr. Brady."

Brady grunted at the sound of Mendelov's voice. For the first time he noticed that he was fastened in his seat by a shoulder strap. He released the belt catch and stretched slowly. His limbs ached; he judged their soreness from too many hours of inactivity. To his left he saw Dianne Sims, who favored him with a quick

—and apologetic?—smile. Brady sighed. He would learn where he was in good time. Mendelov's presence made it all too clear that Brady exercised not a whit of control over his immediate situation.

"Headache?"

"What?" He turned to Dianne.

"How's your head?" she asked, not unkindly.

"It's been better."

She smiled again and rose to her feet. He watched her open a sliding panel behind which there was a bar of some sort. She handed him a glass.

"What is it?"

"It's a head-straightener," she said. "Please drink it, Mr. Brady. It will help, I assure you."

Brady drank quickly. There was a faint lemon taste, almost bitter-sweet. He couldn't recall anything similar to it. He closed his eyes and took a deep breath. She was right; he began to feel better almost immediately. Among other things, he judged, the drink must contain a stimulant. Suddenly he craved a cigarette. He returned the glass to Dianne. "All right if I smoke?"

She nodded and slid back a panel in the chair armrest, revealing an ash tray. Brady lit up and dragged deeply, savoring the taste. He felt almost human again.

He looked at Mendelov. "Okay. I give up. Where am I?"

"That will become clear soon enough," the scientist said curtly. "First, it appears necessary for us to continue our conversation." Mendelov's eyes were steady and piercing.

Brady didn't miss the change in Mendelov's tone, or the difference in mood. The last time they had faced one another Mendelov had been the congenial host. That man had vanished. In his stead was a man accustomed to power and totally in control of the situation.

"I would appreciate your relating—without holding back, please—the entire story of the discs as you understand them,"

165

Mendelov said. "This time, however, I want your thoughts to their final conclusions. No matter how unlikely they may seem. Your life may depend upon your answer, Mr. Brady. Especially the sincerity, the honesty of that answer."

Brady licked dry lips. Not for an instant did he doubt what he heard. He took a deep breath and leaned forward. Without hesitation, he began. Added together—Brady ticked off one point after the other—one conclusion only withstood all examination. The discs, Brady said carefully, *had* to be real. Even before the shattering experience of encountering such a vehicle, he had believed this to be so. Now all events led him inevitably to the conclusion that Blackburn Aero and those involved, including Mendelov, *must* be related to the discs. He was through. He leaned back in the chair and gazed steadily at his adversary.

"Remarkable," Mendelov said quietly. "However, we still have need of sharing our thoughts." The smile vanished as if Mendelov had turned some switch within himself. He leaned his great bulk forward, his eyes burning into Brady.

"I wish to ask you something," Mendelov said slowly. "Why are we doing all this?"

"Doing what?" Brady countered.

"Assuming everything you have concluded is true," Mendelov said, unperturbed, "why are we involved in this, ah, effort of ours?" Mendelov leaned back in his chair, his expression unreadable.

Brady wrestled with his thoughts. Several times he started to speak but changed his mind. He realized that he had no clear idea of the purpose behind the vast expenditure of time and money and energy that must have been required to create the disc he had seen. He would have to guess, to probe, and attempt to draw Mendelov out into the open.

"It's a power play," he announced finally. "You people are obviously in a position to pull off some of the wildest capers the world has ever seen. You've got millions; millions, hell, you've got hundreds of millions to back you up. You've got a tremendous organization, you've got power, brains. All that adds up to freedom of action. What you've got going for you makes all those fiction ideas of an international crime group look like a Sunday picnic. . . ."

Mendelov had relaxed his stern visage and Brady caught the expression of disappointment clouding the scientist's features. He may be the world's greatest semanticist, Brady thought, but he's got a few things to earn about playing poker.

Brady leaned back in his seat and stabbed a finger at Mendelov. "Everything fits into what I've said except one thing. *You.*" Brady smiled. "You're the fly in the ointment. Someone like Wilkinson could be in this up to his teeth for power to control things. Groups, people. Taggert's the kind of scientist who'd follow his holy grail anywhere. That makes him easy to understand. But *you're* not," Brady stressed. "You're the antithesis to money, or even power, when it comes to complicated involvement and risks. I just don't think you care one way or the other about it."

"Why is that, Mr. Brady?" The voice rumbled from deep within the chest of the huge man.

Brady didn't answer at once. He reached for a cigarette and glanced at the woman with them. She hadn't made a sound. She sat easily in her chair, completely relaxed, following every word of the two men. Brady made a mental note to find out just where she fitted into the picture. He turned back to Mendelov.

"Because of time, Dr. Mendelov, because of time," Brady said slowly, convinced he had his man pegged. "Time is too precious to you to throw it away." Brady didn't miss the glance that passed between Mendelov and Dianne Sims. Finally she had reacted to something. What could there be in what he had just said that would bring her out of that cool composure? He *had* to be right. . . .

"For you there's not enough time. Every week, every day, is fleeting. You don't have enough time. I think you're more the philosopher than the scientist. Maybe they're both the same; I don't know. I've read your works. Pretty thoroughly, too. You're an evolutionist and you're worried the human race is going to cream itself all over the map and you haven't got time to screw around. So there's only one conclusion left."

"Which is, Mr. Brady?"

"You're a zealot. Like other zealots, you've got great dreams." Brady allowed an edge of sarcasm to enter his voice. "You think you've found the miracle cure. Some new way to keep the world from destroying itself.

"It's not hard to figure, I suppose," he said after several moments of silence. "Somehow you people have put together a new drive. From what I've seen, it makes anything else in the air look like a bark canoe. Maybe it's a weapon. If what happened at Kennedy and MacDill is true, then obviously it *is* a weapon." Brady made a weary gesture. "And your little club figures now it's got the upper hand and maybe it's time to step in, right?"

"You have emphasized time, Mr. Brady." Mendelov spoke slowly and carefully. "But I doubt you understand its true meaning as it relates to the present moment. Nature often arrives at critical junctures in the survival pattern of any race. The race of man is right now at such a crossroads.

"What road we take will determine," Mendelov said, "not whether man moves into a future where certain forms of prosperity are guaranteed, but whether or not man survives. Whether or not he selects or avoids the massive devastation he is preparing to wreak upon all peoples."

Mendelov shook his great head in a gesture of sadness. "You think you know the weapons, don't you? No, hear me out. I'm aware of what you know and I say that you know all too little. That's why we have Hoffsommer with us, why we also have in our midst a Soviet air marshal. . . ."

Brady felt a mild shock. Stanley Hoffsommer? He was the number-one man in nuclear-weapons development . . . a brilliant

Israeli scientist. And a Soviet air marshal . . . ! Until this moment he had never thought that Mendelov and those about him might include within their group opposite numbers of other countries. Jesus, how big was this thing? He listened with complete attention.

". . . because we *know* what we're facing. You're aware that years ago the Russians tested bombs as powerful as a hundred million tons of high explosives. But the hundred-megaton bombs, Mr. Brady, are *toys!*" For the first time Mendelov revealed the intensity of emotion for which Brady had waited. "Toys, I repeat. The weapons now available, that have already been emplaced . . . they are a hundred times more powerful than a hundred megatons. Do you understand what I'm saying, Brady? *Think,* man, *think!*" Mendelov slammed a huge fist against his armrest.

"They are so powerful they cause a gravitational warp where they detonate. Do you realize the enormity of that statement, Brady? They are disturbing the space-time continuum. They are literally shredding the fabric of space itself. I told you these weapons were emplaced, and so they are." Mendelov's powerful voice shook. "More than thirty of these monsters are ready for use. In five years there will be more than a hundred of them ready. Can you possibly comprehend the energy we are preparing to unleash upon ourselves? These are planet-busting forces, man! Planet-busting! And we—the United States and the Soviets—are preparing to use such monstrous devices in the name of self-defense!"

After a long silence, Brady felt compelled to respond in some manner. "From everything you've said"—Brady chose his words with care—"I take it you, and whoever forms your organization, believe there's an alternate solution?"

Mendelov nodded. "Not merely an alternate solution. There's only one course to pursue."

"Sure," Brady said. "Take away everybody's guns. Then no one blows up anyone else."

169

Mendelov frowned. "You seem flippant about it."

"Who, me?" he asked, his voice mocking the scientist. "That's an old refrain you're playing. Disarming everybody puts all the guns in the hands of one group. That group—I take it this means you—then watches everybody so they can't build any more bombs. The next question is easy. Who watches the watchers? Who decides who's to play God?"

Mendelov grimaced with distaste for Brady's choice of words.

"Of course, of course," the scientist said after a pause. "Whenever any one nation has attempted to practice what you've just preached, it was with the heaviest hand possible. They used the same weapons available to everyone else. The result was inevitable. Wholesale slaughter. In this particular respect history has only repeated itself." Mendelov's voice became grim. "We choose not to build upon a repetition of past tragedies."

"That's got a nice sound to it, I admit, but—"

"Be still for a moment," Mendelov snapped. "Do you understand what is meant by an ultimate weapon, Mr. Brady?"

Brady waved his hand. "I'll defer to your description. I have the feeling anything I said would be wrong."

The scientist ignored the barb and went on. "Simply stated, it's a weapon vastly superior to anything that may be arrayed against it. But its superiority exists only within a limited time. In other words, the weapon must be used when the time is opportune. That weapon, Mr. Brady, includes destructive power as only one—*one*, I repeat—facet of its strength. It is a weapon combining many strengths—easy availability, flexibility, psychological impact to achieve a desired effect, virtual immunity to the user—all of these are important criteria of the ultimate weapon.

"And, Mr. Brady . . ." Mendelov paused. "We possess that ultimate weapon . . . now."

Brady didn't speak, didn't move.

"Do you understand why I've told you all this? Why I have

asked you to respond so carefully to the questions I've asked?" Mendelov's face was impossible to read.

"Frankly, no," Brady said.

"Because in our, ah, organization," the scientist said, "I believe there's a vital place for you."

"Me!"

Mendelov nodded, a half-smile appearing. "Yes, you. I confess my colleagues don't share my opinion. However, I think they may be persuaded to—"

"Now you wait just a moment!" Brady shouted, half out of his seat. Brady stuttered in his sudden rush of anger. "If you th-th-think for one moment you can shanghai me into joining your holy-rolling, save-the-world crowd of do-gooders, you're out of your fucking mind!"

Mendelov held up his hand as a light flashed on the wall. "Later, Mr. Brady, later," he soothed. "Perhaps before too long we can bring about a change in heart. In the meantime I have a surprise for you."

"Go to hell!" Brady growled.

"Please sit here next to me," Mendelov said, his voice suddenly warm. He gestured to the seat to his left. Brady shrugged and took the chair. The scientist turned his own chair on a pedestal and motioned Brady to do the same.

"Settle yourself well, Mr. Brady. This often comes as a shock, I daresay, to those exposed for the first time." Laughter boomed from the scientist. "You're a pilot, aren't you, Mr. Brady? Yes, of course. Um, how high have you flown?"

"About seventy thousand feet. Why?"

Without answering, Mendelov depressed a button. In front of them, steel plates began to slide back from wide, clear ports.

Brady gasped, his stomach twisting.

He looked down on the earth.

Sixty miles down.

CHAPTER XVI

BRADY STARED IN WONDER AT THE CURVING PLANET THREE HUNDRED thousand feet beneath him. Questions surged to his mind but what he saw told him more eloquently than could any words the awesome power that surrounded him. Sixty miles high, they rushed through wispy atmosphere without sense of motion. Brady was struck with the clarity of the stars, like those at sea or on the desert at night. The stars did not twinkle but shone with a steady, faultless gleam. Then, in the awesome silence of the void stretching before him, a star moved. He watched it rise from the distant horizon, gaining in brilliance as it drew nearer. A star made by man, a satellite spinning its orbital web as it plunged around the world. Deeply impressed, Brady watched the gleaming orb moving across the star field.

The faintest orange glow on the horizon brought his attention down once more. Lower than the gently curving rim of the world he saw the scalloped edges of clouds snaring the first light of the coming day. The horizon brightened swiftly, the orange deepening until finally it glowed red with yellow-orange shadings. The clouds reflected pink and then whitened swiftly. Brady saw for the first time the massive skeletal ridge of the South American continent, the thundering march of the Andes, a huge tidal wave of stone absorbing the dawn light.

Still cloaked in silence, Brady looked upon an expanded dimensional map of the upper regions of South America. He needed no questions to supply what his eyes and memory brought to him. In the brightening shades of the early day he watched the reflection of rivers snaking through still darkened jungle and plains. Far to his left he saw the ocean becoming richly visible.

"Careful of your eyes. Watch out for the sun." Mendelov's voice was a thousand miles away. "Here." Brady paid no heed. A hand jostled his shoulder. "Here," Mendelov repeated. "Take these." Brady accepted dark glasses and turned his eyes back to the miracle about him. Barely soon enough, he realized. Savage light flared above the horizon. Above the protecting atmosphere the stellar furnace stabbed wickedly at the unprotected eye.

A bell chimed. Mendelov glanced up at the speaker. "Mendelov here."

"Sir, we're starting descent," said the voice from the speaker.

"All right," Mendelov replied, his voice carrying to whatever part of the disc—Brady assumed it was the upper dome—contained the controls and the crew. "Take the course I ordered."

"Yes, sir."

Brady took a deep breath and exhaled slowly. He nodded toward the sight beyond the viewglass. "It's quite something," he said simply.

"It sobers a man," the scientist replied. "It's a shame the sight has been shared by so few. There's something about the perspective from here . . ." Mendelov's voice trailed off in a mental shrug.

"Mr. Brady." He hadn't heard Dianne's voice for some time. "Your belt, please."

173

Brady joined the others in fastening the belt across his lap. He smiled awkwardly. "According to the science-fiction stories I've read," he said, "people in discs don't need belts. They're surrounded by electrogravitic force fields or something."

"Something is as good a description as any," Mendelov said dryly. "Unfortunately we haven't yet learned how to repeal the laws of motion and inertia." The scientist tapped his own belt. "A good thunderstorm—if we ever blundered into one—could give you a good knocking about."

Brady ran his thoughts backward. "Speaking of force fields," he said, "what makes this thing go?"

"All in due time," Mendelov said. "I'm not being evasive, Mr. Brady," he explained. "Bear with me a while longer, however."

Brady shrugged. "Forget it. Let me try another. I've never been, obviously, anywhere this high. How fast are we moving?"

Mendelov thought over the question. "Much less than optimum," he said finally. "Umm, the Mach numbers don't apply at this altitude. Insufficient density." Brady nodded; he knew that. "In more familiar terms, then . . . oh, I'd say about eighteen hundred miles per hour."

Brady's face remained blank. "And that's much less than optimum?" he asked.

"Yes, yes. We've been holding back. I didn't want to start our descent until dawn." Mendelov pointed. "Ahh, there. We're on our way now. I recommend your undivided attention to this, Mr. Brady."

Brady didn't need further prompting. His eyes were already glued to the view straight ahead. The flanks of the Andes splashed back the sun now well above the horizon, and Brady could discern the different hues of jungle green and the browner stains of the higher plateaus. The horizon lifted in a smooth, flowing motion as the forward rim of the disc lowered to match the path of flight. Brady was astonished with the smooth move-

174

ment despite their tremendous speed. He dismissed the mechanics and threw his attention into the exhilarating sensation that swept before his eyes.

The mountains expanded swiftly as the disc plunged in a heady swoop toward the earth. The planet closed in from all directions as their height vanished, the we̅ n coast of South America sliding beneath the uprising flanks of the now tremendous peaks. Almost as swiftly the disc shredded its way through growing cumulus clouds. For the first time the disc rocked gently from strong vertical air currents.

The peaks appeared now at eye level. The forward motion of the disc increased as the thick jungle carpet expanded into individual details. Then the peaks were well above them and they plunged forward in a dizzying rush low over the thick matting of trees. At two hundred feet they hurtled across miles of raw jungle. The disc eased into a shallow ascent. Brady noticed their height above the ground remained constant. They had swung to the southeast and now, he judged from the shadows, the disc raced along a southwestern heading as it came upon a vast plateau. Clearings in the thick growth appeared more frequently and scattered native villages flashed into sight.

Brady was astonished to see the natives in clearings look up as the disc burst into sight and *waving at the disc*. Not once did he see a single action he might interpret as fear. Few natives, he judged with growing wonder, even seemed surprised at the sight of a great disc tearing along almost directly overhead.

The disc moved deep within a valley, great mountainous walls flanking them on each side and directly ahead of their course. Their speed diminished steadily. Brady judged their forward movement at no more than a hundred miles an hour. Still they slowed, the flanking mountains closing to narrow the valley until, after twisting along a gorge, he knew peaks surrounded them from every side. There was no way for him to know where they might be. Brady saw a huge waterfall. Along the sheer sides of a mountain appeared the power lines and other facilities of a hydroelectric plant. Brady studied the scene carefully, noting the generating plant was set well back from the slope within a cavelike depression. From a distance it would be virtually invisible. More signs of vast work; the depression had been gouged out by some terrific force. Brady looked about the area. No roads led away from the hydroelectric facility. Whatever equipment had been used here had been brought in by air.

Still their speed fell. Directly ahead lay a towering pinnacle of rock. The disc hovered, a startling sensation. Brady leaned forward and saw a faint blue ionization of the air along the rim of the disc.

Obviously the crew was waiting for some signal or—suddenly the massive stone walls directly before them split, the rock outfacing slid aside, and Brady looked into a cavernous opening. The disc eased forward. Brilliant lights stabbed into life within the cavern and Brady saw a landing cradle with flashing approach lights. He felt a slight rocking motion and then nothing. They had landed.

Moments later he felt new movement, a service tractor drawing the landing cradle farther into the cavern. Brady looked ahead and to the sides. Overhead floodlights made the vast interior almost as bright as day.

By now Brady had ceased to be surprised by anything he saw. He counted a flight line of eight discs similar to the craft he had seen over Arizona. Far to one side was a single disc at least twice the size of the others. The forward movement stopped. Brady heard air hissing from valves. His ears popped slightly as pressure equalized and a green light flashed in the cabin.

Part of the curving cabin wall slid away to form a ramp to the cavern floor. Brady unbuckled his seat belt when he saw Mendelov and Dianne release theirs. The girl started along the ramp and Mendelov motioned for Brady to follow. Brady left the disc, his eyes trying to take in everything at once.

Then he heard his name. "Mr. Brady."

He turned. Dr. Kenneth Taggert greeted him with a broad smile.

"Welcome to Condor, Mr. Brady."

CHAPTER XVII

"No guards," Taggert said. "Until you know your way around, you'll need a guide. But no one will be, um, standing watch over you." The scientist smiled. "Really, it makes it much easier on all of us."

Brady shook his head as they walked along a wide corridor. "I don't get it," Brady admitted. "You can't tell what I might do."

"Brady, we don't *need* guards. Do you know where you are?"

"Somewhere in the northern part of South America," Brady said. "From what I saw on the way down, we're east of the Andes. That puts us in the plateau that, well, it could be Brazil or Colombia along this latitude."

"That's good enough," the scientist said. "The point is, you're isolated. By more than simply distance. We don't believe a white man has ever crossed this part of the continent. Not"—Taggert smiled—"that they haven't tried it. You're in the midst of dense jungle," he explained. "You saw the mountains around here, the rivers. The natives for two hundred miles in every direction serve us. Our organization is on excellent terms with them. There are no fences or other barriers. Just impassable jungle, rivers, savage animals, dozens of different types of poisonous insects."

Brady forced a smile of his own. "I'm convinced!"

"I didn't finish," Taggert warned. "The natives will kill anyone who leaves this base on foot. *Anyone*. You, me, Mendelov. It doesn't matter. If anyone attempts to leave here under his own power, he's as good as dead. No exceptions. It's the best security system ever devised."

"Yeah, hurrah for you," Brady said.

A frown crossed Taggert's face. "I'm sorry you had to come here the way you did," he said. "I know it must have come as a shock—"

"Think nothing of it," Brady said airily. "I'm used to being suckered in by beautiful blondes and being knocked out by drugs and kidnapped. Happens all the time."

Taggert hesitated.

"Forget it," Brady said. "It's not your worry. Besides, I have no intention of leaving. I wouldn't miss this for the world."

Taggert nodded. "Thanks. This has bothered me, I admit."

"I said forget it."

Taggert motioned toward the main chamber where Brady had seen the discs. "I'm supposed to give you the grand tour," he said. "Would you like to start now or would you rather clean up? You look tired."

Brady glanced down at his clothes and rubbed his chin. "I do feel sort of gritty," he said. "Cleaning up sounds good. Besides"— he smiled—"I'm not going anywhere. All this can wait."

Taggert slapped him on the shoulder. "Okay, let's go. This way." He turned off along a side corridor. "All apartments down here," he explained. "Number Fourteen is yours."

"Apartments?"

"That's right." Taggert glanced at Brady's stocky frame. "What size flight suit do you wear, by the way?"

"Thirty-eight. Why?"

"We'll get your clothes cleaned for you and you'll need some-

179

thing to wear in the meantime. We use jump suits," Taggert said. "Much more sensible."

The scientist opened a door marked "Number 14" and motioned Brady in. The newsman looked around a comfortably furnished living room, bedroom, and kitchen bathed in a pleasant artificial light. "Neat," he said. "All the comforts of home."

Taggert showed him the bathroom. "Everything you need is here," he explained. He glanced at Brady's shoes. "What size?"

"Nine D," Brady said. "More of your haberdashery service?"

"Sure." Taggert laughed. "Flight boots coming up. You smoke, ah . . ."

"Luckies."

"Anything else?"

Brady shook his head. "Just that shower and a shave."

"Go ahead. I'll phone in for the suit and boots. And the cigarettes," he added. "I could put some coffee on while you're getting squared away, if you'd like."

"Great." Brady looked at Taggert. "You're quite the host."

"Took a Dale Carnegie course," Taggert replied. Brady laughed and turned on the shower.

Well, Brady thought, a couple of wars prepared me for anything. He tried to be objective about his reactions to the events of the past twenty-four hours, events that should have overwhelmed him completely. But after a while the mind refuses to absorb any more and creates a natural defense against the unexpected. Something like this had happened to him during the Korean War when he was a prisoner of the Chinese. After being kicked and punched and tied with barbed wire for hours in excruciating positions, he had reached the point where fear vanished. It wasn't that he had gained courage. He just didn't care anymore. He couldn't do a thing except die. Once he felt that he *would* die, they couldn't reach him anymore. You stop caring about events you know you can't control.

Obviously he hadn't been very much in control of his actions for quite a while now. And what Taggert had told him about the natives enforcing a zone of death for two hundred miles in every direction had sunk home. Brady was a realist. He accepted the fact that someone else was calling the shots.

He turned the shower to hot and felt the steaming needles against his skin. Anyway, he laughed to himself, this was being kidnapped in style. Brady scrubbed his body and rinsed off.

Ten minutes later he was dressed in a flight suit and boots. Taggert had produced new underwear and socks as well. They must have a complete quartermaster and commissary to support the many people working here at—what had Taggert called it?— *Condor*. The name fit, Brady thought.

Taggert waited with a pitcher of steaming coffee. Several packs of cigarettes lay on the table.

"I understand you may be joining us," Taggert said.

Brady looked up slowly. "Who told you that?" His voice came out flat, unfriendly.

"Why, Vadim. He—"

"Next time try asking me, huh?"

Taggert was flustered. "I didn't . . . I mean, Vadim said you and he . . ." Taggert put on the brakes. "From what I understand, you and Vadim discussed this organization."

Brady knew how to keep someone off balance. "We discussed it," he interrupted. "That's a long way from signing on the dotted line."

Taggert nodded slowly, confused by Brady's hostility. "Apparently I misunderstood."

Brady fixed his gaze upon the scientist. "Look, Taggert, I'm not holding you responsible for my being here or even the way I got here. I know that's out of your bailiwick. Let's get that straight. But as for joining up with this crowd"—Brady shook his head—"uh-uh. I still don't know what makes all of you tick or what you're really doing with all this talent, but I'll tell you one

181

thing straight out: I'm a long way from agreeing with self-appointed cops."

"Just a moment, Brady," Taggert said. "You've got to understand—"

"I've got to understand nothing," Brady snapped. He rose to his feet. "I don't want any fights with you," he said. "I told you I don't figure you in the fun-and-games department. Let's leave it at that." Brady reached for a fresh cigarette. "Are we ready for your grand tour?"

Taggert came to his feet slowly. He took a long breath before replying to Brady. When he did, it was with a definite coolness. He wasn't out to make anyone happy. Not anymore.

"Yes, I'm ready," Taggert said. "It's rather a long walk, and we can discuss any technical questions you may have."

"Long walk to where?"

"The servicing area for the discs," Taggert replied, opening the door and stepping into the corridor.

Brady followed, walking at Taggert's side down the hallways. "That hydroelectric plant I saw on the way in," he said. "All that for here?"

Taggert, relieved to change the conversation, nodded. "Yes. The hydroelectric facility supplies all our base power. For housekeeping. There's another plant about a mile to the east; you couldn't see it the way you came in. It's an alternate source in the event of failure. We use two nuclear generators to provide the energy feed for the discs. They—"

"Two nuclear generators?"

"Yes."

"I don't understand. What is—how did you put it?—energy feed for the discs?"

"We feed energy to the drive unit in the discs," Taggert said. "Whatever we direct into the energy storage system provides a return outflow directly proportional to the—"

"Whoa there!" Brady halted his stride and held up his hand. "Right then and there you lost me."

Taggert smiled in understanding. "I know it sounds difficult at first," he admitted.

"Look," he said, "I understand propulsion systems pretty well. I can tell you how piston, turbojet, fanjet, solid and liquid rocket engines work. I'm even pretty good on balloons. But maybe you'd better go *all* the way back."

Taggert nodded. "It's a long story."

"I don't want the nuts and bolts and especially I don't want the math," Brady said quickly. "I've already had more than my share of headaches this week."

Taggert laughed. "Yes, I can well believe you." He motioned down the corridor. "Shall we continue?" They started up again.

"You know my background, don't you?"

"Pretty well," Brady said. "I did a biog search on you before I went to Flagstaff. Rocketdyne, Lockheed, AEC. I'm fairly well grounded. Before you joined Blackburn, that is."

"Right. I think it's best to give you my philosophy on power systems first," Taggert said. "Not a long story, though."

"Shoot."

"Well, the long and short of it, Brady, is that for years I was convinced the power systems we employed were hopelessly archaic. Were you aware that the most efficient form of transportation is the steel wheel on the steel rail?"

"The railroad?"

"Strangely enough, yes." Brady noticed the rising enthusiasm of Taggert as he moved into his narrative of power-systems development. Brady had pegged Taggert perfectly in his discussion with Mendelov. Dr. Kenneth Taggert cared little or nothing for politics as he pursued the holy grail of science.

"I knew," Taggert went on, "that sooner or later even the most advanced propulsion we used would become extinct, like the dinosaur. You're aware I left Nerva after only one year, aren't you?"

"Uh-huh. Any particular reason?"

"Good Lord, yes. It was a dead end from the start," Taggert replied with a grimace. "Nerva was simply a nuclear application of large rocket engines. Trying to squeeze hotter gases through a smaller throat nozzle about summed it up. It was a better rocket. Period. It was still a giant with feet of clay."

"So you quit?"

"Not quite that way," Taggert corrected. "When I saw the dead end, I moved on to what I'd always believed was the key to energy control. I discovered I'd been on the wrong track all the time. It was like trying to make the piston engine more and more powerful when the answer was to get rid of pistons and go to jets. I drew the same conclusion for all propulsion systems. They were hopelessly archaic. Nothing was really new, including the jet. What we needed was a complete breakthrough. So I undertook some studies of force fields, magnetic fields, subnuclear structures, such things as the effect of supermagnetic fields against electron orbits. That was really the key, and I—"

"I hate to bust in on you again," Brady said, "but just as your audience of one, I don't know the first thing about supermagnetic fields against electron orbits. Would you believe I never even heard of it?"

"I'm sorry," Taggert said. "No nuts and bolts, right?"

"Right. And no math."

"Difficult to do without it, but I'll try." Taggert chewed his lip. "I made certain never to lose sight of the first law in this business of power. In any power system the key factor is your efficiency in extracting energy. For example, you can burn a mixture of crude oil and you get heat. Burn high-octane gasoline and you get far more heat. But everything then depends on how well you use that heat. You can burn gasoline to heat water to operate a steam engine. Not terribly efficient. It makes a lot more sense to burn gasoline in a piston or jet engine or use it as fuel for a liquid rocket engine. That will use the gasoline's energy with the greatest efficiency." Taggert glanced at Brady. "All right so far?"

"Fine," Brady said with enthusiasm. "I like to keep things in my own mind in the form of analogies. In my business I fall back on that pretty heavy. You're doing great," he emphasized.

"Well, then. We have the basic law: maximum source, plus maximum efficiency, equals maximum power. When you understand the law as we've simplified it, you know in what direction you must move. Do you realize that power exists all about us in quantities that strain the imagination? But we don't know how to use that power. Again—to use an analogy—you can burn a lump of coal in a stove or, if you know how to go about it, you can split the atoms of that coal. Let's say it's a lump weighing about two pounds. Handled efficiently, as nuclear fuel, that amount of coal would give you a power return of something like twenty-five billion kilowatt hours of energy! That's about equal to all the energy produced by every power plant in the United States running at maximum output, day and night, for six weeks without interruption. So there it is. The problem and the road to its solution, I mean. Find a way to really use all the tremendous energy that's always about us."

"You make it sound simple," Brady commented.

"It *is* simple," Taggert replied. "Everything is simple, once you know how to go about it. Few things were easier for the American Indian than making fire. But put an inexperienced man in a field of flint, stone and dry brush and he wouldn't know where to begin to make his fire. To the Indian it's simple."

"What happened after you found the right road?" Brady asked.

"Force fields started me off," Taggert said. "Energy fields invisible to the eye can contain other forms of energy. Again, going to analogy, you can have a forced draft of air within an enclosed space to keep out air."

"I know what you mean," Brady said. "They call those air

185

doors. High-speed fans blow air downward in a doorway. It keeps out bugs. Air, too, I suppose."

"That's right," Taggert said. "You're using air to contain air. A better analogy would be ice. It's a form of water that's also used to contain water."

"So this set you off?"

Taggert chuckled. " 'Set me off' is an excellent way to put it. I was doing theoretical studies of force fields when I was introduced to some new work involving the collapse of electron fields. In effect, this meant being able to compress or reduce the diameter of electron orbits about an atom. The key was that the atom wasn't broken up."

"Wait a moment," Brady said. "Orbital mechanics—maybe that's the wrong phrase, but it'll do—is the same for electrons or planets. When you tighten up an orbit, you increase its speed, right?"

"Exactly. The moon orbits the earth at just over two thousand miles an hour. A satellite at a few hundred miles above the earth has orbital volocity of about seventeen thousand miles an hour. Let's say this satellite was first put into a very high orbit. If we then bring it closer to the earth we increase its speed—along with its mass, of course—but the nature of the satellite itself doesn't change at all."

"This apply also to electrons?"

"I thought it would," Taggert confirmed, "and as it turned out, it did. That's why I spent so much time working with the bevatron at Cal Tech. The experiments I was able to do there, along with theoretical calculation—I rather hogged a computer for several months—established that I was on the right track. There was a lot of trial and error, of course. But I moved closer and closer to the answer. I discovered I had to use a certain alloy, a metal of absolute purity that—"

"What kind of metal?"

"Sorry." Taggert smiled quickly. "Very few people know that, and we believe it's wiser to keep it that way."

"I can see that. Forget the question."

"Thanks. Anyway, I found out, in theory, that electron orbits could be reduced in size. Tremendous energy would be needed to create a force field, a super force field—you might call it a field of compression—but finally"—Taggert shrugged—"I put all the right pieces together. It worked."

"What happened next?"

"Oh, I wasn't quite out of the woods yet. It was one thing to arrive at a theory, but something else to prove it in repetitive demonstration. That took some doing, but we managed to get the funds.

"The next breakthrough came when I discovered that if we poured energy into the compression field, and then halted that energy input, what we had poured into the field would be returned in precisely the same quantity."

"Could you break that down?"

"Look at it this way," Taggert said, drawing figures in the air as he spoke. "You put a thousand tons of fuel in a rocket. When you light your fire you burn that fuel within a few minutes. You get heat and thrust for a specific period of time. You're operating with relatively low efficiency, of course, but it works. If you could burn that fuel with three times the efficiency you have, you'd get three times as much energy. In other words, if your big rocket could put thirty tons into orbit, just by burning the fuel with more efficiency you could triple that payload and orbit ninety tons without using an extra drop of fuel."

"No sweat so far," Brady said.

"All right. In essence, we discovered that the compression field was acting as a . . . consider it a storage battery. If we put in x quantity of energy to collapse the electron orbits, we discovered that over a certain period of time we got back that same x quantity in power outflow. It was like putting energy into a bank. The moment we stopped pouring it into the bank, the bank started to return the deposit. We found out that if we primed the force field for a period of thirty-eight days, we would get back thirty-eight days of equal output of energy. The moment we stopped feeding the compression field, the electrons, still within the force field, remember, began to return to their normal paths. That meant they were giving up the energy required to collapse their orbits in the first place."

"I see," Brady said slowly. "And you were there to catch all that outflow in your own bucket."

Taggert chuckled. "Not a bucket, exactly. Let's say a paddlewheel. As the energy began pouring out from the force field, our drive unit—the paddlewheel—was there to be turned."

"You said a period of thirty-eight days. Does that mean you can charge up your system and have power coming back to you for thirty-eight days?"

"Exactly," Taggert said. "The energy outflow is constant. For thirty-eight days we get energy at a maximum rate. Whatever we don't use is lost. Or we can use that energy at maximum rate for the full thirty-eight days."

"And that's where your nuclear reactors come in?" Brady asked.

"Right again. We use the hydroelectric plants for housekeeping, as I said. But we can't take a chance on a power interruption to energize the disc drives, so we decided to ship nuclear reactors here. There are always a few discs in the chamber, being energized."

"Can I see that being done?"

"Certainly. We're on our way there right now."

"Good. Can you translate your energy output—what's coming out of the force field—into normal measurements of power?"

"It wouldn't be completely accurate," Taggert cautioned.

"Use a ball-park figure," Brady urged. "If you had to translate it into pounds thrust or horsepower, how would it add up?"

Taggert thought for a few seconds. "All right. It would work out something on the order of two million horsepower."

"Two mill—"

"Difficult to accept," Taggert said to the astonished Brady. "It's true enough. However, that's an equivalency we're using. Six pounds of oranges don't make six pounds of apples, even though in both cases you're dealing with fruit. In the same way, pounds thrust, or horsepower, can't always be translated accurately."

"I know, I know," Brady said quickly. "But, Jesus Christ, you're talking about—" He shook his head. "I can see now how the discs get such tremendous performance. Can I ask you some other questions?"

"I'm here to serve," Taggert said with a smile. "In your own idiom . . . shoot."

"That ionization—the blue glow around the discs, I mean. Is that a result of your energy outflow?"

"Yes. We use—no, let me back up a moment. I consider the disc drive an electrostatic-field drive. Some people here feel the proper term is electrogravitic or perhaps purely electromagnetic. What's important is that the disc operates through resistors incorporated around the entire rim of the disc. We not only control the energy flow at any given level, but also with a positive or a negative field. What we do, in its simplest form, is to have two different electrical fields, each of tremendous disparity, on opposite poles of the disc. It operates as a giant magnet chasing itself. I realize," Taggert explained with an unhappy expression, "that doesn't explain it too well. I can show it to you much more clearly with the formulas that—"

"Perish the thought," Brady said quickly. "What you've said is fine. Would I be correct in saying your energy field pushes against itself?"

"No, you wouldn't," Taggert said. "But the effect seems to be that, just as much as a rocket pushes against itself."

"Let me ask you another. Does your drive leak?"

"Leak?"

"Well, there must be some leakage. I mean, your energy output is so great there must be electrical discharge of some kind beyond the disc." Brady sought for another analogy. "What I mean is this. You've driven your car, when your radio was playing, alongside power lines, or past a truck with poor shielding in the engine, haven't you? The result is static in the—"

"I see what you mean," Taggert said, nodding. "Yes, you're right. We can't always contain all the energy outflow perfectly, so leakage is sometimes present."

"Would that account for airplane radios and ignition systems going out of whack?"

"Certainly."

"Could the disc be responsible for car engines conking out? I mean, if it was low enough?"

"Oh, yes. It could blanket out just about any electrical system within its field."

Brady told Taggert the story of Barstow Air Force Base. Taggert explained the incident. A disc overflying Nebraska at more than a hundred thousand feet had suffered a failure in the drive. The energy pouring from the partially collapsed force field had been enormous. With the collapsed force field, the energy had penetrated hundreds of feet through solid objects. Including radio equipment of the underground missile complex and the power station in the town.

"I've got an idea why there haven't been any sonic booms from the discs," Brady ventured. "The ionization effect . . . is that it?"

Taggert confirmed what Brady had deduced. The electrical field broke up the air molecules before the moving disc. The turbulent ionized air was unable to form a clear shock wave. Therefore, no sonic boom reached the ground. One more puzzle solved.

They climbed a metal stairway, passed through doors entering the huge, hangarlike cave, and walked down a catwalk that

190

curved along its upper walls. Brady marveled at the size of the cavern below and the ingenuity with which complex machinery, astonishing in its variety, had been installed and was in use. Taggert led him away from the main hangar through several air-locks, each time opening and closing the doors with ship-type dogging handles. Finally they stood before leaded glass viewports.

Brady leaned close to the glass. Within a giant metal chamber a disc rested on its landing cradle. Access plates had been removed and four cables led into the bowels of the machine.

"This one's been here for just about a month," Taggert said. "Another week and we'll remove it."

"And it's got power for thirty-eight days after that?" Brady asked. Taggert nodded.

"What are all the radiation signs around here for?" the newsman queried.

"We're working with tremendous energies," Taggert explained. "There's some ionizing radiation involved."

For an hour Brady studied the disc carefully and questioned the scientist closely on details of the scene spread out before him. When he had absorbed as much as he could, he turned to Taggert. "Is this a natural cavern?" he asked.

"You mean this chamber?"

"That's right."

"By no means. We did this ourselves."

"Christ, this must have taken a lot of explosives." He couldn't believe they had hollowed out so vast an area without spending years at the job.

"Not dynamite," Taggert said.

"Then how . . . ?"

"Two men were responsible for this," the scientist explained. "Harry Boener and Wayne Priest. You'll have a chance to meet them if you like. They determined how to channel the energy output of the disc drive into a beam—"

191

"The missile at Cape Kennedy!" Brady exclaimed. "And the bombers at MacDill . . ."

"Yes." Taggert frowned.

"You mean what your two geniuses did was to turn the drive into a weapon, right?"

"It can be either a weapon or a tool," Taggert said, "just like any other device or implement or force. Boener and Priest adapted the drive system to create a beam. It acts something like a laser beam, but its power is increased by a very high multiple. Directed against a solid object, like the rock here"—Taggert swept his hand through the air—"it causes complete molecular disruption. Not destruction, although the physical effect seems to be just that. The energy beam slices through rock as if it were so much fog. We used it to hollow out this cavern. It was really quite simple. We—"

"Simple, my ass. It took more energy than building the Panama Canal."

"Yes, but that's a matter of utilizing the energy that's available," Taggert insisted. "We had high utilization. We used two discs, hovering outside the mountain, to start the job. The entire task was completed in a month."

"What's the range of your little toy?"

"Well, it's affected by inverse law, of course. If—"

"Just the range, Doctor. Please."

Taggert sighed. "Yes, of course. The extreme effective range would be about a thousand yards. Close up, for the job we had here, we could expand the beam to a width of about two feet. It cuts through rock quite nicely."

"It certainly looks like it," Brady observed. "Where to next?"

"My office," said Taggert. "This way."

"Just what are you people trying to do?" Brady resumed, coffee cup in hand. "You've performed a scientific miracle with the discs. You can revolutionize global transportation. *Global.* Christ, you could go to Mars on one of these babies. Half the people in

192

this world are on starvation diets—not because we can't produce enough food, but because we can't get the food to the people who need it. The discs could wipe out the logistics problems or colonize another planet. And instead you're off on this half-baked crusade Mendelov seems to have started. Surely, one of the first tenets of science is that you can't turn your back on a new frontier. Seems to me"—Brady grunted contemptuously—"you're doing just that."

"You through?" Taggert said.

"Yeah. I made my little speech for the day."

"Then let me clarify something for you," the scientist said, thoughtfully. "I'd like to go to the moon. Personally, I mean. The idea fascinates me. Good Lord, to walk the surface of the moon . . . and *Mars*. I'd give almost anything to do that."

"Then why—"

"Because, for one thing, Brady, we don't *know* if the discs can operate safely above ninety miles. We don't know what will happen when we're out of the electromagnetic field of the earth. We have to make tests first. Extensive tests to eliminate the margin of error. All that means time. We don't have that time. And as far as using the discs for revolutionizing transportation, for food, as you put it, that's nonsense."

"That's debatable. If—"

Taggert didn't give him the opportunity to reply. "Maybe from your viewpoint it is," he said with a touch of anger, "but not from mine. The people involved with us, Brady, include some of the best minds in the world. Not only in the physical sciences but in sociology, economics, geopolitics; we cover the range pretty well. Do you know Robert Kroot?"

"I've heard of him."

"Kroot is a first-rate politicometrics scientist," Taggert said. "Whatever there is to know about the matter of food and world population, including logistics, Kroot knows it. Don't you think we've thought of, and examined, at great length, every pos-

193

sibility that you brought up? When I first became involved in this with Dr. Mendelov, I sounded a lot like you. That's not an insult, Brady. I believed the drive would provide power anywhere in the world, help lift that part of the world that's still in the dark ages to new levels. I was wrong," Taggert said harshly. "I was wrong because I looked at things from a restrictive viewpoint. The solutions I thought of were the same old solutions. Their effect would be temporary. The point is *survival.* People with full stomachs and television sets in their front rooms die just as easily as people who are hungry and don't even know how to read."

"Sounds like the master planner himself." Brady laughed without humor. "Your Mendelov is brilliant. I'll admit that. He's more than brilliant. He's pure genius. But I'm not sure if he's an evolutionist or a benevolent Genghis Khan."

"He's a long way from that," Taggert said angrily. "But even if he were. . . well, I'll tell you this, Brady: The worst that man could do, and I mean the *worst,* would be a damn sight better than what the world is heading for."

Brady's reaction came instantly. "Who the hell says so, Taggert? You? Him? His entourage? Who appointed him God?"

Taken aback at Brady's response, Taggert didn't answer immediately. When he spoke, his voice was calm. "It's not a case of anyone playing God," he said.

"The hell it isn't!" Brady shouted. "I don't know all the answers yet, but I can sure figure some of them. This drive, the discs, the energy beam—all this gives you and Mendelov and this whole bunch absolute power, doesn't it? Aren't you thinking that way, Taggert? You've got something so powerful no one can touch you. Right?

"Absolute power corrupts absolutely, mister, in case you've never heard that phrase before." Brady slammed his hand on the armrest of his chair. "Do you really think you're original about this business of saving the world from itself? Jesus Christ, man, every tyrant who's ever been in business has used that line!"

Taggert had become ice. "You seem certain of what we're trying to do."

Brady gave the scientist a scathing look. "Don't give me that," he shot back. "Just show me where I'm wrong."

"Don't lecture *me*, Brady!" Taggert shouted suddenly. "You're insulting. It's clear enough that this is quite *different!*"

The newsman laughed harshly. "It's *always* different."

"But it *is* different, damn you!" Taggert cried. "Mendelov's found an answer that's evaded us all." He stopped when he saw the sarcastic smile on Brady's face and struggled visibly to control his temper. "You're hardly the objective type, are you? It must be wonderful to draw such perfect conclusions before you've heard a man fully. Saves time, doesn't it?" Taggert rose to his feet. "Sometimes I wonder what Mendelov sees in you or why you're here," he said. "He must have his reasons. I'm willing to wait and find out. Do you realize you're the first man who's ever come here, knowing what you do, before he's even been accepted as a part of what we're doing?"

Brady smiled bitterly. "I'm touched. I really am. A bunch of megalomaniacs get *me* branded as a lunatic, thrown out of my job, blackballed in my profession; they drug me, drag my ass out of the country, hold me a prisoner, threaten to cash my chips for me, and *you* think I should be grateful! Har-de-har-har!"

"Sometimes, Brady, one man isn't that important in the—"

"Shove it," Brady snarled. "That's the easiest thing in the world to say when that 'one man' isn't you."

CHAPTER XVIII

BRADY FACED DR. VADIM MENDELOV ACROSS A LOW TABLE. THEY were alone. Mendelov might have been comfortably at home in his Princeton study. The huge scientist wore an open-necked shirt, and his booted feet rested comfortably on a hassock. On the table to his left stood a pitcher with cool wine and glasses. Mendelov smoked a calabash, with obvious relish, Brady noted sourly. Even the room rubbed Brady the wrong way.

"Damn it, Mendelov," Brady said, "it's time we stopped beating around the bush."

Mendelov blew smoke from his nostrils and gestured with the pipe. "Have we forgotten something?"

"Yes," Brady said angrily. "How long do you intend to keep me here?"

Mendelov swung his feet from the hassock and faced Brady. "That depends."

"Thanks a heap," Brady said caustically. "Upon what?"

"On many things," Mendelov said with open good humor. "I thought I'd made it clear . . . You're being considered for this organization."

Brady waved his hand in a gesture of disdain. "*You've* got big plans for my joining your circus. But not me. Saving the world isn't my cup of tea."

"Isn't it? I should think it would be the avowed interest of any sane being."

"Goddamn it," Brady raged, "it's not a matter of 'could' or 'would'! To hell with you and your games. I just don't for one damned minute believe you could prevent a nuclear war if that's what the major nations of the world decide to get into. Not you or anyone else. This circus of yours is very impressive. But do you really believe you've got the power to affect what countries like the United States or Russia or Red China intend to do?"

The scientist shrugged. "You realize what you're trying to do? You're saying, Brady, that what always has been will—must—always be. That history is repetition without hope for change. Really! It's not so, not so. You've ignored the saturation factor." A sad smile appeared on the scientist's face. "Everyone, it appears, struggles desperately to ignore the saturation factor.

"You won't admit that war has reached its point of saturation. The popular idiom refers to doomsday weapons. Their power is so great that casualties mean nothing anymore, simply because there won't be enough of us left to compile the casualty lists. Sad to say, that possibility is no longer remote."

Brady glared at the other man. "And you've got the answer to all that right here?" he said. "Is this the big speech you've been building me up to? Because if it is, you sure haven't—"

"No, Mr. Brady," Mendelov broke in. "This is not 'the big speech,' as you put it."

"Then what are you waiting for?"

"The right moment, Mr. Brady. You haven't had sufficient conditioning yet. You see, I—"

"The Chinese tried that 'conditioning' long before you showed up," Brady snapped.

"Forgive me. I had no intention of compelling a change of heart. My beliefs don't run that way. I don't want to alter your basic convictions. No pressure is being placed on you, Mr. Brady. I have much more confidence in your native intelligence than you think."

Brady waved his hand to cut off Mendelov. "Never mind the bouquets. Taggert tells me you've discovered the flaw in everything the human race has ever done. That's a tall order"—he laughed without humor—"even for you. He claims you've found the key to world peace."

Mendelov was suddenly brusque. "You have never heard anyone here say our interest is in world peace. Bah! Peace as it's commonly defined is literally impossible. Man is incapable of existing without strife."

Brady stared at Mendelov. What he had just heard baffled him. "You're right," he said. "I *don't* understand."

"Obviously," Mendelov retorted. "We're not searching for an emotional nirvana that doesn't exist. You must understand that we're not pursuing unattainable goals. Nor is our interest the imposition of global peace—an impossible task. Our interest, Mr. Brady, lies in preventing the destruction of the world civilization. Do you understand? The two concepts are wholly distinct from one another. You must distinguish between the two, or you'll never understand what our effort represents."

Mendelov laid his pipe on the ash tray. He leaned back in his chair, both hands on the armrests, facing Brady like a judge passing sentence. "Nothing is ever black and white," Mendelov said. "Nothing. Neither in nature nor in the affairs of men. But every sign, every indication, every lesson from the past fairly screams its warning. Man is headed for a final conflict with thermonuclear weapons. We have the chance to avert this mass suicide. The means at our disposal, some of which you've seen, much of which you have *not* seen, give us the hope we pursue so urgently."

A thick finger stabbed in Brady's direction. "That is what we're after. It has nothing to do with peace—as you've been using that most imprecise word."

Brady sighed. "Look, don't get me wrong," he said. "No doubt what you're trying to do is . . . well, I don't want to use the word 'noble' because I don't think it would sit well with you."

"Bloody well right," Mendelov growled.

"All right, so you've got good intentions. But everything you've told me avoids the crux of the matter. You—and this includes everyone with you—believe you've come up with the right answers. You also believe you've got the means to enforce what you feel is the only way for the world to behave. So you're all convinced you can rule better than anyone else. *You* know what's best for—"

Mendelov's roar filled the room. "Rule! Good Lord, man, are you blind?" The giant had come bolt upright in his seat and was staring at Brady. "The *last* thing in the world we want is to *rule* anyone!"

Mendelov cut himself short with a sudden laugh. "Never mind," the scientist said. "I believe we've gone far enough for the moment. Let me change the subject. You'll be told what you need to know in good time. In the interim, Brady, I do wish you would think deeply on what we've discussed. Because we need you—your knowledge of the public mind, the press, the world of the well-informed laymen. We need that knowledge for what we have in mind."

"You need *me*? Very flattering." Brady laughed. "You got off to a hell of a start. Do you go after all your help with knockout drops?"

"Spare me, Brady. Your ego's been damaged. You're supposed to be a realist," Mendelov said with no attempt to conceal his irritation. "What we did was necessary because of your persistence in tracking us down. That interested me, and I can see great value in recruiting a man who managed to do what no one else has accomplished. But we've gone over that ground before. It's done.

199

Don't confuse my interest in you with weakness. That would be stupid." Mendelov's eyes gripped Brady. They were cold and heavy-lidded. "If it becomes necessary . . . You may as well hear this without any room for doubt . . . If it becomes necessary, you will be killed."

CHAPTER XIX

BRADY WAS LUCKY. HE WAS OUT OF THE CITY WHEN IT HAPPENED. He drove along a narrow country road edging the Neversink River near Fallsburg, New York, about a hundred miles northwest of New York. It was about three o'clock in the morning and Brady was returning to the city when the night tore apart with a soundless scream of light. One moment the road was clear in his headlights and the next instant everything vanished from sight. Light, all-pervading, intense beyond description, blinding the universe. New York was a hundred miles away, but in that split second Brady knew what was happening even as the savage glare from a hundred miles away clawed at his eyes. With the pain ripping upward through his sockets, everything took on the false tones of a photo negative with the glare behind it.

Instinct brought his foot slamming onto the brake pedal, his hands clutching the wheel. But he was going too fast and the turn rushed at him. The car bounded into the ditch and flipped crazily over and over. When everything came to a stop and the sound of metal tearing ended, the car lay on its side and something wet and sticky ran down his face. He tried to clear his head. He knew he was bleeding, that he had been hurt. He struggled from the wrecked car. Despite the dancing lights in his eyes and the needles of pain, he could see. Ignoring the pain, he turned to the southeast. Toward, he realized with a sickness in his belly, where New York *had been*.

In the sky writhed something monstrous, boiling and writhing within itself, twisting upward. A flowery head disgorged itself from the glowing stalk. Brady remained numb, strangely calm. He realized he was watching the funeral pyre of what had been millions of human beings. He started walking and looked at the spreading sky glow that filtered down through the trees and illuminated the clouds. When he had climbed a small hill and could see for miles there came another terrible glow in the sky from a much greater distance, this one to the northeast. A steel fist grinding into the bowels of a city. Then, dimmed by an even greater distance, still another. Then the heavens took up a slow, uneven pulsing, a throbbing of nuclear hells that no longer faded completely. Slowly the shock ebbed from his body and the pain, stabbing more deeply, brought the distant nightmare into focus. He heard the sound of a car, the engine racing. Brady turned and signaled with his hands, but the car rushed past, a glimpse of white faces within.

Twenty minutes later he reached a small crossroads village. People milled about the streets, many carrying rifles, all of them grim, listening to a car radio blaring loudly. The man in the car turned up the volume and still the throng pressed closer. Brady joined them. No one seemed to notice the blood caked on his face or his torn clothes. Brady knew the emergency networks had come into action. He heard what he expected to hear. Confused, angry, frightened men behind the microphones, themselves lacking hard information to pass on to their millions of invisible listeners. The voice blaring from the car radio spoke falteringly of mass nuclear attack. There were no reports from the cities that had been attacked. How could there be, Brady queried himself, when there isn't anyone left to report?

Brady listened to the pleas for the public to stay off the roads. The announcers were more hysterical, Brady noticed, than the grimly calm people about him. Those who weren't calm would do what they pleased or felt compelled to do. Those close to the cities who saw the leaping flames and the spreading clouds downwind would run for it. They'd run madly, impelled by years of fright building to this moment. They wouldn't have anywhere to go, but they'd run there in cars and on foot and any way they could move. The highways would swiftly become clogged. The man nearest Brady blurted suddenly, "Thank God we're off the main roads." The others nodded, and Brady noticed a tightening of hands around rifles and guns.

The radio was reporting massive tidal waves along the Pacific Coast. Brady felt it was true enough. One of the recognized dangers for many years had been the threat of the Russians sinking monster hydrogen bombs along the sea bottom from fifty to two hundred miles from the West Coast, and then setting them off by remote control. Brady closed his eyes and shuddered. He thought of tidal waves a thousand feet high, rushing inland from the sea with a roar such as no one had ever heard since man first walked the planet: a wall a thousand feet high and moving at eight hundred miles an hour, boiling with radioactivity. He thought of the massive radioactive clouds and the steam that would cross the high mountains and flow inland, drifting for hundreds and even thousands of miles, a sticky blanket of slow death.

Brady felt a hand on his arm. For the first time since he had arrived, someone took heed of the blood on his face. A man tugged him away from the crowd, led him to a doctor nearby. Brady remained only half conscious as the doctor attended his injuries. Two broken ribs, lacerations, bruises, one deep cut requiring sixteen stitches. Brady remained with the doctor for the better part of an hour. Then the lights went out. The doctor lit two kerosine lamps. The old man lit two cigarettes and passed one to Brady. His hand paused as the deep roar of passing jets bounded from

203

the sky. The hand continued its motion. Brady sucked greedily on the cigarette.

"Well, it's come finally."

Brady didn't have any comments for the end of the world.

"They must be hitting everywhere." The old doctor talked as if his words gave him release. "Everywhere. Whole country is being torn apart. . . ."

The words came from Brady without bidding. "At least the Russians must be getting it three times as bad. There won't be a city standing anywhere in the Soviet—"

In the flickering light of the lamps he saw a strange expression come over the doctor's face. "Does it make you feel better? What's the difference, mister? Does it do them"—he pointed in the direction of New York—"a damn bit of good? Why don't you go down there and tell everybody that we're really giving it to the Russians? Why don't you . . ." The doctor's voice trailed away.

Before dawn the first white ash fell from the sky. A ghastly pallor appeared over the trees and on buildings, on the ground, on cars and animals and people caught outside. A warm snow that wouldn't melt. They all knew what it was. The fallout. The deadly ash from the bomb. It was everywhere, drifting before the wind, swirling along the breeze. It wouldn't be so bad, Brady thought, if it thundered or roared or did something. But it doesn't. It doesn't make a sound.

The invisible death brought with it the signs of fear. Widened eyes, spasmodic movements, high-pitched voices, tight lips. The doctor had returned with Brady to the village center. With many others they collected in a small diner. The owner kept it open "because I wouldn't know what else to do." They were in the diner when the ash came from the sky.

The wind piled it against buildings, on street corners. It lay everywhere, weighing almost nothing but pressing against them all with a terrible finality. Brady sensed the first waves of hysteria. The shrill laughter, sudden cursing. He, they, all of them;

they were helpless. You always thought of mass death with violence and horror and the world crashing down all about you. Outside, not a single twig was broken. Not a window shattered. Still the death flowered down from the sky.

It fell for hours. No one remained near the windows any longer. The doctor smiled to himself. He knew the diner was no protection. He didn't say that aloud.

Later, they saw someone walking in the ash, an alien creature in a rubberized suit and hood, wearing a mask and heavy boots, in his hand a shining metal-and-glass instrument. Measuring the radioactive count. They didn't need the man and his goddamned instrument to tell them what the vomiting was telling them better. The weaker among them were feverish, nauseous, wide-eyed with fear. They knew they were all walking dead, everything so quiet and peaceful, the ash raining softly in its death kiss from on high. They saw the hooded, caped, booted, masked figure gesture in anger or disgust, they couldn't be sure, but he flung away his Geiger counter and tore off the hood, threw away the cape, kicked off the boots, and walked toward and into the diner. They shrank away from him because the ash was on him. Brady tried to see his face, but too many people were in the way. He heard the stranger's voice. ". . . goddamned counter's no good anyway. Right off the scale, right—off—the—scale; it's so damned hot out there, that stuff is so hot!" The figure paused, framed in the doorway, and Brady moved to see him. "You're all dead!" the man laughed, the laughter swelling into a cackle. "Dead, dead, dead! In a day or two, you'll all be dead!" He roared with mirth, his arms spread out and his head thrown back, a standing crucifix, then he brushed the ash from his body, swirling it through the room toward them. Abruptly he reached up and with a wet, sucking sound ripped the mask from his face. Brady knew a shock of horror. There was no face: He stared into empty skull sockets, heard the jawbone clattering as the cackling laugh roared at him. Cursing, Brady hurled himself

205

at the skeletal thing in the radiation suit. He heard himself screaming as he clawed at the thing, but he couldn't raise his arms or batter with his fists; he struggled to rip and tear and destroy but he couldn't move and the laughter swelled like a balloon inside his brain, calling *Brady, Brady, BRADY!*

He stared wildly, gasping, trying to focus his eyes, the grinning skull a fleeting retinal shadow mocking him as it faded slowly. Brady jerked himself to an upright position, perspiration matting him everywhere. "Brady! Are you all right?" Mouth open, he looked up. Taggert. Bending down over him, grasping his arm. "Are you all right?" Again the question. Brady nodded slowly. "You've been having a nightmare."

"Uh-huh." Brady's throat hurt, he was hoarse. He swung his feet to the floor, the sweat-salt stinging his eyes. He shuddered. It had been so goddamned real! He looked up at Taggert, saw the concern in the other man's eyes. "I—I'm all right," Brady stammered. "Just let me get, get my wits about me." He couldn't shake the dream. It came back in spasms, breaking waves of horrible memory. Brady stumbled into the shower, jolted himself with a stream of icy water, turning it hot until steam billowed about him. He sagged against the wall as the water washed over him, cleansing him.

Christ, how had it started? He remembered now. He had left Mendelov to visit with several of the top men in Condor—Wilkinson, Kroot, the others. It had all been too much for one day, for the night before. Crammed from beginning to end, thoughts, conflict, anger, all of it churning in his mind.

He didn't stay long with Drew Wilkinson. To the financier the situation and events necessary to meet that situation were cut and dried. Within several years there was every chance his entire financial empire would crumble in ruin. "Because," Wilkinson told Brady, "financial structures collapse just as readily as mortar and stone when a nuclear shock wave arrives." Wilkinson gave Brady the impression of being involved with Mendelov strictly for his own purposes. Personal interests spurred on the man, not a sense of avoiding war, as Mendelov judged the matter. Brady spoke his thoughts to Wilkinson. The financier laughed in Brady's face.

"For the life of me I can't understand what Vadim sees in you," Wilkinson lashed out. "You fool! You put *your* values into everything! Isn't that it, Brady? You've bitched and complained about the dangers of do-gooders. Yet I've been flatly honest with you and told you I was committed up to my ears for personally selfish reasons. And what does that call for me to do? To risk everything I have so that we might avoid a total nuclear disaster. Because if the country is destroyed, I go down with it. And because I *am* honest with you, and because I detest dishonesty in these things, because I agree with you that do-gooders are a dangerous breed, you still insist we're misguided zealots wasting our time.

"Let me ask you something, Brady. You're aware that even the most optimistic computer studies give us barely three chances in ten for staying out of a total nuclear war. You agree it appears inevitable. You know it means the destruction of everything in the world that's meaningful to us." Wilkinson slammed his hand against his desk. "Just what the hell have *you* done to prevent its coming? As far as I'm concerned, you're a blind fool with a loud mouth. You can harp and snipe and wallow along with the rest of the world, wailing about the savagery of man, but you're not *doing* a goddamn thing. You make me sick. Get the hell out of my office."

Brady was still brooding over Wilkinson's words when he first met Robert Kroot. The economist was worlds removed from Wilkinson. Retiring almost to the point of physical discomfort, he seemed to fade into his surroundings. Yet the small man looked upon his visitor with eyes that were electric. They moved almost constantly, darting about, reassuring their owner that nothing would escape his notice. Kroot didn't have any speeches for Brady. He responded to Brady with adding-machine efficiency.

From Brady's point of view, Kroot made more sense than everyone else put together. He lacked the high-flown idealism of Taggert, he remained remote from the calculating self-interest of Wilkinson, he had nothing of the philosophical depth of Mendelov. What Kroot did have was a dispassionate and calculating appraisal of the facts of life. He was a scientist of applied economics, and in clipped sentences he stated flatly to Brady that the industrial-economic society of the world had accepted that nuclear war could not be avoided.

"Accepted," Kroot repeated. "The international community has geared itself to a nuclear war economy. Hard business has been corrupted with a compelling need to increase the capacity for mass destruction. I use the term 'corrupted' advisedly. Once you achieve an industrial goal, a senseless repetition of that goal, resting on national debts of prohibitive proportion, is a corruption of all logic." Kroot shrugged as if none of it mattered beyond his evaluation. He was totally impersonal. "It's simple enough," he went on. "There exists the capacity to destroy civilization many times over. The hair-trigger balance has lost its stability. With the introduction of nuclear weapons to new countries, beyond France and China—and I know at least eight other nations now developing their nuclear arms—the whole delicate structure is set in quivering motion. It has the substance of jelly. It's impossible by any normal means to stop the vibrations now sweeping the mass. One day"—Kroot shrugged again—"it comes apart at the seams, like a bag of water split down its side. There are many signs attesting to this."

"Are you referring to specific items?" Brady asked.

Kroot looked with disdain at Brady. "I deal only in specifics," he said coldly. "The sum of national knowledge is microfilmed in underground vaults. Redundancy and lead-shielded vaults are the theme. Vast stores and stocks of materials, weapons, the like, are cached. There are secret deep underground shelters that can withstand anything save exposure to the nuclear fireball. The select members of our society to occupy these human vaults are aware of their role. They number in the thousands. The public, however, can't be told of the existence of such facilities." Kroot smiled as Brady started to interrupt. "You of all people, Mr. Brady, are aware of the ramifications of such news being made common property.

"Did you know that at least twenty nations have sperm banks in cryogenic storage? Those sperm banks are buried far beneath the sea, in underground caverns, high in mountains. They have only one purpose, Mr. Brady, and it has absolutely nothing to do with economics. They have been prepared for the day when all mature males left alive will have been rendered sterile by radio-activity."

A smile flickered on Kroot's face and fled, the grim humor of a man who sees the future and cannot help smiling at the madness of man.

"Dr. Mendelov and our associates, Mr. Brady, believe the world is rushing into an accidental nuclear war that's inevitable. I don't agree with them."

Kroot's words startled Brady. "No, Mr. Brady," the economist said in that same quiet voice. "There's nothing accidental about it. *The world is preparing deliberately for that war.*"

After his meeting with Kroot, Brady had returned to his apartment and had fallen asleep. And had dreamed. Even now, after running the shower alternately cold and hot to sting him fully awake, the nightmare haunted him. Maybe Mendelov and the others were right, he thought wearily. Maybe anything they did was better than waiting to be trampled under a rain of atomic hell. Every time Brady fought back from whatever rationale he could muster that an all-powerful group meant the greatest of all dangers, he heard Kroot's words that the world was preparing deliberately for its own self-destruction. The dream swirled through his mind. He could ignore the scenes of the terrible light, the towering mushroom stalks that punched their way far into the stratosphere. But he couldn't push from him that silent, terrible rain of lethal ash. The silence of that horror pounded in his ears.

He dried himself quickly and dressed. Taggert studied Brady's face as he came into the living room.

"You all right?"

"I'm fine now," Brady replied, managing a weak smile. "That was like nothing I've—" He cut himself short and dropped gratefully into a chair.

Taggert nodded. "I think you could use something a bit stronger than coffee this time," he said. He reached into a zippered pocket and withdrew a flask. "Scotch?"

"Christ, yes," Brady said with relief.

Taggert unscrewed the cap and handed the flask to Brady. He drank long and slowly, letting the fire settle in his system. Finally he lowered the flask and took a deep breath. "Thanks. It helps."

Taggert replaced the cap. "I've got some news for you," he offered.

"Oh? What about?"

"Your fiancée."

"Who?"

"Why, Miss Dallas. Ann Dallas. She is your fiancée, isn't—"

Brady's eyes narrowed as he came upright in his chair. "What about her?" he demanded.

Taggert was taken aback by Brady's intensity. "Mendelov told you about her, didn't he?"

"No. What about her?"

"You should be proud of that young woman, Brady. She's a wildcat."

"Goddamn you, get to it, Taggert!"

"Sorry. She showed up at the Blackburn office in Flagstaff."

"Oh, good Christ."

Taggert's smile was friendly. ". . . and when she discovered you'd checked out of your motel, and she couldn't find you, she tore the roof off."

Brady eased carefully back into the chair. "How?"

"She threatened to tell the police that the Blackburn company had kidnapped you."

"She'd be dead right."

"Yes, of course. But Miss Dallas didn't *know* that. Either way it could have been embarrassing to have the local police tramping through the building."

"Never mind. Where is she? What's happened to her?"

Taggert held up his hand. "She's on the way here."

"*Here?*" Brady echoed.

"Yes."

"But why in the name of God did you have to—" Brady came angrily from the chair.

"Please. She's perfectly all right. Will you let me tell you what happened?"

Brady sat down again and waited.

"Miss Dallas threatened to go to her father."

"Her father?" The whole thing was mad.

"Sam Dallas, it turns out," Taggert said with a wan smile, "has some very powerful friends in Washington. In the White House, in fact. We couldn't permit that."

"Don't tell me you—"

"No, no, of course not," Taggert said, anticipating Brady's words. "No abduction this time."

"Then how could you—I mean, how did you get her to agree to come here?"

Taggert couldn't resist the grin. "Love is a powerful force, apparently. We simply told her the truth."

"You mean . . ." Brady stared at Taggert. "And she just went along?"

"That's right."

Brady didn't know what to say.

Taggert glanced at his watch. "It's six now. Your, ah, fiancée will be here in about six hours or so. About midnight, I should say."

"Hold it, hold it," Brady said as the question occurred to him. "How can you cover up a second disappearance? The airline will be looking for her, and if she's reported as missing, and her old man's got the friends you say he has, you've got a can of worms on your hands, haven't you?"

Taggert laughed and stood up. "Not at all. She's not missing. She called the newspapers and told them you and she had eloped."

CHAPTER XX

BRADY WALKED THROUGH THE DISC SERVICING AREA WITH DIANNE
Sims and Dr. Kenneth Taggert. Mendelov, called away for the
night, would see Brady the next morning. Brady glanced at his
watch. The disc would be arriving within minutes, descending
almost vertically from high altitude.

"When do I find out just where we are?" He addressed the
question to both Taggert and Dianne Sims. They exchanged
glances and Taggert picked up the query. "He has a good idea
right now," he told the woman. "It's all right. Vadim said to tell
him what he wants to know."

Dianne smiled at Brady. "Have you ever heard of Palenque?"

He searched his memory. "No," he admitted.

"Palenque is a form of quasi-statehood," she said. "Not really
a country in the legal sense, but a country in practice. Its existence is neither recognized nor challenged."

"Challenged by whom?"

"Palenque forms part of Venezuela, Colombia, and Brazil.
The countries involved look the other way as far as Palenque is
concerned," Dianne went on. "We're in the high plateau and rain
forests east of the Andes chain. You had a good look at the terrain

on the way down. You can see why it's considered the most inaccessible region anywhere in the world. The winds that blow off the mountains make this entire area very difficult for airplanes. Several have been lost, in fact."

"It's what you'd call an atmospheric trap," Taggert broke in. "The currents are strong and no one has any idea of their flow. Most aircraft couldn't stand up under the turbulence."

"There are about a hundred thousand natives in Palenque," Dianne continued. "To outsiders they're the most hostile savages anywhere in the world."

"You seem amused about that," Brady noted.

"I am," she said. "That's why I was so careful to say 'outsiders.' Among themselves they're a peaceful and gentle people."

Brady laughed. "That isn't the story I got."

Dianne smiled gently. "That's because you haven't lived with them, Cliff. Otherwise you'd know better."

Brady stared. "*Lived* with them? I thought no white man had ever gone through this country."

"They haven't," Dianne said. "My mother was part of a missionary group attacked by the natives. She was the only survivor. One of the chief's sons took my mother as his wife."

"So you're, I mean . . ." Brady halted, embarrassed.

"That's right. I'm half-Jicaque."

"That's why we're on such excellent terms with the natives," Taggert said. "As far as the Jicaque are concerned, Dianne's one of them."

"But how did you—I mean, you speak English so perfectly and . . . and . . . just *look* at you," Brady said, still baffled.

"Have you heard of Dr. Francisco Valdivia?" Dianne asked. Brady shook his head.

"Dr. Valdivia—that's his name in Brazil, not his name among the Jicaque—became a great friend of my mother. She taught him to speak Portuguese, Spanish, and English. He learned so swiftly, she convinced Ah Tutul that Valdivia should be sent to

214

school in Brazil. He saw that the modern world was bound to encroach upon this territory and that the Jicaque would need several of their own people who understood civilization. He—"

"Wait a moment," Brady broke in. "Who's Ah Tutul?"

"Ah Tutul is chief of the Jicaque Indians. He has been as far back as I can remember. His word is law throughout Palenque."

"Right," Brady said, keeping track. "And what happened with Valdivia?"

"Mother was right," Dianne explained. "Francisco fulfilled the promise Mother saw in him. With the languages he commanded, besides Mother's instruction in other subjects, he had no difficulty in school. While he was attending the university, he struck up a close friendship with Carlos de Landa and—"

"General de Landa?" Brady asked.

"Yes. Have you heard of him?"

"Heard of him? I've known him for years," Brady said. "He was a Brazilian Air Force observer with us in Korea. I even flew him on a few missions. Is de Landa tied in with all this?"

"Only indirectly," Dianne answered. "Francisco became close friends with General de Landa. They were pretty much agreed about Palenque. Francisco became the liaison between the outside world and the Jicaque, and General de Landa worked closely with Francisco. There are some things about civilization Francisco felt could benefit our people.

"The Indians were happy to receive medicines," Dianne continued, "and Francisco felt that the outstanding Jicaque should receive an education on the outside."

"Sanitary engineering; that sort of thing," Taggert added. "But Ah Tutul's a wise old bird. He won't permit anything to interfere with the sanctuary of Palenque. The natives will still slaughter anyone who tries to penetrate this area."

"If that's the case," Brady said, "how come this place is here?"

"Francisco Valdivia and Vadim Mendelov are close friends," Taggert replied.

"Dr. Mendelov," Dianne explained, "met Francisco during a study of different tribes in South America. Mendelov had been warned not to travel within Palenque. So, having heard of Francisco, he arranged a meeting. That was many years ago," she explained. "All this, the discs and this base, I mean, came much later. When Dr. Taggert developed the drive for the discs, and the group began to form—"

"Mendelov plans to fill you in on that tomorrow," Taggert interjected. Brady nodded.

"The discs must be pretty impressive to savages—"

"Indians," Dianne corrected gently. "Not savages."

Brady grinned ruefully. "Sorry. But what I meant is that for people who've lived the same way, apparently, for thousands of years, the discs are rather overwhelming, aren't they? I should think the natives—Indians"—he smiled at Dianne—"must look on you as gods."

Dianne shook her head vigorously. "Absolutely not," she said quickly. "You mustn't underestimate the intelligence of these people. Once the Jicaque ruled much of the northern part of this continent. A long time ago they accepted the white man. They paid for that trust." She bit her lip. "They won't make the same mistake again. The position the Jicaque take is they must rule within their own territory before mixing. They're quite prepared to die first."

Brady thought over what he heard. "Then what's the position of Ah Tutul with Mendelov and the rest of you?"

"Mendelov persuaded Francisco to set up a meeting with Ah Tutul," Dianne said. "During that meeting—it was after the first discs had flown secretly—Mendelov arranged for this base to be set up here. To protect the sanctuary, they agreed upon the rule that no one ever enters or leaves here by any other means save the discs."

"That's what I meant when I told you no one, including Mendelov, can ever move through this country," Taggert said. "Dianne's case is different. This is her home."

"You said Ah Tutul doesn't regard Mendelov or anyone else as gods," Brady persisted. "What brought him to accept this base right in the middle of his home grounds?"

"Ah Tutul's an Indian," Dianne said quietly, "but he has great wisdom, and he's not unworldly. I've never confused his lack of what we call schooling for ignorance on his part. Francisco acts as his ambassador to the outside world, but Ah Tutul judges for himself. After Dr. Mendelov first met Ah Tutul, Francisco went with Mendelov to Princeton. It was then that Mendelov told Francisco about the discs and his plans. After all," Dianne said with a quick smile, "if the world is covered with radioactivity, Palenque also will be affected."

"I suppose," Taggert said, "Ah Tutul considers what we're trying to do as a holy mission. Not in the theological sense, of course. He—"

Taggert broke off as a warning horn echoed through the great chamber. Red lights flashed over the huge sliding doors.

"They're here," Taggert said briskly, motioning for them to move inside, away from the doors. Moments later the bright floodlights winked out and guide lights for the disc crew came on. The doors rumbled aside to reveal a starry night. Several hundred feet away, motionless, glowing in the night air, the disc waited for the doors to open fully. Brady heard a low hum as the disc pilot increased power and the machine glided forward to settle on its landing cradle.

Moments later Ann was in his arms.

"But what made you go to Blackburn and start screaming I'd been shanghaied? How did you know?"

Ann placed a finger gently against his lips. "Shh. You're not letting me tell you." She kissed him and pressed her body close

217

against his on the couch. She sighed and placed his hand by her cheek. "You feel so marvelous. . . ." She let her words trail off and held him tightly for several moments.

"Anyway," she sighed, picking up her story, "when I called and the motel told me you'd checked out, I just *knew* something was wrong."

"Woman's intuition?"

"I just had this awful feeling, Cliff." She shuddered. "I called the airlines in Flagstaff and they didn't have your name on any reservations, and I knew you wouldn't have taken the plane you rented somewhere else—"

"How'd you know that?"

"Silly. I know what they cost to rent. Remember, no more expense account?"

He kissed her on the nose. "Go on."

"I even called all the car-rental agencies in Flagstaff. Nothing," she said sternly. "Absolutely nothing. As far as I was concerned, you were either still in Flagstaff, or . . . or, well, or you'd been taken away against your will."

"That sounds pretty grim," he said. "Against my will, huh?"

"Cliff, stop it. I was frantic. I took the first flight to Flagstaff and went straight to the motel.

"I asked the motel desk when you'd checked out. They showed me the time on their ledger and I asked the man what you were wearing."

"What I was *wearing*? Why would you—"

"Cliff, shut up! I knew what I was doing," Ann continued. "The man, the one at the desk, thought about it for a few moments, and *then*," she said with a note of triumph, "he said he didn't know. I asked him if he meant he didn't remember, but he said, no, he couldn't possibly know because you hadn't checked out personally, that another man had checked out for you." She looked at him with her eyes bright. "So I *knew* you were in trouble," she exclaimed. "You didn't know anyone there, you went

218

to Flagstaff alone, and . . . well, that was it. I went straight to Blackburn and demanded to see Dr. Taggert. You know the rest."

Brady exhaled slowly. "What a woman."

"Cliff, when I—I mean—when you were gone . . ." She threw herself into his arms. "I was so afraid. I love you so much. . . ."

"Say that again." His voice was dry and husky.

She clung tightly to him. "I love you so much . . . and I was so worried. . . ."

He pressed her close to him. "Yeah. And so you put yourself into hot water right with me."

She sat straight, studying him. "I don't understand."

He told her of his conversations with Mendelov and the others. "And the long and short of it, honey, is that it's a one-way trip down here."

Her eyes widened. "You mean . . ."

"You don't think the friendly giant is going to turn us loose after what we know, do you?"

"Turn us loose?"

"Yeah. Or else . . ." He drew his finger across his throat.

"But why would he want to do that!"

He squeezed her hand. "At the risk of using an old cliché, Ann, we know too much."

"Know too much? But you're part of them now!" She shook her head. "I don't understand."

"Hey, hold on," he said harshly, "I never told you I'd signed up for the crusades. Where'd you get that idea?"

Ann was flustered. "Why, after what they told me at Blackburn about your being somewhere, at a secret base, I mean, and the *way* they said it, I assumed . . ."

"I haven't agreed to a thing."

"But Cliff! What they're doing is wonderful. A chance to prevent a nuclear war. How could you *not* want to help?" She stared at him in disbelief.

"Oh Christ," Brady groaned. "Not you, too."

"You mean you won't help?" she blazed.

"Sure, sure I would," he said soothingly. "If I believed in how they were going about it and if they really had a chance of making it stick. Now, hold on," he said quickly as he saw another outburst starting. "All you know is what you've been told so far and that spectacular little ride down here. You don't *know* anything else. Remember that. You don't *know*. So far it's all been their story, and no one else has come up with any arguments. I'd say that was good cause not to take everything they offer at face value."

He rose and stretched, smiling down at her. "But right now, sweetheart, no more. I want you in that bed."

"Oh, no, you don't," Ann said, rising to her feet and placing her hands on her hips. "Not so fast."

"Ann, it'll wait until tomorrow."

"Why can't we talk about it now?" she demanded.

"I *told* you," he said, vexed. "I don't want to talk. I want to make love to you! *Now* will you shut up and come to bed?"

CHAPTER XXI

MENDELOV AND ANN WERE STILL EXCHANGING SMALL TALK. BRADY chewed his lip, trying to force from his mind another period of subconscious terror. Last night, Ann in his arms, he had dreamed again. The same dream, everything the same. Ann told him he was thrashing wildly and screaming. He snapped out of it again soaked from head to foot in perspiration. He left her in bed, puzzled and alarmed, while he went into the next room to smoke in the dark and wrestle with himself. Later, in bed, he spent most of the night awake, afraid to drop off, afraid he'd return to the terrible white ash drifting silently from the sky.

Today Mendelov would get down to cases. The longer Brady thought about the organization and the people who were involved, the more he realized that both his and Ann's lives *were* at stake. Vadim Mendelov would not give a signal for execution with a wave of his hand, but there were other ways to ensure a person's silence. Drugs or a wire-thin needle in the brain would do it. Hell, they needn't kill anyone.

Ann took to Mendelov. What he and the others were attempting appealed tremendously to her. Brady looked at her with affection and smiled to himself. He wondered if she had ever marched in student demonstrations. The way she had snapped at him last night for not leaping into Mendelov's schemes had surprised him.

Mendelov and Ann finished their pleasantries and the scientist fixed his gaze on Brady. "Mr. Brady, I've told you that our organization neither wants nor feels capable of ruling the affairs of men. What we do want for all men is a guarantee of freedom from nuclear war. Everything we're doing is directed toward this one purpose. The world needs a reprieve from threatened self-destruction. A reprieve; time. Time for the social sense to mature, for mankind to mature, for nations to engage in competition without brandishing nuclear arms. We need—this is empirical, of course—not a single power to control all governments, but an enforced international conscience whose sole responsibility is race survival. *Survival* only. And we need your help to bring this about."

"You have said your outfit," Brady replied, "doesn't want to rule." The scientist nodded slowly. "You have also said," Brady went on, "that it is impossible to achieve peace because man is determined to fight no matter what."

Ann looked on with astonishment. She was even more bewildered when she discovered the scientist nodding agreement with what Brady was saying.

"You also made the point," Brady ticked off the items one by one on his fingers, "that man's most precious commodity is time. You keep bringing that up. You insist the world needs time for the social sciences to catch up with the physical sciences."

Brady wasn't certain of his conclusion, but he took a deep breath and plunged ahead. "What it all adds up to, I *think*, is that you and your crowd *have* figured out some way to influence governments with nuclear weapons. I don't know how, but you hope to make them give up their nuclear weapons. I don't see how you could accomplish this, but for the sake of argument . . ." Brady shrugged and glanced at Ann, who sat silent

222

through the exchange between the two men. "At the same time," Brady said, returning his attention to Mendelov, "you're restricting yourselves. Your intent is to influence or to force the action you want, but not to go any further."

"Precisely," Mendelov said quietly.

"Then are you going to enforce your demands? Because that's what it amounts to, isn't it? None of the world powers are going to listen to what you say but to what you can do." Brady scratched his chin. "You must have a lot of muscle I haven't seen yet," he mused aloud.

Mendelov nodded. "We do."

"And you're prepared to use it even if people get hurt?"

"In view of the alternative," Mendelov confirmed, "yes."

Brady glanced at Ann. He was glad she had heard that from Mendelov directly. She seemed to have the cock-eyed idea that Mendelov could accomplish what he wanted without bruising people.

"All right," Brady said, more confident than he had been for several days. "When do you take the wraps off your little toy?"

"Very soon," Mendelov countered. "But not yet."

"That still leaves *you*," Brady said slowly. "You are the last man in the world I would expect to get into something like this—a barefaced power play with nuclear hardware. I don't care what the stakes are; I haven't changed that opinion. So something more important than your entire lifework is involved. What is it? Why are you in the picture?"

Mendelov ignored the question and motioned for him to continue.

"So you're not trying to stop man from fighting, and you've said time is critical . . . in essence what you want to do is to keep everyone from killing themselves off." Brady was talking to himself, deep in thought. "That also means that as far as you're concerned, war is inevitable, but there's no real harm in letting people hack at one another. Man's ability to reproduce far outstrips any damage he can do to himself. *Just as long as nuclear weapons are out of the picture*. Is that it?"

"It is." Mendelov said only those two words and then fell silent.

Brady ran his fingers through his hair, searching for the answer that lay at the edge of his thoughts. "There's still more to it than that," he persisted. "You're looking beyond all this, because whatever *you* do is temporary. Sooner or later things would return to where they are now, everyone getting ready for the big bang. So you're looking for a change that will be effective after you're out of the picture." Brady looked up at Mendelov. "Something that will last for a long time."

Mendelov's features were frozen.

"You're waiting for someone to take over from you."

"Yes." The word was an intense whisper from the scientist. Mendelov's eyes seemed aflame. His huge hands gripped his chair, knuckles white from the pressure. "What we have found, Mr. Brady—I hope you can comprehend the significance of this discovery. What we have found is . . . the missing link!"

"The missing link," Brady repeated softly. "Man and the apes are supposed to have descended from a common ancestor. Science has been looking for the place where they branched . . . but they've never found . . ." Again his voice trailed off. He returned the unblinking gaze of Mendelov.

"They've been wrong all these years, haven't they." Brady made his words a statement.

Mendelov sat like a granite statue.

"We are the missing link," Brady breathed. *"The missing link is man himself."*

Mendelov's voice came from a great distance. "And man stands in the way of the next step in evolution."

"Homo superior?" Brady queried.

"Some use that term," Mendelov said. "I don't. I believe that we are the predecessors of the first *humane* beings that will be seen on this planet."

224

". . . so you can see," Mendelov was saying, "there's a purpose that transcends all our own lives. An intellectual compassion for the first time in history spurs us on."

"That's great," Brady said dryly. "But most of the human race doesn't agree with you."

"How could they!" Ann protested. "They don't even know what Dr. Mendelov's been telling us."

"They don't know directly," Mendelov interjected. "But there is some sensing of all this. Man isn't a sane creature. Conflict is as necessary to him as eating and sleeping and reproducing. It's nature's law; man must conquer all his adversaries, take over and prepare the planet for the next phase in evolution. That's why we'll never see peace in our time. Man hasn't any choice. He's condemned by instinct to fight. *Not* to fight goes against the very nature of man.

"We're certain that various members of the next race—*homo superior* was the term you used—have already made their appearance. Aristotle, da Vinci, Michelangelo, Newton, Lorentz, Galileo, Plato, Kepler, Steinmetz, Einstein; many, many others of which we know. Perhaps Christ was one; I like to think so. But there must have been many denied the opportunity to flourish. From here on, it's critical they have that opportunity. It's even more critical that those of us who realize the facts take every step to assure that we'll be—"

"Replaced?" Brady offered.

"It's not a very nice word, is it?" Mendelov replied, looking from Brady to Ann.

She shook her head. "No, it's not."

"However"—Mendelov sighed—"that's the crux of it. We believe the racial sense of man is somehow aware that the next step has already begun. Man—*men*—won't consciously permit this to happen. They'll crush anyone who shows the first sign of being superior. Indeed, they'd rather drag the entire world down in nuclear flames than yield willingly to a superior animal. Have you ever considered why sane men should drive inexorably toward the ultimate holocaust? They can't help themselves. They aren't aware that racial instinct spurs them on. They'd rather die in a howling pack than to step aside gracefully. They can't help what they do.

"For more than a hundred thousand years," Mendelov said, "there hasn't been any change in the size or shape or the capacity of the human brain. Man's up against a stone wall. I believe that man, as a race, is aware of this. Because he can't get any more out of his own brain, he desperately builds artificial replicas, the advanced cybernetics systems, to compensate for his own deficiencies. The beneficial effects are unfortunately limited because man himself teaches his computers and they simply reflect man's own fear and promise of self-extinction." Mendelov spread his huge hands palms down on the desk before him and lapsed into silence.

Minutes later, Brady shifted his position impatiently. "All right," he said briskly, "there are things we've got to do."

Mendelov chuckled. "Then I take it you've joined us, after all."

Brady's words died on his lips. Damn Mendelov! Brady couldn't even recall making a conscious decision, but he knew he was in. He looked at Ann, who beamed a smile back at him. Before Brady could collect his thoughts, Mendelov thrust again.

"You didn't enjoy your dream?"

"That's one way of putting it," Brady growled. "How'd you know about it? I didn't think Taggert was reporting to you whenever I . . ." The expression on Mendelov's face ended his words. Brady took a grip on himself. "Mendelov, you've got canary feathers all over you. If I didn't know better, I'd swear you expected me to have that damned nightmare." Even as he said it, he knew he had hit dead center.

"Of course," Mendelov agreed affably. "You see, your apartment was subjected to low-frequency signals of six to twelve cycles per second. Perhaps you're aware this affects the natural fre-

226

quency of the brain. It excites the alpha rhythm which, Mr. Brady, is your carrier of ideas, how you conceive mental pictures, and—"

"You mean you had me set up?" Brady was incredulous.

"No, you're wrong," the scientist corrected him. "The radiated signal assured us only that you'd dream. What's been on your mind these past days? Nuclear destruction. All we did was to prompt your subconscious fears and bring them to the surface of your dream mind. The dream, however, was yours entirely." Mendelov half smiled at the newsman. "I don't imagine it was pleasant."

"Damn you, you act awfully sure of yourself."

"I am," Mendelov admitted. "I rarely make a mistake in my choice of men."

CHAPTER XXII

Vadim Mendelov filled in the gaps in the history of the development of the discs for Ann and Brady.

"One evening in Princeton, twelve years ago now, Taggert spent several hours with me," Mendelov related. "During dinner with a group of my colleagues he'd listened to our discussions of nuclear war. We also spent some time confirming our conclusions that identified man as the missing link in the evolutionary chain. I knew," Mendelov said, nodding his great head slowly, "that something was tearing at Taggert. He was a classic example of conflicting inner emotions. Later, of course, I learned the details. If Taggert were to pursue the course that beckoned so strongly to him, he knew he'd be branded by his own country as a traitor —there's no other word for it from the nationalistic sense. We've all faced that decision. You two," he said to Ann and Brady, "have yet to realize the impact of what I'm saying. No," he said quickly, with a motion of his hand, "listen to me carefully. You haven't had time to reflect. You must understand that making the decision to serve the best interests of mankind can be diametrically opposed to the best interests of your country as they judge your actions."

"Had Taggert developed his new drive yet?" Brady queried. He was ignoring Mendelov's warnings about his conscience. Brady figured that was up to him and no one else. As for Ann, well, Brady already knew she had decided with Mendelov.

"Yes," said Mendelov.

"I couldn't help but notice Taggert was containing something ready to burst free. Finally he revealed to me he'd perfected the propulsion system we now refer to as the Taggert Drive. He received my word that our conversation would remain between the two of us. It was then he described the Drive and added that he'd kept its details secret.

"Taggert kept returning to our conversation of what was needed to prevent the war we were all so convinced was inevitable. What steps would I take? How could such an organization be formed and controlled? Would I prepare for him a list, known only to myself and him, of those individuals I felt were vital to such a concept? With all that Taggert told me of his Drive I was also aware he hadn't revealed anything to implicate him beyond a point where he could extricate himself from our relationship. He was testing me, of course, and I could well appreciate his caution. Taggert on his own part was already striving to bring his concept to working reality. I'm referring to the Drive. Theoretically it should work, but between the laboratory and actual flight there lies an abyss of unknown dimensions. Taggert had enlisted the aid of two men he trusted implicitly: Harry Boener, a brilliant aerodynamics engineer, and Wayne Priest, an electrical genius. Those two men applied Taggert's theory, and to the three of them we owe the discs. It was Priest who adapted the Drive as an energy beam. Not even Taggert had seen the implication of the weapon during his theoretical work.

"The next steps essentially were mechanical. I handpicked the first group, the cadre, if you will. They had requested me to direct the effort. Little by little we expanded the group. Each person brought within the fold was himself convinced, beyond all doubt, that the future promised only total ruin unless the nuclear conflict was avoided. Taggert had given us the miracle we sought and the rest lay in our hands.

"Such a venture, as I'm sure you both understand, presented critical problems in organization, management, security, financing, industry, communications, and even administrative control within our expanding numbers. Drew Wilkinson has been invaluable and without his genius at organization and financing I doubt we would ever have progressed as we did. He's worth at least two or three hundred millions, and he turned over to us his entire resources. Frazer Blackburn also is a multimillionaire, but far more important than his finances was the full spectrum of Blackburn Aero which responded to all our needs.

"I'm certain you've wondered how we managed to produce the discs right under the noses of the United States Government. Actually, it was less difficult than we anticipated, thanks to Frazer Blackburn. Once the design was completed, different Blackburn plants around the country produced various components. No one element produced in Michigan, for example, could be related to any other element without knowledge of the basic design. We used Blackburn's aircraft plants, steel mills, shipbuilding yards, forging plants, engine factories, power-generator plants —well, let's just say that Blackburn was able to bury completely within his own organization and his subcontractors the major elements of the discs. The components were delivered to the Colorado Plateau where assembly was carried out.

"Frazer Blackburn's own son was our chief test pilot," Mendelov continued. "The rest of the story is, I suppose, prosaic in its telling, but critical in its actual involvement. I understand Miss Sims has told you of the relationship with Dr. Francisco Valdivia? Good. You can imagine the roles played by Wilkinson, Blackburn, Kroot, Valdivia, and the others. Um, you've met Professor Walton from the University of Colorado? He's been with us from the outset. Yes"—Mendelov boomed with laughter—"I can see that you have."

"You mean he's part of this, too?" Brady asked.

"Of course," Mendelov confirmed. "He's a splendid actor."

"Son of a bitch," Brady muttered.

"He's been vital to us. As the scientific head of the Air Force's UFO research effort, he's created a very effective smokescreen. Confusion is his forte, and he's been helped a great deal by the people who see all sorts of things in the sky. The discs are camouflaged neatly within the many reports. Officially the discs don't exist, which makes it difficult for the Air Force to lend credence even to those sightings when there seems absolutely no question that an artificial craft is being observed. Of course, incidents like the Cape Kennedy affair have convinced a certain element within the government that the discs—"

Brady broke in. "That film we had of the Minuteman, the one that was stolen. Did . . . ?"

Mendelov nodded. "Yes, we arranged the theft. We felt the dangers of the film on television would outweigh the normal confusion we could associate with the story."

Ann reached over to rest her hand on Brady's arm. So many things were falling into place now.

"Let me mention a few more of our key people," Mendelov said. "Perhaps it will allow you better to appreciate the scope of this effort. Do you know the name Adrian Ramsey? I thought you would, since he was formerly the director of British Intelligence. Ramsey is our security chief. Thomas Carmody? Um, of course. Our inside man of policy at the United Nations. He has no confidence in the UN but his eyes and ears there are invaluable. Warren Young? A top administrator. He's one of my oldest friends and is in just the right position in the Pentagon to keep us in close touch with events there. Carl Renick. You may not know him, but he's about the best civil engineer in the business. He created this base and others like it. Well. Enough of that. Now to business.

"There's an urgency in our operations I can't exaggerate. We're about to reach the most critical juncture in our plans. . . ."

CHAPTER XXIII

Brady finished his coffee and lit a cigarette, getting his thoughts in order. He still had unanswered questions and the beginnings of a plan to carry through with Mendelov, but he didn't want to reveal his hand. Not yet.

"All right," he said to the scientist, "let's lay it out. You've got something like thirty discs, right? Each disc mounts an energy beam and can operate about one month—plus a week's emergency reserve. If you're using double crews, you can maintain a steady operation. That is, if you don't get knocked out of the air. And something else. If I remember correctly, the maximum effective range of the energy beam is about a thousand yards?"

Mendelov nodded.

"That means you haven't got any long-range capability."

Mendelov didn't react immediately. When he did, his words were guarded. "No," he said. "Nor are we in need of any weapons of long range. Our plans—"

"What *are* you going to do with the discs?" Brady broke in. "You can tear up airplanes on the ground or even missiles in their silos and you can chew up a lot of equipment and real estate. So what? Where does it get you?"

Brady watched Mendelov carefully. For the first time since he had been face to face with the scientist, he detected less than unwavering confidence. Brady was a damned good poker player, and he knew Mendelov held something less than a sure hand.

"Our strongest weapon is psychological," the scientist replied finally. "We intend to use the discs and the energy beam with full effect in selected areas. However, that's more for demonstrative purposes than anything else."

Mendelov linked his fingers and laid them across his expansive middle. Brady recognized the gesture and felt dismay. Goddamn it, he thought angrily, don't lecture. Get your feet wet. . . .

"Over the years we've created an aura of mystery with UFO's," Mendelov went on. "Officially, as you know so well, no one sanctions the concept that any UFO is an artificial device. We have staged, deliberately, many phenomena in the air to add to the confusion surrounding UFO's. Obviously we could never operate the discs without detection, so we managed the next-best thing. Let them be seen but with the assurance that officially their existence would be denied. Again, as you know better than anyone, we accomplished our purpose.

"Everyone has an opinion about UFO's. It doesn't matter if they believe or they ridicule; they have an opinion, and they've voiced their opinions to the point where most people react to UFO stories with weariness. Our campaign has given us extraordinary freedom of movement."

Brady gestured with impatience for Mendelov to get to the issue at hand.

"So"—the scientist pursed his lips—"our weapon is of a psychological nature. The psychology of demonstrating in the most exotic and dramatic fashion that the discs—which will suddenly appear and in great number—*are* real. But no one will know where they come from. No one will know if they originate on this planet or come from somewhere in space, perhaps from another galactic system. We can see to it that the issue remains clouded in doubt. The flight performance of the discs also will generate a great psychological impact, for they will *demonstrate* a performance which on the basis of even the most advanced scientific theory cannot be of terrestrial origin. This demonstration of overwhelming performance in an astronautical science far superior to anything known on earth, coupled with the energy beam . . . well, the impact will be far-reaching and attended with a real and growing doubt. A mixture of doubt and of fear."

Brady was not satisfied. "All right," he said. "Then what?"

Mendelov looked carefully at the newsman. He couldn't help but notice the furrows that reflected a conflict within Brady. Was it resentment?

Keeping a weather eye on Brady, Mendelov continued. "We plan a carefully timed sequence of appearances," he said. "Each designed for its overwhelming psychological effect. The discs will appear in different parts of the world, simultaneously. They will hover over major cities. Each disc is equipped to display flashing lights in a pattern that will indicate it is unquestionably intelligent. However, the codes will remain indecipherable. Random sequences, so to speak, but in patterns which the viewers cannot possibly *know* are random. The intent is deliberately to confuse, and to breed fear. When the authorities are unable to prove what the discs *are*, people will react in a predictable manner. They will endow the discs with an alien—extraterrestrial—origin. Some will of course reject such a belief. But most people won't. They'll believe with religious fervor that the discs come from somewhere out there"—Mendelov shook his head—"heaven-sent to warn the earth of its nuclear folly."

"Where do you go from there?" Brady's skepticism was plain.

"We have planned a method of communications with—"

"You're going to *communicate*?"

235

"Of course."

Brady couldn't believe it. He forced his words back and waited.

"As the discs make their second appearance around the world —everything coordinated to Greenwich mean time—they will broadcast a message. Again, the transmissions will be carried out simultaneously. This won't be evident immediately, that everything is taking place precisely at twenty-four hundred GMT, but it will be discovered soon enough to have its effect. Each disc will broadcast its message in two languages. One will be the language of the particular area or country involved. The second will be a computer language, again intended to create serious doubts by being indecipherable. We'll broadcast on at least two frequencies. One will be a main radio or television frequency and the other will be on a major communications band, such as airport towers or air-traffic control, which are always monitored and recorded. The Taggert Drive, incidentally, provides enough power to overcome any local transmitters.

"We, um, will not broadcast with human voice." Mendelov smiled briefly. "We'll feed a message directly into a computer, where the words will be rearranged in speech electronically so that a mechanical-electronic voice will be heard. The actual broadcast won't have any tones that can be identified with a human voice. Inflection, tone, timing, well, everything will be done to create the impression that this *could* be a nonhuman voice.

"Let me go back to that artificial language I mentioned. A brilliant linguist has been running a computer program for some time to create the alien language which we believe will have a pronounced psychological impact. Hentsch has worked it out to the point where the message will be decipherable only in part. This should enhance the desired impression in the governmental and scientific community that the discs may be, ah, extraterrestrial. I'm convinced the public reactions will generate widespread fright

236

of the power of the discs. We *want* this public consternation. We want as much controversy and tearing of hair as we can possibly generate."

"You've talked about the message," Brady interjected, "but you haven't said what it is."

"I should think that would be obvious," Mendelov chided.

"Nothing's obvious," Brady retorted.

Mendelov didn't reply for a moment. "The message will be a warning and a threat," Mendelov said. "The warning will be that the entire planet is endangered by the preparations for nuclear war. Unless the nuclear weapons are struck down, unless the missiles are removed from their silos and the submarines recalled from their positions beneath the sea, unless the planes are stripped of their nuclear bombs, unless all nuclear arms are banished—"

"You'll clobber everyone in sight. That's it, isn't it?"

"Not quite so crudely, but in essence, yes," Mendelov affirmed. "We've had under consideration some overwhelming demonstration of the power of the discs. First, no defense will be made against any attack against a disc. I'm convinced of the ability of the discs to outperform any weapon—"

"Including an antimissile missile like the Spartan? Have you ever seen that thing *move?*"

"Including the Spartan." Mendelov nodded. "Demonstrating the ability to evade any interceptor aircraft or missile without destroying the attacking weapon is more effective than direct action. The very act of disdaining to strike down the attacker has the greatest possible impact because it's our intention to demonstrate clearly that the discs are invulnerable to whatever weapons may be brought against them."

"That's a tall order," Brady said.

"The discs are quite capable of fulfilling it." Mendelov's voice was edged with arrogance. "We may use the energy beams to destroy selected military installations, again to make it absolutely clear that the discs represent a science far more advanced than anything known on earth. We would want such demonstrations before the largest possible audiences—either directly or through mass-communications media. In fact, it's in this very area that you fit in."

Brady raised his eyebrows but held back his comment.

"Immediately after the appearance simultaneously of the discs throughout the world, we intend several other demonstrations to establish beyond all question the vastly superior performance of the discs. Our pilots will seek out airliners everywhere to pace them in flight and then streak away with maximum speed. We'll do the same with the bombers of several nations. Since the discs are capable even in lower atmosphere of more than seven thousand miles per hour, their maneuvers will show just how helpless the most modern aircraft are in comparison. As a next step—"

Mendelov's voice stopped abruptly. Brady's features were contorted as he struggled to hold back his words. "Apparently there's something wrong, Mr. Brady?" Mendelov said, glancing from Brady to Ann and back to the newsman.

Brady jerked himself to his feet. "Wrong?" he shouted. "No, there's nothing *wrong*, as you put it. That'd be easy. That would even be simple. *Wrong?*" He stabbed a finger at the scientist.

"Jesus *Christ*," Brady cried. "That's the most asinine, juvenile . . ." he sputtered as he sought the words.

"Cliff!"

Brady spun around to Ann. "Shut up and stay out of this," he snapped. He turned back to Mendelov.

"Do you know what you'd be doing if you followed such a plan? You'd be playing right into their hands! You'd lose everything you've achieved so far!"

While Mendelov and Ann stared, Brady struggled to recover his composure. When he spoke again, his voice carried a reflection of his inner torment. "Do you realize what you're doing?" he cried. "You're going to *threaten* them! The men who control the most awesome power this planet has ever known! Threaten *them*? Christ, man, you can't frighten those people! They've lived in the shadow of the atomic cloud for so long, they have *accepted* its inevitability. They're the merchants of megadeath, every last damned one of them. The Russians and the Americans and the Chinese and the French and the British and whoever else is going to get the bomb. And you're going to shake them up? The hell you are!" Brady roared, shaking a fist at Mendelov. "You're going to make electronic speeches and buzz airliners and tear up a few installations and you think that's going to frighten them into standing down their weapons? Don't be childish!"

Brady's tortured breathing filled the room. He was so angry he failed to see tears running down Ann's face. Strangely, Mendelov remained silent. Brady paced furiously back and forth across the room, fists clenching and unclenching. He fought to control the rage that had erupted so unexpectedly. He spun on his heel to glare at Mendelov.

"The first goddamned moment you even *attempt* communication," Brady said, his voice cold, "you're dead. Finished. *Kaput*. The first time you try to communicate, to *deal* with these people, you and this whole damned outfit have bought the farm. You'll be playing right into their hands. I know, I know," he sneered, waving his hand to forestall an interruption from Mendelov, "you don't believe they can penetrate your disguises and your camouflage. Horse shit, they can't. They wouldn't even *care*. Don't you understand that? They wouldn't even care what or who you are or wherever the hell you're from. They're tough, determined men. They control the greatest power in history, a hell of a lot more than the fancy toys you've got here. Christ, this isn't a drop in the bucket compared to what they'll throw at you. You're offering them a *challenge*? The hell you are. You're coming down to their level, where they can get a good grip on you. Psychological impact, huh? In that kind of confrontation you'd blow it all in a few hours.

239

"The first time you condescend—and that's the only word for it—the first time you condescend to communicate with them, you get yourself in the position of a man trying to make a deal. You're showing them you're not nearly as strong as you look. They'll grab you and this whole outfit by the balls so fast you won't know what's hit you."

Mendelov could no longer remain silent. "Aren't you forgetting the tremendous influence of public opinion? The whole world will be aroused. There'll be great pressure brought to bear—"

"For Christ's sake, Mendelov, will you come down from your ivory tower!" Brady shouted. *"You're turning public opinion away from you!* The only time the public becomes a force is when it becomes a mob. That's the *only* time. Public opinion, my ass!"

Brady slammed his fist on the desk. "So long as you communicate," he said, "you blow every advantage you have. You become *identified.* It doesn't matter if they *know* where you're from. If you let people have a good look at you, you're going to be identified as an enemy, a threat, a danger. You're giving the men who control power the most beautiful target they could ever want. Then you'll see public opinion, all right," Brady said bitterly. "They'll scream for your blood at any cost."

Suddenly Brady stood rock still. The change was startling as he spoke slowly and carefully. "You're dealing with a species that's psychotic. Those are your own words. A species that's compulsively bent on self-destruction, right?" He waited until Mendelov nodded confirmation.

Brady pushed the issue. "A race that's cast logic into the garbage can. Haven't you said as much?" Again Mendelov nodded.

"Then how do you expect us to behave like reasoning creatures?" Brady paused to let his words sink in. "You've told me again and again that logic and reasoning have been rejected by the human race, and then you set up your plan anticipating a reaction with the very logic and reasoning you know we don't have!"

Mendelov's voice came out flat. "You're ignoring the motivating factor. You're ignoring the introduction of a wholly new source of fear. You're—"

"Is what you're offering any more fearful than Hiroshima? Is it worse than the hundred-megaton bombs we already know about? What are you threatening us with that we haven't got worse a hundred times over?"

"The discs have the element, Brady, of the unknown. They're half-seen. The intense initial reaction is what we're after. The last several years of creating an atmosphere of unknown phenomena, of distrust—"

"Initial reaction, huh? What happens *after* that initial reaction? Don't you realize you'll be considered heaven-sent by the same people you're trying to manipulate?" Brady was pleading with Mendelov to grasp what he was saying. "You yourself told me the human race would rather drag the whole civilization down in flames than allow themselves to be replaced by whatever it is in the back of their skulls that's waiting to be born. Now you're offering them an honest-to-God physical enemy, a superior being from outer space. The men who run this show would go to hell in a basket before they'd bend to any such demands, no matter how much damage you do."

Brady leaned forward, with both hands on the desk. "Mendelov, you've got to understand you're presenting them with a common enemy. You're a blessing in disguise. You're giving them every reason in the world for joining as a single force to attack . . ." Brady spread his arms and took Mendelov's huge shoulders in his grasp. He shook him for emphasis. ". . . You. They'll go after you, us, all this," Brady said, sweeping his arm through the air, "with everything they've got.

"They'll know the discs are real enough. You're bending over

241

backward to make certain they understand they're real. They'll also *know* you're not extraterrestrial. Not that they care. Oh, for a while there'll be panic and a lot of running off at the mouth, but they'll know you're not from somewhere out there because the space-surveillance systems will never have given them the first suspicion that you came here to the earth. So they'll eliminate the possibilities one by one until they'll know that someone right here on earth has made the quantum jump in a new drive, and then, look out.

"*You're playing all your cards face up on the table.* You don't understand that they don't need to *know* all the answers. All they need is something on which they can act. The moment they suspect there's a major base or a couple of bases for the discs, do you know what they'll do? Think about it!"

Brady paused as he watched the changing expressions on Mendelov's face. "That's right," the newsman said, almost savagely. "They'll go after every suspected base. They'll let loose their biggest guns. What have they got to lose, Mendelov? You'll have given them every excuse there is for shooting the works. They'll use those super hydrogen bombs you've been talking about and they won't give a damn one way or the other if they wipe out half the world in the process.

"And you know something else?" Brady was shouting again. "*The whole goddamned world will agree with them!*" Brady laughed harshly. "The world will agree with them, cheer them on, because you'll have given them a danger greater than their own dictators, worse than their miseries, more frightening than all their fears. An Alien. Something *different. And* superior. That makes it the most hideous, dangerous, terrifying foe of which man can conceive. Every mother's son will be doing his best to tear the heart right out of your chest.

"You wouldn't stand a chance because they've got nothing to lose."

Silence fell heavily between them. For the first time in many minutes, Brady thought of Ann. She sat stiffly in her chair, staring at Brady as if she had never seen him before. Several times she started to speak, then shook her head and pressed her lips together. Brady agreed with her in silent sympathy. What the hell was there to say? The minutes went by and Brady poured coffee. It was barely warm, but he drained the cup without hesitation. He took his seat, trying to let the anger subside.

A sad smile appeared on Brady's face as he spoke again, this time his voice at its normal level. "You know, this sort of thing has happened before." He glanced at Ann and was pleased to see the surprise on her face. "You told me about it yourself," he said to Mendelov. "During World War Two, when our top scientists petitioned the President not to use atomic bombs against Japan. Remember? They wanted us to invite the top Japanese military leaders to a barren island in the Pacific, where we would demonstrate the power of the bomb. It looked great on paper. It was just chock-full of logic. But it wasn't realistic. The hard heads in government had a fit when the scientists made their proposal. Maybe the Japanese would have told us to shove it and refused to come. Maybe they would have shown up and the bomb might have fizzled. Or maybe they'd see it explode and be unimpressed by it because they'd be watching it explode from ten miles away. Whatever the reasons, we threw out the idea and we hit Hiroshima and Nagasaki with the works, and we saved a few million lives that would have been lost in the invasion set for a few months later. It was a tough decision, and it cost the lives of thousands of Japanese civilians, but it was the inevitable decision. My point is that the best scientific minds in the United States got together, just like you're doing with your associates, and they came up with something that looked beautiful but was harebrained in reality."

Brady cracked his knuckles and looked steadily at Mendelov. "Maybe that's one of the dangers of being on top. You lose perspective. I always try to think of what happened at Singapore before the Japanese clobbered the British and took the island with hardly a struggle. The whole north shore of Singapore didn't have a single gun or bulwark or even a log for protection, although there was plenty of time and manpower and the weapons for the job. You know why that happened? Because the men commanding Singapore used logic. They said that to expend all that energy in building fortifications to resist a land invasion would be bad for the morale of their troops. They were dead right, I suppose. But it was a lot worse for their morale when the Japanese chewed them to ribbons."

Brady rubbed his eyes; he seemed to be looking for a resting place for his hands. He fidgeted for a while and then grasped the armrests of his chair. "I've spent my life studying and writing about science and scientists. You awe me . . . all of you. But who could have figured two bicycle mechanics named Orville and Wilbur Wright would prove all the experts wrong? Five years after the Wrights were flying, the best brains in the world still said an airplane couldn't fly and that the whole concept was ridiculous. Scientists in 1940 said it would take five hundred years to develop an atomic bomb and the Germans even quit at the end of 1944 because the whole thing was impossible. I remember when the biggest brains in science said it was impossible to fly faster than the speed of sound. After that was out of the way, they said man would never survive in space. Now we've been around the moon, and walking on it isn't enough. We're talking about building moon bases and going to Mars."

Brady tried, wanted to reach out to Mendelov. "I suppose," he said with a heavy voice, "I forgot that you're sometimes fallible. Maybe I shouldn't be surprised. You may know man, Mendelov, but I know *men*. What you propose to do . . . You'll be setting off a nuclear avalanche and standing right smack underneath it."

Brady stared unseeing at the floor. He was aware that Ann had come to his side, was sitting on the armrest of his chair, that she had taken his hand in hers. Brady had nothing else to say for the moment. He wasn't aware of Mendelov speaking to him until the scientist repeated his name several times.

"Cliff? You have something else in mind," Mendelov said slowly.

Mendelov had never used his first name before. Brady noticed the change and yet he felt tired. He knew Mendelov had been shaken, but he no longer felt the energy to press the other man. Finally Brady looked up, nodding.

"Yes," he admitted. "I've something in mind. You told me before, when you were talking about your meeting at Princeton, that you realized that scientists would have to shed their moral and ethical principles. I thought you meant it. Perhaps you did.

"In any case, the only way you're going to prevail is to deal with the world on its own terms. I'm afraid that means you're going to have to hurt people and kill people and possibly kill a great many of them. Unless you're prepared to go that route, I advise you to quit right now."

"Why do we—why is it so necessary to kill people?"

"Because if you don't, you're not going to get through." Brady wanted desperately to use the right words.

"I've listened pretty carefully to you. What you've told me has sunk in. I think it will take an insane man—insane men—to save the world from itself. The cure is drastic. It's got to be drastic or it won't work. No sane man can deliberately slaughter innocent people. But if you want a world left for that next step in evolution, you've got to do a job that's nasty, vicious, and"—Brady faltered—"insane."

He locked eyes with the scientist. "Are you prepared to do that, Mendelov? You're going to have to give orders that will result in the deaths of men, women, and children. Don't answer me yet. A few hours ago I couldn't have faced this myself. But if everything you've been telling me is true, then hundreds of millions of people, maybe even most of the earth's billions, are going

245

to die in a nuclear war we both know is inevitable. If we *don't* do something, when we've got a chance to prevent that war, our very inaction is equivalent to permitting the holocaust to take place.

"Do you understand what I'm saying? You're going to have to sacrifice perhaps a few million people to save all the others. For once, the end is going to have to justify the means. And I don't like it any better than you do."

Mendelov's sigh was almost a soft cry of pain.

"Tell me what you propose."

The newsman shook his head. "Uh-uh. Not yet. First you've got to level with me. You haven't been doing that."

For a long moment, Mendelov paused. Then the words came. "No, I haven't."

"Unless you're prepared to be completely honest with me," Brady said, "I want out."

"What do you want to know?"

"I want to know why Stanley Hoffsommer is mixed up in all this. I think—I'm sure—I've known for a long time. But I want to hear it from you. If I'm right, then you've tried in every way possible not to use what Hoffsommer and Taggert have come up with."

Mendelov's face was contorted. The effort to answer, to unlock a doomsday's secret was a struggle.

"Yes," he said hoarsely, "you're right."

CHAPTER XXIV

It began exactly at four thirty on a Sunday morning . . .

The darkness shrouding the plains of eastern Montana vanished. Thirty feet beneath the surface of the rolling plains, beneath massive steel doors, the warhead of a Minuteman missile detonated.

The explosion was impossible. The warhead was on full safe. Acceleration triggers and other devices installed to prevent such a disaster were working perfectly. The warhead couldn't explode. It did. The warhead was designed to produce an energy yield equal to the explosion of a half million tons of TNT. Full efficiency was not achieved. Scientists later estimated the blast effect as only one tenth of design. But a blast equal to fifty thousand tons of high explosives is still an awesome event. The fireball punched up and outward in all directions. A seering gout of flame ripped nearly six hundred feet above the earth. It vaporized the missile silo as well as three other silos within reach of the fireball. The earth shock wrecked another dozen facilities for launching intercontinental ballistic missiles.

The nearest town, fifteen miles distant, suffered the blinding light, a deep rumbling thunder, and smashed windows as the shock waves tore across the ground. The earth shock collapsed more than two hundred buildings. Worst of all were the panic and the radioactive fallout. The explosion, nearly three times more powerful than the blast that destroyed Hiroshima in 1945, hurled out millions of tons of radioactive dirt and debris. Before evacuation could be started in the nearest communities downwind of the explosion, a massive fall of radioactive materials had settled onto the towns.

Outstanding emergency work by local, state, and military authorities helped evacuate communities farther downwind, and prevented heavy casualties. Considering the power of the explosion, casualties were surprisingly light. Authorities expressed gratitude that the missile silo was located in a comparatively isolated area.

Scientists were completely at a loss to explain the terrible blast. They repeated that theoretically the warhead explosion was impossible.

The news media, quick to point out that had the bomb exploded with full power the casualties would have been substantially higher, raised the question about other nuclear weapons exploding despite their being allegedly "foolproof."

Congressman James McIntyre (D. Montana) promised a full-scale investigation by the Congress, warning that atomic bombs that had been stored for long periods of time became "unsafe" and were liable to go off without warning.

The Pentagon denied that there was any further danger.

The second bomb exploded less than forty-eight hours later, at a secret military air base in southern France. On the flight line the French Air Force kept a strike force of six Mirage III bombers armed with nuclear weapons at combat readiness. Each Mirage carried a bomb with an energy yield of one hundred thousand tons.

Shortly after three o'clock in the morning, one bomb went off. There was no way to tell which bomb was faulty. The crater was 400 feet wide and nearly 250 feet deep. As in the Montana blast, the French weapon exploded with only partial power, estimated at 15 percent of design. The force of fifteen thousand tons of high explosives in a single detonation obliterated the French air base and destroyed a nearby town. Casualties in the area immediate to the air base exceeded thirty thousand dead and nearly a hundred thousand injured or suffering from radioactive poisoning. The light of the bomb was seen for hundreds of miles.

Fortunately the prevailing winds carried most of the radioactive cloud across the Mediterranean, but it was still "hot" by the time it started drifting across North Africa. Hundreds of thousands of Arabs swarmed the streets of their cities in violent, fear-ridden demonstrations against the French, sacking embassies and other offices.

Several representatives to the United Nations rose in the General Assembly to demand the dismantling of all nuclear weapons as unsafe and of terrible danger to people everywhere. Fail-safe systems had barely prevented the triggering of an attack on equivalent bases in the Soviet Union.

The French premier assured its allies and Moscow that there could be no reoccurrence of the accident.

". . . interrupt this program to bring you a special news bulletin. Britain's largest nuclear plant, producing electricity for the northwestern industrial region of England, exploded today in a mystery blast that completely wrecked the atomic installation. Witnesses said the blast was like a huge bomb going off. First reports indicate that the nuclear pile, which contains plutonium, exploded without warning. This was not an atomic explosion like that of a bomb. However, the force of the blast was equal to the explosion of several hundred tons of TNT. The power plant was completely destroyed. Radioactive debris was scattered by the blast throughout nearby communities. Nearly three hundred persons are dead or missing, and a mass evacuation of the area is under way. . . ."

". . . and latest reports indicate that the explosion of an atomic bomb on the edge of Moscow has the entire Soviet nation on edge, especially after the mystery blasts in the United States, France, and England. Russian officials have clamped tight censorship on all news leaving that country, but the presence of anti-missile bases with atomic warheads in the Moscow suburbs is well known. The blast wiped out an area estimated at one square mile and caused heavy damage for another mile in all directions. Casualties are reported to be heavy, as a giant new apartment complex was caught within the blast. Foreign observers estimate anywhere from twenty to fifty thousand people killed. Soviet authorities have clamped martial law on Moscow as panic swept the Russian capital in the path of a radioactive cloud drifting across the heart of the city.

"Scientists believe the explosion to be another failure of an atomic bomb similar to the mysterious explosions in Montana and southern France. The warhead exploded with only a fraction of its full power, but due to the heavy concentration of population the casualties have been high.

"The United Nations is in an uproar with demands that . . ."

"A giant explosion seen for hundreds of miles, confirmed by Japanese scientists to be nuclear in origin, devastated a Chinese city in . . ."

". . . confirmed that the fission warhead of a hydrogen bomb in a B-52 bomber stationed on Okinawa exploded shortly after midnight, only two weeks after the first accidental blast of a missile warhead in Montana. Scientists say only a miracle kept the atomic trigger from setting off the hydrogen bomb aboard the B-52. It is well known that the hydrogen bombs carried by B-52 bombers are equal in power to thirty-two million tons of TNT, a blast that would have destroyed part of the island of Okinawa. However, only the atomic warhead exploded, with a force estimated as equal to the old bombs used against Hiroshima and Nagasaki in the Second World War. The military air base and an adjoining community of twelve thousand people have been completely destroyed. The radioactive cloud has been drifting to the north and it is feared it will brush the southernmost island of Japan. Hysterical demonstrations and widespread panic are sweeping the major Japanese cities. At an emergency session of the United Nations today . . ."

"Two more missile atomic warheads exploded in their silos in the western part of the United States. The radioactive fallout is headed toward . . ."

"There have been at least five known nuclear explosions within the Soviet Union. Reports indicate . . ."

"Wild demonstrations and panic continue to rock Spain. All American strategic bombers have left that country after threats of direct attack on bases used by the United States . . ."

". . . unconfirmed reports that two nuclear-powered submarines carrying Polaris missiles with atomic warheads have been lost in mystery blasts at sea."

". . . atomic energy plant built only two years ago in the Union of South Africa exploded, killing hundreds of people. Local authorities report they are helpless to control the crowds demonstrating in the streets. All atomic energy plants are being shut down immediately. It's reported that . . ."

" . . . top Japanese scientist said that an unexplained increase in cosmic radiation, which is sweeping the earth with high-energy neutrons, is the cause of the mysterious explosions of atomic bombs as well as at nuclear reactors for commercial power plants. To date, nuclear reactors have exploded in the United States, England, Russia, India, South Africa, Brazil, Sweden, and Australia. Reports indicate that all remaining nuclear plants throughout the world have been closed down. Many of these were, in fact, destroyed by wild mobs who broke into the installations with . . ."

" . . . and NASA reports that none of its satellites in orbit about the earth have shown any indications of unusual activity from the sun. A new radiation-detection satellite is being rushed for immediate launching from . . ."

"Atomic bombs exploded in England and France during the last weekend. There were reports of strange glowing shapes in the sky immediately before the explosions. Authorities have identified these as plasmoids, collections of energy caused by the unusual outflow of radiation from the sun reacting in the earth's atmosphere, as was recently described by Dr. Tadashi Hashimoto of Tokyo University . . ."

"The Atomic Energy Commission denies emphatically the report from Japan that increased cosmic radiation is responsible for the nuclear explosions that have been encountered in recent weeks. There still is no valid explanation for these accidents. At the same time, as a safeguard, all research reactors in the country have been shut down. The industrial facilities producing nuclear weapons are temporarily closed and are manned only by caretaker staffs. The AEC wishes to reassure the American public, and all the peoples of the free world, that the situation is under control, and that . . ."

"You don't trust them mothers, do you? Do you? Lissen t'me, all you people! Lissen to what I say to you! Them's white man's bombs! Them ain't been no accidental explosions! Accidental nutthin! You know what's gonna happen next? Do you know? Next time there's gonna be another accident and one of them white man's bombs is gonna land right in the middle of where we all live! You hear what I'm saying? Are we just gonna lay back and wait to be wiped out like dogs? Are we dogs or are we black people? I say we don't wait no more! I say we tear down this fence and we burn them goddamned airplanes what's carrying them bombs! I say burn them! You ready? You ready? You got your guns and dynamite and Molotov cocktails? Let's go! Go, go, go!"

". . . unconfirmed but reliable reports that two more atomic bombs have exploded somewhere within the Soviet Union."

". . . don't care *what* your goddamned scientists tell you! General, I'm telling you my men have been seeing these discs, or saucers, or whatever they are. They've been *seeing* them. There's something way out of line—"

"Colonel, shut *up*. Jesus, all we need now is a damned UFO flap on our hands! Do you realize that mobs have been storming SAC bases throughout the country? That bands of people are roaming through the hills trying to pour gasoline down missile silos and set them afire? And you come in here with harebrained stories about flying saucers. . . !"

". . . another nuclear explosion, this time from Alaska. Reports indicate the United States and the Soviet governments are near accord on an agreement to dismantle all nuclear weapons, and that the other atomic powers will follow suit. Following Red China's refusal to join in any international agreement, mobs sacked the government buildings in Peking and the country

253

stands on the edge of revolt. The Russians have moved up armored divisions along the Chinese border. The United States is reported to have assured Moscow that if it becomes necessary to . . ."

". . . riots sweeping the major cities of almost every nation in the world. Martial law has been imposed throughout the Soviet Union, and in this country the National Guard and Army Reserves have taken up positions surrounding military airfields, missile launching sites, and nuclear submarine bases. Violent clashes are being reported as an aroused and frightened citizenry tries to remove nuclear weapons from . . ."

". . . so far the world has seen more than ninety atomic explosions in less than four weeks. Radioactive fallout is spreading rapidly and scientists estimate many millions are being affected. No one knows when the next bomb will explode or . . ."

"But we've got to put the blame on *somebody!* For years all our nuclear weapons have been absolutely safe. Then, suddenly, just like *that*, they start blowing up all around us. Not only us but everyone else. Maybe it *is* those damned flying saucers!"

"Are you out of your mind? You heard that scientist, that Professor Walton, from the University of Colorado. He's been studying UFO's for more than twenty years, and for all that time this country has insisted, absolutely and emphatically, that there isn't a damn thing about UFO's that's real. Now, all of a sudden, you're going to blame flying saucers for those bomb explosions! I tell you you've lost your marbles!"

"All right, all *right!* So we can't say anything to the public. But what if those discs *are real?* There's been enough of them seen the last—"

"Discs? You mean glowing shapes, don't you? *Glowing*. They're plasmas and corona discharges."

"Maybe they are and then again maybe they ain't. What do we do if they *are* real? Goddamn it, we've got to do *something*."

"Okay. I'll buy your argument, but only behind closed doors. Not one lousy word gets out about this. I want full security right on down the line. Send out these orders. All fighters with guns and missiles hot. Anytime anything shows up in the sky, no matter what, I want it identified. Immediately. If we can't identify it, shoot it down. And tell the pilots if they can't shoot it down they're to ram . . ."

CHAPTER XXV

THE CITY HAD BEEN THRUST UP FROM HELL. ALL ELECTRICAL
power was out. Yet light heaved and tumbled everywhere, the
deep orange and flickering crimson of flame diffusing the boiling clouds of dust and smoke, tossed every which way by a
gusty and capricious wind. Cliff Brady and Ann Dallas pushed
forward, handkerchiefs pressed against their faces, staring wide-
eyed at the maelstrom about them. The bomb had exploded on
the outskirts of Lincoln, Nebraska, nearly twenty hours before.
It hadn't been one of the larger weapons. This time the warhead
of an antimissile rocket had detonated. The fireball ripped
through the earth, racked the ground with a hammering earth-
quake shock, and then sent the shock wave punching along one
edge of the city, pulverizing buildings and other structures as it
heaved through the stunned metropolis. In its wake of broken
gas mains and shorted electrical systems and overturned stoves,
fire crawled into being. No single huge blaze, but tens of thousands of small fires. Unchecked for lack of water, the flames fed
eagerly on the twisted and tossed debris of the shock wave until
fully one third of the city lay awash in a sea of growing flame.

Strangely enough, the city enjoyed a measure of fortune. The prevailing winds that night blew away from the main section of town, away from the more heavily populated areas. The winds snatched at the angry cloud mushrooming from the earth, massive and pregnant with intensively radioactive debris; snatched and pushed and bulled the cloud away from the fearful people, sending the greater part of the lethal fallout into the open countryside. Fifty thousand human beings owed their lives to that incident of wind that night.

None of them, in the hours following the ripping explosion, were aware of their "good fortune." None of them understood that a powerful warhead had exploded with only a small fraction of its power. Measurements are relative. The force of ten thousand tons of high explosives is on the low end of the nuclear-blast scale. But it is on the higher end of hell for those within the embrace of the savage shock wave.

Brady and Ann were in Omaha when the bomb explosion knifed along the edge of Lincoln. Minutes later, they knew there had been a terrible blast in the Nebraska capital. They were in the best place to receive such news—just outside Omaha, at headquarters of the Strategic Air Command. For several weeks Brady, Ann always with him, had been traveling at a nonstop pace throughout the country. Milt Parrish at World Press still didn't fathom the telephone call from Drew Wilkinson to return Brady to the WP staff. He didn't care. Parrish was still bent out of shape from his last encounter with Brady, and he took pleasure in welcoming Cliff back to the fold. When the bombs started exploding in the United States and around the world, Cliff was worth his weight in any ten men. The stories he filed during his rapid trips to the explosion sites were the best in the business. With Ann at his side, Brady covered the nation from coast to coast, seeking not only the effects of the weapons tearing up cities and countryside, but especially the reactions of people. He wanted the public pulse beat and he sought out the official reactions. Not their statements. To hell with the words. He wanted the taste and the shock and the smell of it; he wanted to be right in the middle of it. He got what he sought: the dust and the stink of fear and the aftermath.

But never this close. Brady didn't waste a moment. He and the other newsmen got the word from a tight-lipped SAC officer. His words were cryptic, as impersonal as he could make them. Brady listened to the words and concentrated on the man's eyes, on his facial expression. He found what he wanted. The un-spoken questions of the man. The thought, betrayed in his eyes. Where would the next bomb go off? Who was next? What city might die tomorrow? Brady observed and made his notes and then he was asking hard questions about the latest metropolitan victim. He learned that the winds were pushing the radioactive cloud to the northwest of Lincoln. They could take a helicopter to the east of the stricken city, they could approach from either the east or the southeast and they'd be upwind of the lethal, fall-ing cloud. The closer their approach to the city—delayed nearly fourteen hours by martial law clamped on the area, until they received permission to move into a city from which thousands were fleeing in panic—the greater reality came home to them. They saw the orange glow from miles away. With each decreas-ing mile the flames reached higher until visual definition emerged from the glow. Finally they were so close the super-heated air smacked and chopped angrily at the helicopter and the pilot refused to go any closer. He brought the machine to ground as near as he dared. Brady and Ann continued on foot, their official passes taking them through the police barricades, the frightened and angry officials who thought they were crazy for wanting to move into hell.

They pushed their way forward no more than a mile, their path blocked by wreckage-strewn streets, abandoned automo-biles, people with eyes wide and shocked. Every so often they encountered disaster forces at work, fire engines for the most part helpless, the water mains severed by the rolling earth shock of

258

many hours before. Yet the municipal services, the police and firemen and the public-works crews, were doing their best. Which meant to save as many lives as possible, to render any vehicle as a makeshift ambulance or an evacuation vehicle. Anything to get the people away from the fires roaring out of control, spreading steadily, feeding easily on the masses of wreckage that lay everywhere.

A street sign hung awkwardly, the metal plate reading "Jackson Avenue" hanging askew. All about them smoke and dust whirled and surged like a sandstorm from a Daliesque painting of hell. Flame crackled explosively as it chewed through wreckage. Buildings collapsed in fiery cascades. Ann's ears hurt from the constant pounding of fire-noise, from sirens screaming helplessly, from shouts and cries. People emerged as ghostly wraiths from the smoke shifting before the wind. At times the clouds were so thick flame would spear a deep shaft through which blazing houses and automobiles could be seen like volcanic pits.

Ann stumbled, gasping for air, and Brady clutched her arm, kept her from falling. "Cliff . . . I—I can't take . . ." more coughing . . . "this can't . . ." Her voice trailed off in a new spasm. Brady knew they had to get out. They weren't doing anyone any good, and now their own lives were endangered. He supported Ann and they turned to retrace their steps. For a moment fear swept through him as the billowing smoke obscured the street. Then he saw the searchlights, one after the other, a serried row pointing straight up, showing the evacuees the route to safety. One street, cleared by frantic workers to provide an avenue of retreat, with every light they could commandeer from the fire engines and the police vehicles, vertically beckoning fingers. The heat-laden smoke burned Cliff's eyes and fouled his lungs and he thought they might have come too far. Sparks and firebrands whirled through the air, great glowing eyes mocking him, streaking the flame-splashed darkness.

The thought wouldn't leave him. This was their answer, their solution to the fear for tomorrow. *This?* He stared gaunt-eyed around him, helping Ann, who fought off another spasm of coughing, stumbling together, leaving the fires. *This was their solution? This was the answer? This hell they had visited on people . . . Good God!* He told himself again and again that this *had* to be the right way, that what they endured about them would be a million times worse if ever the world plunged into full-scale war. He repeated the words to himself, over and over and over. They failed to dent the rising horror, the sick helplessness that refused to leave him. For he, Cliff Brady, he and the others, Mendelov and all the rest, were responsible for this hell. Couldn't there have been another way? Wasn't there some manner to avoid suicide without *this?* They wound their way through wreckage, past bodies strewn in the streets, the broken glass crunching beneath their feet. A firebrand spun out of the air and in seconds a tiny spark of flame showed in Ann's hair. Brady cried out and thrust his hands against that tiny fire and his heart hammered within his chest.

"Come on!" he shouted. "Faster! We may be cut off!" He had to shout to be heard, and he moved more quickly now, half dragging Ann with him. Ahead of them a light jabbed through the boiling smoke, a mindless Cyclops that showed the path to safety. Then there were people all about them. They looked up and saw firemen, grimy, tired, listening to the firetruck radio bellowing instructions.

"Fall back . . . fall back . . . all units . . . fall back immediately to Foster Boulevard . . . regroup . . . acknowledge and . . ."

"They're all getting out," he said to Ann, unnecessarily, wanting to hear his voice, wanting to talk with her. She nodded, swallowing the pain. Brady turned down the street, along the fire-limned avenue, people moving like cloaked figures all about them in the new-flowing tide of complete evacuation. The wind had found new strength and the heat rolled over them in successive waves. Brady took off his jacket and placed it over Ann, using it as a hood to protect her against heat and swirling sparks. They had gone only two blocks when a man rushed into their midst. "The children! For God's sake, help me! Someone help me!" he cried. They stared at him until he pointed to what remained of a house, through which flames crackled like tributaries seeking a common flow. "My children!" he shouted hoarsely. "Trapped! I've got to get them . . ." Brady and several other men ran to the wreckage, coming up short as fire leaped upward. No one could be alive in there! Then two others were pulling at wooden beams, heaving wreckage, digging with cut and bleeding hands. Brady joined them, working frantically. He heard words of a collapsed floor, children in the basement. He thought he could hear a thin scream of fear, a keening sound through the fire. The flames crackled explosively, throwing them back. Brady lost sense of time. He thought he saw a dress, a print, beneath tumbled wreckage and he hurled himself at the debris, unknowingly cutting his hands. His world resolved into saving a life, into the redemption he might find here and now. Arms pulled at him, tried to drag him away. "No use!" cried a voice. "It's no use! We're too late, too late. . . ." Brady jerked himself free, shouting incoherently, wincing from the heat and the pain stabbing through his arms. He remembered only the sight of a small body, and somehow he was there, shouldering aside the wreckage, and he had the frail, unmoving form in his arms, stumbling, lurching back to the street, Ann guiding him, walking as quickly as he could, cradling the small girl, trying to protect her. He walked forever, his sense of time numbed, his awareness blunted. He knew only that he had saved the child, saved her, saved her. . . .

"Oh, my God."
She whispered the words.
Someone, a white coat, helping arms took the child from Brady. Ann watched, disbelieving, as the doctor shook his head slowly.

"Oh, my God."

The little girl was dead.

The last thin line cracked.

Brady wept.

Ann cradled his head in her arms as it spilled from Brady, racking him, deep shuddering sobs. She held him to her breast and he cried.

There was nothing else she could do.

"Physically he'll be all right," the doctor said. "But he's not trying. I mean, his body is responding and he's strong. There's no concern there." He looked up and met Ann's gaze. "But there's something else. . . ." He shrugged; they both knew the rest.

Ann nodded.

"What?"

Ann looked up with a thin, humorless smile. "Nothing, Doctor. Is there anything else I can do?"

"No, no. Just be sure he has his medicine at the times I've prescribed. Here's my number. Call me if you need me."

"You're very kind."

"I can afford to be," he said with a faint tone of mocking himself. "His office said . . . well : . ." He shrugged again. "Anything he needs, they said."

Except, she thought, what he needs the most.

She was right. Their intimate exposure to the hell racking so many of the nation's cities had been the start of it. Repetition, horror piled upon horror, the knowledge that hundreds of thousands of human beings, helpless and innocent, had been killed, millions more injured grievously . . . all this, the inescapable, driving fact that he was one of the men responsible for the agony and the terror and the deaths, shattered the certainty of his convictions. It was not a thing of suddenness. Each successive exposure to what they had wrought chiseled deeper into the granite of his confidence, his beliefs that this was the only way. Until, finally, the granite showed the first cracks, the pieces fell willy-nilly about him, and Brady began to accept the torment of the victims as his own. As self-punishment.

The dead girl broke him. Even that, Ann knew, would have been but a passing agony. But not the hypocrisy of what happened several days later.

Another newsman had seen Brady emerge from the flame-illumined street, seen Brady stumbling, weary and cut and burned himself, carrying the little girl. It was a personal facet of a story of mass horror, and the newsman seized upon the opportunity. It made the wire services. It made Brady one of the heroes.

Cliff Brady wanted personally to kill the man who had written the story. Ann watched him, speechless with rage, as he read of his "heroic rescue" of the child. Nothing was said in the story about the girl's being dead.

It was the last straw.

"That was the moment," she later told Vadim Mendelov, "when Cliff learned to hate himself."

For more than a month, always together, so that she knew the fiber of the emotions tormenting him, they had been witness to and part of violence, naked fear, vast suffering. And death. For weeks she and Cliff poured out to one another their feelings. They both knew they sought in and through their words the self-justification that this was the only way. Survival of the race depended upon what they might do, on the measure of success they might all achieve.

They moved through a planet different than what they had always known. A world made up of many nations, but which they now saw as a single entity, struggling through agony. The world endured the terror of bombs exploding without warning, of death always present or threatening. Only they knew why this was happening, why it was needed. But they could tell only themselves and in the logic of words between them they sought to pacify their consciences.

"It's like the pain of birth." Ann voiced her thoughts to Cliff Brady. "That's what it is to me. Pain that's necessary, that's birth, or"—she looked up, hoping he could share her thoughts more than the words for which she groped—"or rebirth. I don't know," she whispered. "I keep telling myself over and over that this is the only way." She shuddered. "But then I remember and . . ." Her words trailed away.

Yet, if not directly, then in ways similar or parallel, people everywhere, without knowing what Ann knew, shared her thoughts. They were letting it soak through their consciousness. The exploding bombs were giving the world a grim foretaste of what the threatened nuclear cataclysm would be like intensified thousands of times. Men who could think clearly, no matter where they might live on the globe, struggled to imagine the effects of thermonuclear bombs going off at full power.

Hiroshima was twenty kilotons.

Some bombs were detonating at a hundred kilotons.

The bombs waiting in the wings for World War III were set to explode with energy yields in the hundreds of millions of tons of high explosives.

It didn't take a scientist to realize that the few craters several hundred feet wide could just as easily be fifteen miles from one radioactive edge to the other. Mendelov's hopes were coming to pass. The European peoples, most of them packed even more closely together than the city populations of the United States, had rallied to the cause. Not of world peace, that nebulous goal always beyond men, but of self-preservation. There was a demand for the immediate destruction of nuclear-weapons stockpiles and emplacements that toppled governments and swept outward in the form of an irresistible tide. In the United States they were slower to react but no less severe in that reaction when finally it ripped free of its restraints.

264

The toll of cities grew. Lincoln, Miami, St. Louis, Pittsburgh, Los Angeles, Seattle, Oklahoma City, Dayton, Buffalo, Charlotte, Fort Worth . . . to say nothing of the bombs that went off in open countryside, in missile silos, aboard submarines, at air bases scattered throughout the nation. San Diego felt a bomb gut its innards and then, in the aftermath of a night without wind, the scattered flames fed greedily on the debris of the city and joined into a dreaded firestorm. It was the aftermath of Hamburg and Hiroshima all over again. A single fire monster nearly three miles high that howled with the throats of a million demons. The fire was visible for over a hundred miles. It burned beyond all control through the night. By ash-choked dawn more than 110,000 human beings had been consumed.

The public wanted, demanded, screamed for only one response: Dismantle every nuclear device and installation. Not next week. Not tomorrow. *Now*. Don't waste a moment, a second. Brady and Ann had seen the mobs, mixed with them, had been carried along in the smell of fear and the howls for the blood of those charged with guarding the now-dreaded nuclear machinery. The mobs stormed military installations and defending soldiers refused to fire on the throngs that often included their own families and friends. Brady and Ann watched the mobs blowing up and burning airplanes and pouring flaming oil and gasoline into and over and around anything involved with nuclear weapons.

The fear of stripping the nation of nuclear defenses had been banished. The danger of leaving the United States open to nuclear assault from her possible enemies was a tenet no longer to be endured. The bombs were exploding everywhere. No one lay in danger from anyone else. They were *all* endangered.

By the bombs right in their own backyards.

The world was stripping itself of its means to commit nuclear suicide.

But all Cliff Brady could see was a dead child in his arms.

265

The summons to meet with the others in Arizona came as a blessing. With Ann by his side, Brady stared through a wide picture window at the tall pines stretching across the hills and mountain slopes. His face reflected none of the serenity of the Flagstaff countryside. Brady's eyes had become sunken, his face gaunt and etched with his inner suffering. He and Ann had arrived early and waited for Vadim Mendelov and the others.

Brady knew nothing of someone else with them until he felt the hand on his shoulder. He turned to face Dr. Stanley Hoffsommer. For a long moment the two men gripped hands, stared unblinkingly at one another. Hoffsommer's face was the same, his eyes untroubled. The scientist saw within Brady what he had known himself a long time before. But he had forced from active memory the camps in Europe, and he refused now, as he had all these years, to heed the call of the suffering he had himself known behind the high barbed wire. . . .

The last time Brady and Ann had seen the weapons scientist was in Condor, deep within the caverns of the South American mountain. Brady had been told they would all be here for this meeting. No; not all. Robert Kroot was dead, victim not of a bomb explosion but of wild panic that had exploded through his neighborhood.

Sometimes you paid the price close at home.

They gathered in the conference room, uncomfortable at first with one another, troubled by what they had all seen, what they knew, what had stemmed from the power they wielded. Dr. Mendelov ill concealed his shock at Brady's appearance. The newsman, whom Mendelov had known as a volatile, energetic individual, seemed withdrawn, embittered. At the first opportunity he drew Ann aside. She told him what had happened.

The huge man nodded slowly. "I understand," he said heavily. "I wish I could say something, but . . ." She took his hand in answer. He squeezed hers in return and left to take his seat. She wondered if Cliff noticed what had happened to Mendelov, if he realized how loosely the man's clothes hung on his big frame, how much weight he had lost.

Brady sat in silence. Frazer Blackburn opened the meeting with a question thrown to the group.

"It's been more than a month," he said slowly. "Has anything happened? I mean, do any fingers point to us?"

Dr. Hoffsommer shook his head slowly, a pleased smile on his face. His sigh was audible throughout the room. "No," he said at last. "We're still entirely in the clear. They're mystified, of course," he added with a chuckle, "but immediate events have trampled under the authorities. They haven't time to do anything but attend to the task at hand. Dismantle the bombs. That is the outcry everywhere. People are demanding protection from the explosions. It is like living under an overhanging rock. No one knows when the avalanche will start and everyone is afraid to move." Hoffsommer paused to light his pipe. In the midst of a world torn and frightened, he was a stark contrast of calm and assurance. No one spoke, no one wanted to interrupt. He took his time, bringing the pipe to life slowly.

"The important thing," he continued, "is that no one relates the explosions to the discs. Not directly, that is. Oh, some people are suspicious, of course," he said, gesturing with the pipe. "There's a group within the Air Force, in this country, I mean, that's convinced the discs must be involved. Other people, in Europe, feel the same way. But their policy isn't official. They haven't any idea of how the relationship would exist. They have even less of an idea of where the discs might come from. And since, despite their vociferous convictions, they lack proof . . ." Hoffsommer shrugged.

"Something else has happened in our favor."

Heads turned to Vadim Mendelov. The huge man was evidently pleased, but nothing could bring him to smile. His plans were successful beyond his wildest dreams. But the deaths of millions, with millions more maimed and suffering the effects of injuries and the long-term effects yet to come from radioactive exposure had suppressed within Mendelov any jubilation. He glanced at Brady, who met his gaze with almost a vacant stare. Troubled by the newsman's detachment, Vadim Mendelov forced himself to the issue at hand. "The fact that the discs were sighted by so many people," he went on, "has brought about something we apparently failed to anticipate. Brady"— he nodded to the newsman—"has seen the effects. Many people believe the sightings represent some form of divine intervention in the affairs of man. Remarkable," the scientist mused aloud. He turned his gaze to Brady. For a moment he frowned, questioning the wisdom of trying to evoke a response. "Your suggestion," he said after the pause, "certainly bore its fruit."

For a long moment Brady's eyes kept their vacancy. Finally he nodded his acknowledgment. One of the ideas he had proposed was deliberately to increase the leakage of energy from the discs. It resulted in a powerful ionization effect that caused the discs to glow brightly. People no longer saw a clearly defined artificial object, a mechanical device. They saw what they had often observed when plasmoids or corona discharges were present. A glowing shape in the sky. Scientists were convinced they *were* plasma or some other electrical effect in the atmosphere.

Mendelov picked up the conversation after waiting for Brady to speak. "It's all worked out as we hoped," the scientist continued. "They know nothing of the true nature of the discs and they're completely unaware, of course, of the Taggert Drive. Neither do they know anything of the energy beam and even less—that's a paradox, isn't it? Forgive me," he said with the same humorless smile. "Well, obviously, then, they know nothing of the modification made to the energy beam."

They accepted his words without comment. The pain endured by Mendelov, one of the most gentle of men, they knew, showed clearly. He held himself more responsible than any one for the terrible casualties. Brady, wrapped in his own bitterness, had forced the issue, had demanded that Mendelov face squarely what Dr. Hoffsommer and Taggert had developed—which Mendelov had refused to countenance for use.

They made a further modification to the Taggert Drive. Instead of a destructive beam, the Drive was altered to project a loose stream of nuclear particles. Included within that invisible energy stream was a high proportion of neutrons. That would have meant little to them except for Hoffsommer's intimate knowledge of nuclear weapons.

"The nuclear devices," Hoffsommer had related to them, "operate ·on the implosion principle. Essentially, each bomb's energy source, its plutonium, is kept porous. The bombs contain different ingredients, such as gold cones, to soak up stray neutrons and prevent an accidental explosion. To set off the bomb you must implode, squeeze together, the plutonium, so that it forms a dense mass." Hoffsommer sketched rapidly the mechanism of the bomb as he talked. "Now, if we can generate a flood of neutrons from an outside source—the modified Taggert Drive, operating as an energy stream, so to speak—we can create what you might call an accidental explosion." Hoffsommer tapped the sketches with his pencil. "See what happens here? The plutonium remains porous, but we introduce so many neutrons that the fission process begins. We will get a partial explosion. The bomb, in other words, goes off with only a fraction of its designed power. But," he added significantly, "it goes off."

The modified beam produced a stream of nuclear particles no more visible to the eye than X rays. But they penetrated the thick bomb casings just as easily as X rays flash through the human body. Their effect on the plutonium was disastrous. Partial fission took place.

A bomb with a designed energy yield of one million tons of TNT went off with only a small fraction of its potential.

Only a small fraction.

But a blast of one hundred thousand tons of high explosives was still five times more powerful than the bomb that wiped out six square miles of Hiroshima and killed one hundred thousand human beings.

This was the weapon from which Vadim Mendelov had recoiled. Brady argued it was the only course on which they might embark with any hope for success.

They could detonate nuclear weapons anywhere they were found.

The only destruction they would cause would be from existing weapons wherever they were located and set off.

The modified energy stream was effective over a range of several miles. Only they knew that a glowing shape in the sky, regarded by scientists as a natural phenomenon, a plasmoid, could bring on the "accidental" explosion of nuclear weapons.

The pattern was clear. Atomic bombs throughout the world exploded in mysterious, "impossible" blasts at fractional power. Even nuclear reactors could be made so "hot" from the flow of neutrons that they blew themselves apart.

From one end of the world to the other the bombs exploded. Completely "safe" reactors erupted in localized but violent blasts.

No one trusted the safety of the bombs or the reactors.

Next time the bombs might go off with full power.

One hydrogen bomb could explode with a force equal to eighty or a hundred million tons of high explosives.

There were air bases and storage depots throughout the United States, where anywhere from a dozen to one hundred hydrogen bombs were kept at readiness.

It was no secret that at certain bomb-storage sites the total energy contained within a few square miles was equal to *trillions* of tons of explosive force.

270

The bombs could explode. At any moment. Without warning. One such blast would wipe out virtually an entire state.

The danger of nuclear war was forgotten.

Dozens of cities throughout the world counted their dead, feared their fallout, gathered in sorrow. The specter of nuclear disaster, perhaps annihilation from existing stockpiles and weapons emplacements, was immediate.

Scientists warned that the radioactive fallout from the accidental explosions of bomb-storage centers could poison the planet.

Millions of people were already dead or living dead from the nuclear blasts and the subsequent fallout.

No one knew who would be next.

A city thirty or forty miles distant from an air base with a hundred hydrogen bombs was as good as dead.

Cities hundreds, even a thousand miles downwind of such an explosion, and all the countryside between, and for miles to each side of the death zone, would be blanketed with radioactivity so intense it would be lethal for months afterward.

No one knew who would be next.

The specter of nuclear death crawled into every home, every office, every bedroom. It hung, invisible but terribly real, over cities and open countryside. It was there in the shadowy fear of night and in the morning light it remained.

No one knew who would be next.

Throughout the world people reacted as they could only react. Impelled by fear, compelled by survival, they rioted. They stormed through their cities, attacked military installations, searched in frenzy for bombs to destroy.

They had nothing to lose. They were right.

No one knew who would be next.

At precisely that moment, when the fear, the tension, and the violence reached its peak, Vadim Mendelov ordered the discs out of sight. They were sealed off from the world. They ceased to exist. Nothing moved into or from the secret Condor base in the South American jungle.

The UFO reports, the strange glowing plasmas, had plagued governments throughout the world. Almost always they were dismissed because of the immediacy of the exploding bombs and their effects and the horror of still more weapons going off. Yet, in the struggle for political survival, nothing could be overlooked. Every attempt was made to identify the glowing shapes that moved in such ghostly fashion through dark and stormy nights.

But there were no discs to be found. There were sun dogs and meteors, plasmoids and corona discharges, reflectional dispersion and inversion layers, balloons and planets.

But no discs.

The pressures mounted to rebellion, to open revolution. The United States and the Soviet Union assured the world they were standing down their nuclear arms. They had no choice. Even without terrified and rebellious populaces there was still the constant, impersonal, stark danger that more and more bombs would explode. Around the world the bombs were removed from planes and missile silos and submarines. The bombs were dismantled, broken down.

Few people believed the nuclear powers could be trusted.

It didn't matter.

The nuclear powers dared not trust their own weapons not to destroy them.

Delegates to the United Nations shouted for international inspection teams. The United States and the Soviet Union agreed. Why not? Neither retained their nuclear warheads. Their decisions had nothing to do with world peace. It was strictly a matter of survival, and in mutual survival they could afford to be magnanimous with one another.

Red China stated flatly it would not tolerate inspection teams. The American and Soviet governments announced immediately that unless full inspection was permitted anywhere within Red China, a massive assault would be opened at once against that country, using conventional weapons.

And biological agents.

The Chinese said they would think it over. They were given twenty-four hours.

Thus the conspirators met, finally, in the secret offices of Blackburn Aero in Flagstaff. Vadim Mendelov, Stanley Hoffsommer, Kenneth Taggert, Dianne Sims, Frazer Blackburn, Cliff Brady, Ann Dallas. Several of the others, including Drew Wilkinson, were needed elsewhere.

They left empty the chair for Robert Kroot.

They reviewed what had happened, they brought themselves to the immediate moment. They had achieved success beyond what they had dared to hope. They knew also they lacked the final success they needed. Time . . .

Finally, Vadim Mendelov spoke for them. He glanced at each face, studied the eyes of the other person. For a long moment he looked at Cliff Brady, who looked back. Uncaring. Mendelov closed his eyes, pushed aside the sorrow. "For the moment we have gone as far as we dare." His words rolled slowly, wearily, from him. "The discs must remain hidden. But it is possible, just possible, that we have succeeded. If so, then we've managed to derail the engine of nuclear destruction for this world. Those who would fight to the death of everyone else now have something to fear even more than nuclear attack from one another."

Kenneth Taggert studied his folded hands. He looked up at Mendelov. "What do we do now?"

The scientist closed his eyes. He did not open them when he answered the question.

"We wait."

But there's no waiting for him. There's no time to lose. Cliff

273

is drowning himself in bitterness and self-hatred. He keeps seeing that little girl and he blames himself for her and all the others. If I could only reach him, if I could only let him know that all this has been worth it, the pain and the agony and the dying. They're getting rid of the bombs everywhere. There's a sense of relief sweeping the whole planet. It's as though we all stood at the edge of the cliff and were stopped only at the last moment before going over.

Ann clasped Cliff's hand with a firm, steady pressure. At times he acknowledged her presence. Most of the time he seemed not to notice. She glanced through the window at the trees, the distant hills. *There are so many ways to die,* she thought. *A child died in his arms, and Cliff died inside himself.*

She took a deep breath. Maybe she could still reach him, love him, bring him back.

Let the others save the world.

Her world was the man beside her.

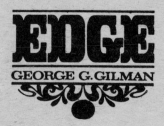

Bestsellers by
William Crawford